FOLLOW HER

ALSO BY ANNA STOTHARD

The Museum of Cathy

The Pink Hotel

Isabel and Rocco

PRAISE FOR ANNA STOTHARD

'The quality of her writing is remarkable.'

—Helen Dunmore

'Astonishingly good . . . Stothard's writing is accomplished and very engaging.'

—*The Times*

'Stothard gets her talons into you . . . read it for its beguiling heroine and sparky prose.'

—*Tatler*

'A stunningly accurate and chilling account of the acquiring of emotional wisdom, with vividly drawn characters.'

—Kate Saunders, *The Times*

'Anna Stothard's third novel cements her place as one of Britain's best young authors . . . Stothard's lush, dreamy prose is given full rein during Eva's frequent flights of fancy.'

—*Literary Review*

'A witty, beguiling and increasingly poignant novel about the scars – physical and psychological – that make us who we are, and about the messy business of love and loss.'

—*The Lady*

FOLLOW HER

ANNA STOTHARD

LAKE UNION PUBLISHING

Published by Lake Union Publishing, Seattle

www.apub.com

EU Product Safety Contact:
Amazon Media EU S.à r.l.
38, avenue John F. Kennedy, L-1855 Luxembourg
amazonpublishing-gpsr@amazon.com

ISBN-13: 9781662529979
eISBN: 9781662529962

Cover design by Jo Myler
Cover image: © Pongstorn Pixs / Shutterstock;
© Maria Casinos / Getty Images

Printed in the United States of America

For Jacob, always.

Some call her a cult leader. Others, their salvation. I used to call her my best friend. In a photo posted online yesterday, she is wearing joggers and a white hooded sweatshirt pulled up over her blonde fringe. Her blue eyes are too bright. 'Have you heard of the drowning instinct?' says the caption. 'It's the time before you drown when you're so busy gasping for air that you can't scream for help. That's the moment you need me.'

I roll my own tired, normal eyes, then go to sit down at the kitchen table, pushing aside kids' colouring books and half-finished homework to frown at my phone.

Ten thousand likes, hundreds of comments.

'Discover bliss,' says another post, with a link to a seminar she is hosting at her spiritual academy in Bali this week. She runs three of them: in Bali, LA and Berlin. Celebrities and royalty credit her with curing their migraines and addictions. There have been rumours of stranger miracles, such as sight returning to a blind follower and a paralysed child learning to walk.

When we were friends ten years ago, she wasn't the curated spiritual guru in front of me today. She was not a girl who could step on to a floodlit stage to a roar of applause and only have to raise one hand for the entire room to fall quiet. She used to bite her lip when she lied, and eat Haribo rings off her fingers. Her teeth were yellow from cigarettes and sugar and her nose was wonky from falling out of a tree as a kid. She did things that summer that she does not want you to know about. In many ways it is my fault all these people follow her. During a heatwave summer when she was seventeen and we were just starting, Frida Rae belonged to me. Now she belongs to millions, and they belong to her.

Chapter One

The morning she returns to my life, the school is buzzing. Parents are trailing strings of bunting or picnic rugs. Dads are balancing cupcake boxes, mothers dragging bags of crochet or parking signage. The field behind the school is filled with deflated bouncy castles and trestle tables, smelling of freshly mown grass. It is too hot for all this commotion.

At first I don't even notice the stranger. My youngest is carrying a box of plastic ducks out of the car for the hook-a-duck stall, which I've been roped into organising. She is too small for the task and spills ducks behind as her pigtails bounce. My eldest is dipping every so often to scoop up his sister's stray ducks. All across the playground, shrieking kids and sturdy PTA mums are battling to be heard while my mind is already drifting towards the solitude of home: fixing the chaos of our morning exit, filling the dishwasher, wiping the surfaces, pressing my feet to the cool tiles under my desk to start work. I exchange pleasantries with form teachers and parents. *Yes, too hot. Yes, the fete is going to be wonderful.* My kids wave and disappear inside.

Back at my car, a man is standing by a lamp post with his hands in the pockets of his jeans. He was in the same spot when we parked, although I didn't give him much thought then. Now I glance at him in passing, and he steps towards me. Maybe in his early forties, he has broad shoulders, a thick neck and greying blond hair.

'Zoe, right?' he says, sticking out an enormous hand for me to shake. 'I wondered if we could have a quick chat?'

'Oh,' I say, not meeting his handshake. My hands stay by my sides. My skin prickles. He lowers his hand with its big, neat, square nails. Kids run around us as the last stragglers make their way into school. 'You have the wrong person, I'm afraid,' I say, fumbling with my car keys. Everything feels slippery and uncomfortable suddenly. 'That's not my name.'

Nobody has called me Zoe for ten years. Since her. The school bell rings and I manage to open the car door, realising I didn't lock it in the first place. Of course not. The windows are all open in this heat and I never lock my car on the school run anyway. He stands too close as I slip in. The car still smells new; it was a present from my husband for my last birthday. The stranger smiles at me through the open window. Take a breath, I tell myself.

'I'm writing an article about the rise of the Frida Rae Academy,' he says. Behind him, parents are climbing into their cars or walking off home. Our picturesque town on the Yorkshire coast is a place where people notice absences and indiscretions. The school only has two hundred children; the entire town has six thousand people.

He rolls up his shirt cuffs to just below his elbows and leans down on my window with a slight smile. Sunlight squeezes in the cracks around his blond hair and white shirt. 'I believe you and Frida were close when Frida was just starting out. She knew you as Zoe. Or Zo.'

I don't react. He smiles, and it is a mean smile. 'Zo-Zo?' he says.

'You have the wrong person. I don't know Frida Rae,' I say, and turn the car on. It idles in park as he drops a photograph casually into my lap, through the car window.

It is of Frida and me sitting together, age seventeen. She took every picture of me off her accounts when I left. She also deleted them from my phone – the trash, the cloud, everywhere – while I slept. She made it so the summer never officially happened. I haven't seen this photo for a decade.

I inhale at the sight of us, almost able to feel the heat that was peeling paint off the windowsills in the photo. We look so much younger than we felt at the time, all freckly and knobbly kneed. Frida is in the middle of the group, as she always was, with crooked yellow teeth and a bump in her nose, both of which have been corrected now. Two other girls, Ava and Grace, are with us. Ava: marshmallow pale and angular, with thin peroxide hair and big glasses. Grace: long black hair down to her bum, breasts straining out of her bikini top, and a tattoo on her inner thigh.

'So, can we talk, now we agree you know her?' the journalist says. He smells of sweat. Not a single day of sweat, either. And his breath smells too minty, as if he's rubbed toothpaste on his gums. 'My name is Oliver Sperling, and I believe we can help each other.'

'I used to know her. I haven't seen these people in ten years and have no interest in talking to a journalist about her,' I say quietly. 'I'm not a follower. We were friends for a few months, ten years ago, long before there was any academy or success. I'm sure there are hundreds more useful people you could be harassing for an interview about her.'

I hold the photo out for him to take back, but he doesn't. He continues to lean his elbows on the edge of my window.

'I need to be getting on,' I say. 'Could you move?'

'No,' he says. 'Because they found Grace and Ava's remains yesterday morning, near the island.'

He pauses, letting the information sink in. My head and tongue throb. It's too hot in the car. I can smell this man's breath in my face. He points at Grace and Ava in the picture and I can hear blood pumping in my ears. 'I've spoken to the police, and early forensics suggest they died around the time this photo was taken.'

He stands away from the window and the sun curls at its edges above his head. My palms are wet and my mouth is dry. I don't move, transported by the photo in my hand. The taste of the seaside heat, the smell of her shampoo. Sweat and salt marsh. Frida's thighs, right there in my hand again, tanned on the outside and creamy on the inside.

◆ ◆ ◆

Frida and I met for the first time on the Northern line, early in the morning on one of those limbo days between Christmas and New Year. Aged seventeen, I had dropped out of school so was on the way to a bleak receptionist job at a digital marketing agency.

The tube stopped at Waterloo, and she got on. At first glance, I took her to be a tall twelve- or thirteen-year-old. She wore white jeans and the same style of plain white hooded sweatshirt that became a sort of uniform later, but with a grubby Nike backpack then. Her long blonde hair was in a tight ponytail, and her fringe was cut straight across her forehead. Her big hoop earrings moved with the carriage. She was holding a bunch of A5 paper. She handed one to a woman in a suit, who ignored her.

The blonde girl handed a flier to some Japanese tourists, a construction worker in overalls, and then paused in front of me. Up close, she was not twelve but more like my age, but skinny to the point of appearing malnourished. Her eyes were set deep in her skull. A slightly rotten, salty smell circled her. Later, we all smelled like that. She had rough patches on her cheeks and acne on her forehead. Her lips were so chapped that the crack had drawn blood, and there was dirt under her nails. I could even see the irritated red circles on her ears from the cheap metal of her hoops. She was not beautiful.

I removed my earphones and came out of my music bubble into scraping metal and thudding mechanics.

'I can help you,' the girl said and handed me a piece of paper. The only thing on there was a grainy and over-photocopied typed URL: *www.AuraLine/chat/FridaRae.co.uk*.

The train stopped at the next station, and she got off before I said anything back. On the platform, she greeted a girl who was also dressed in white jeans and a white hoodie. Ava, I would learn later, with peroxide hair and big glasses. These two walked away together hand in hand, their bright white clothes and yellow hair luminous against the dirty platform.

◆ ◆ ◆

At work, I immediately went to my desk drawer for the relief of a little blue benzodiazepine pill called Klonopin, used to calm anxiety and prevent panic attacks. My tongue touched its delicate indentations with familiar pleasure, pushing it to the back of my throat and down. Even before the chemicals kicked in, my heartbeat slowed. Then, as the chemicals dispersed, I felt happy for the first time since the last pill.

The office was a colourful open-plan space with minimalist furniture. Desks and bean bags were arranged in clusters to 'encourage collaboration'. The walls were covered in framed awards and inspirational wall stickers: 'Engage to Influence', 'Dream, Imagine, Believe'.

There was barely anyone in that day. Most of the office was off living their grid-worthy lives, kissing under mistletoe or wearing branded clothes by roaring fires (#gifted, #ad, #sponsored). So I was there taking stock of supplies, and starting to take down the Christmas decorations to store for next year.

It wasn't until near the end of the workday that I typed the URL from the flyer into my computer. A page opened on the desktop. 'Ask Questions to Accurate Psychics' said a banner in purple loopy writing at the top of the poorly built website. Grainy webcam footage appeared of the girl from the train sitting on an unmade bed. Behind her was a wall with a voile-covered window, and there was a magazine on her lap. Blurred by bad Wi-Fi, she was prettier on camera than she had been that morning.

People could pay for 'private readings' or just ask her questions in a 'chat box'. So, I scanned the page. The viewers were called things like Pennydrop, Littlepny1, Crossgirl. They wrote things such as: 'How will my date with Harry go?', 'Am I paranoid?', 'Will Jordan propose to me in the future when we start a relationship?' Frida's eyes darted, reading the screen, and then she spoke directly to the camera.

'It'll go great, Little Pony,' Frida said. 'Crossgirl, I've told you before you have to forget about Jordan.'

Crossgirl: 'Forget? WHY?! Still don't understand.'

'Crossgirl, come into private chat for a reading if you want any real information,' she said. 'You have a great deal of unused capacity that Jordan cannot appreciate.' She paused.

Underneath her video, there was a grid of photographs of other 'psychics' who were currently either 'live' or giving private readings. Everyone was holding Tarot cards or theatrical crystal balls in their profile pictures. A middle-aged Indian woman with thick-rimmed glasses and a white blouse, calling herself CrystalFairy, claimed to offer 'Chakra Healing, Tarot and Clairvoyance'. A bald white man in a winter scarf called ExpertHati offered 'Angel Communication and Chinese Astrology'. A man named PsychicBob – my favourite – held his fingers to his temples and stared directly out at his audience. His bio said he was from Hull.

I went back to Frida's feed. It was all ridiculous, so I would have closed the site and never looked again if Frida hadn't been saying:

'It was actually with Mickey Mouse . . .' Her eyes were illuminated slightly now, as she talked to the camera. A tiny smile had arranged itself on her dry lips in my absence, and I looked at the chat box to see that someone had asked her: 'when was your first kiss?'

'He worked at the Disney Store, and I kissed him in the parking lot while he was on a cigarette break. If you've been watching for a while, you know I don't often hang out in shopping centres,' she laughed, 'and I've never watched a Disney movie. My mum was a proper hippy at this point. Mickey was very subversive to me. He was wearing his mouse body, but his head was on the floor.'

I leaned forward towards the computer. Frida itched the inside of her thigh and then placed her hands serenely in her lap. Viewers continued to write questions in the chat box ('will he ask me out?', 'will I get my job back?'), but for a moment she ignored this flood of digital anxiety, seemingly lost in the memory of Mickey Mouse.

'He tasted of cigarettes and proudly told me he could get me a job as Cinderella or something if I liked, but that face characters like princesses did not even have lunch with fur characters so we wouldn't be able to date if I worked there,' she said. 'Apparently princesses get demerits if anyone sees them without a smile on their face, but they're paid three times what the animals are. I had no clue.' She leaned back again and stretched on the screen, clicking her shoulders and breaking her claustrophobic gaze into the camera.

I wondered who she was. *Where* she was. Whether this was a joke, a job, or both, and what sort of person had never watched a Disney movie by the time they had their first kiss? Most people I knew had smartphones by eleven, so we watched whatever we wanted. There was an innocence to Frida, then. Even later, after everything I discovered, she had a strange purity.

cradleme: 'will I get my claim paid this month?'

abbeysnooze: 'can I have a breathwork session?'

'You'll get a cheque in February, Cradle,' Frida said. 'Abbey, yes, call any time.'

She continued. 'It's cold today. Isn't it? I feel a lot of sadness out there suddenly. Someone sad has just tuned in. I'm sorry you are sad.'

She paused.

'You're anxious all the time, aren't you?' she said into the camera. Anyone watching psychic webcams between Christmas and New Year is quite likely to be feeling a bit down, so this was a good guess. 'You think you'll be completely yourself and grounded when you fall in love, maybe? From another bite, another sip, another pair of shoes. Another fuck, or haircut, or zero in the bank. Then you'll stop being scared all the time. Stop checking your phone at night. But you won't. Your jaw is tense. You can't concentrate. You have too many tabs open on your computer. You're slouching. You are so scared you can hardly see straight. But I can make it stop. If you call, I will help you find—'

And then, a door slammed in the room she was in. Someone laughed off-camera and said: 'It's snowing, Frida! Come here, seriously, it's snowing!'

There was snow outside my window, too.

The other blonde girl from the tube platform walked past the camera in white underwear. The camera angle changed and I saw a book on the bed called *The Times Crossword Collection: 160 of the Most Famous Crosswords in the World.* This made me smile, because I had the same book next to my bed at home.

'Get out of the way, Ava,' Frida said.

'Sorry,' Ava giggled, and looked directly at the camera for a second. Avaline Thomas, who has now been missing for a decade.

◆ ◆ ◆

Back then I lived above a pub in Kentish Town with my mum and her boyfriend, who saw me as a gauche souvenir from a holiday he hadn't been on. He did not hide his desire for me to move out of his flat. She wanted desperately to marry him so didn't stand up for me.

This was a problem for several reasons. At seventeen I didn't even earn minimum wage. Also, I spent a significant portion of that wage on benzos. They had been prescribed, at first. I'd dropped out of school because of debilitating panic attacks and been given a prescription. But when the panic attacks were no longer frequent, the psychiatrist decided I was 'better' – rather than just 'drugged'. He tapered me off his prescription and I responded in the only logical way I could think of, by buying a similar substance from a drug dealer with tattooed eyebrows who lived in the estate I grew up on. And so, ironically, I found myself not returning to school at all, because I needed enough money to buy benzos. I got a waitressing job at an ice cream parlour on the Finchley Road and started teaching myself to code, then got the receptionist job. My friends drifted away from me.

I started watching Frida at night sometimes, her white sweatshirt hood up over her blunt blonde fringe. Her face was not symmetrical or ideal. Her nose was too long, her eyes deep-set in her face in a way that made me think about her skull. She'd sit in her little box in the bottom-left corner of my monitor while I did coding tutorials or exercises that winter. Sometimes she smoked cigarettes, the smoke curling up around the webcam.

My fingers clacked on the keys while symbols wove together: variables, conditionals, functions. Car headlights swept across my wall from the window, horns honked, my mum and Roger slept on the other side of the wall.

I mostly had Frida on mute. Sometimes though, between calls and monologues, she would pick up her crossword book and I would unmute her. The first time I wrote in the chat box it was because she had been looking for one five-letter word and one seven-letter word that together answered the clue 'theoretical boundary from which nothing can escape'.

I'd watched a documentary about black holes a few weeks previously – I didn't sleep much back then – and happened to know that the answer to that was 'event horizon'. Pretty niche. Pretty top-level geek. The fact that I knew the answer felt neat – almost fated – although to be fair I knew a lot of answers. My brain loved trivia.

I tried to go back to my coding tutorial, fingering my beat-up copy of *Introduction to Algorithms*, but then I enlarged Frida's window and answered her in the chat box under the username Guest72: 'event horizon'.

'Thanks Guest72, what a legend you are. If you googled that I'll kill you.'

Guest72: 'So you can ask strangers on the internet, but not the internet itself?'

She grinned out at me from the screen.

After that, whenever I logged on as Guest72, she would take out her current crossword puzzle and ask me questions, her digitalised face often fragmented into jagged shards because the bandwidth was maxed out: she left a robotic portion of her forehead on one side of the screen, then it caught up with the remainder a few seconds later.

Usually, she was in her bedroom. Painting her nails, brushing her hair. Sometimes a low-ceilinged living room. Sometimes the other blonde from the tube was there. Sometimes a different girl and her boyfriend. Mostly, online, she read people's Tarot cards or just chatted to the camera about stuff: the forest fires, home-made shampoo recipes. Was it some sort of commune, I wondered? She said her mum was a hippy.

One time she spoke more about her mother, and I listened, because mothers are an interesting subject. She described how her mother's identity had always seemed to change according to whichever man she was into at that moment: demure for the churchgoer, vegan for the surfer-boy, anti-capitalist for the guy who lived in a squat. My mum had done the same all my life. We had bags of her shrugged-off former identities in a storage crate somewhere near Brent Cross. The leather jacket from when she'd loved a biker; pencil skirts from the year she'd loved a pilot with a moustache.

When I first spoke to Frida it was near the end of April – the week after Easter. Spring, but a freak heatwave had been building and became a fact that day. 'London wakes up to heat wave hell as Europe battles widespread wildfires,' the papers had said that morning. In the warm street below, a group of kids my age walked with their hoods up, smoking and drinking beer. Across the road, a nurse got on a bus, heading to or from a shift. A stripy cat jumped off a wall and slipped through the yellow puddle of a street lamp.

I'd gone out with some old school friends earlier although I hadn't really been invited – I'd just seen an Insta that they were meeting up. I'd drunk too much to stop myself feeling left out, and ended up throwing up in a Camden Town bin. Nobody had noticed when I left the pub, or asked if I'd gotten home okay. Sober again, I felt scooped out and pointless. Mum and Roger were going on holiday early the next morning, so I would be alone in the flat for a fortnight. She thought he was going to propose while they were away. Which meant that on their return I would almost certainly be asked to move out of the flat. As I sat there in front of my computer, surrounded by textbooks, scribbles, chocolate wrappers and energy drink cans, it occurred to me that if I downed all my benzos, nobody would look for me. Work would send a few emails then move on. Mum, blissed out on holiday, probably wouldn't worry too much if I didn't reply to her texts. I felt sorry for myself about that.

Frida went off the screen to speak to a client. I wanted her back on my screen, looking at me. I tried to concentrate on fixing a broken loop of code but felt an urgent loneliness and touched my pack of pills again. I had nobody to text, nobody who would talk to me this late. I took another pill, then a deep breath. I knew I shouldn't take any more. I ate a Dairy Milk bar in three bites instead, then put in my card details and was given a time slot in ten minutes. I got out my book of crossword puzzles and pencilled in a few answers to distract myself: Diaphanous. Lee Child. Nairobi.

I skimmed Instagram. I hadn't posted anything in two years, but I scrolled through the lives of former friends and strangers. They were whiling away the heatwave outside pubs, sunbathing in parks with lovers or family. Sometimes we shared a DM or a meme but it wasn't much. My friends had distanced themselves when my anxiety became troubling. I didn't turn up to places when I said I would. I would be found crying in toilets. People don't like that sort of shit, long-term.

Soon another window appeared, and Frida smiled warmly at me over a private video conversation.

The boyfriend and girlfriend I saw occasionally were asleep, curled up together on the sofa behind Frida, who was sitting at a table.

'I'm glad you called,' she said. It was odd to hear her speak to me, as if the character in a TV show was breaking the fourth wall. 'You are so tense tonight.'

'It's midnight and I've just called an online psychic. Yes. I'm a little angsty.'

'Are you drunk?' she said. 'What's your name? You're beautiful.'

Nobody had ever called me beautiful. I dressed in baggy t-shirts and leggings to hide a body that I considered ugly. I cut my own thick dark hair, and it was a nothing haircut with no layers, just above my shoulders. A bit plump, a bit short, I walked with zero confidence and was extremely short-sighted. Men didn't stare, put it that way.

'I'm hovering somewhere between drunk and hungover, I'd say. Do people really think you're psychic?'

The couple on the sofa stirred. The guy kissed the girl on the forehead but didn't open his eyes.

'A few charmers want me to take off my "panties" or whatever, but that's another story. Most figure I do what it says on the tin.'

'Worst word. Panties. This is weird. I don't know why I called.'

'Your grandmother wants me to tell you that you are loved,' she said.

I laughed: an unladylike *guffowf* noise. A bit of snot came out of my nose and I wiped it with my sleeve, thankful for the pixelated darkness. I fully assumed she was giving me a joke example of what people called her about. But then she continued:

'Your grandmother wants me to tell you that she left you something when she died and you're not looking after it properly.'

'Oh. You're actually serious? Fuck. Gran barely talked to me when we lived together, she wouldn't bother transgressing dimensions using a teenage internet psychic. You don't need to do all this,' I said. 'I'm honestly just bored and not looking to chat about ghosts. We could do a crossword?' I held up my book.

Gran used to live with us in the flat where I was born, on the tenth floor of a twenty-three-storey tower called Bray in Swiss Cottage. She'd brought up my mother in the same flat. She collected ketchup packets from McDonald's, and smoked Benson & Hedges in the bathtub. She died of her third stroke, each of which had exploded bridges and towns full of memories in her brain until there wasn't much left of her infrastructure when the lights actually went out.

She'd been a librarian at Swiss Cottage Library until her first stroke, and I used to go there most days after school to read and do my homework until she finished her shift. She was a brisk, no-nonsense woman who believed children should be seen and not heard, but she also used to buy me maths workbooks because my homework was too easy, and she pushed me to read difficult books about difficult subjects. She'd been a librarian since the age of eighteen and had a gift for the right book for the right moment. She knew which story would fill whatever void or itch a person had that week.

She didn't leave it to me in her will, but the turtle necklace around my neck had been a gift from her on my fourteenth birthday. It did need a polish. Still, this did not make me believe that this teenager on the internet was psychic.

'I cost two pounds a minute,' she said. 'You know that?'

'I'd pay that for the river that runs through Italy, two letters.'

'Po. What's your name? I can't call you Guest72 now,' Frida said.

I was impressed. It was Po. Impressed and intrigued.

'Zoe,' I lied. It didn't feel right to turn away from online anonymity just yet, even though we were talking face-to-face. This lie kept one foot in a comforting grey area without real-life risk. Later, this lie gave me time to get away from her.

I'd never felt like a Katie. Katie was sweet and approachable. A people pleaser. I was Katie on my actual birth certificate; my mother didn't gift me the gravitas or choice of the name Katherine. I was named the diminutive form of a proper name.

There'd been a Zoe at my school who always seemed effortless. People laughed loudly at her jokes. I once saw her fall down the central library staircase. Instead of being embarrassed, she bowed and everyone laughed with her rather than at her.

'"Po" fits,' I said. 'How did you know that?'

'I'm psychic,' she said, and I laughed. She didn't.

'Zoe, you take prescription medication to calm your mind but your fears are confused and out of control,' she said, and I raised my eyebrows because that actually was a bit impressive, but then I saw a pill packet on a shelf behind me. Observant, but not magical. 'In fact, you are far more powerful than you think. You are limitless. Or you could be if you chose.'

'Is Gran telling me that? I'm definitely not limitless, Gran. I can't spell "daiquiri", or "Edinburgh", and I can't cook. I'm still a bit confused about apostrophes.'

'You hide your fear behind humour. If you want a different outcome, control your habits. You have the power to reinvent yourself and to be something other than what your parents expect. What are you scared of?'

'Oh gosh, lots. Asteroids, and cancer, and deep water, and bad Wi-Fi, and being beaten at chess, and now also my mean grandma returning as a ghost?' I said. I adjusted my glasses. 'My carbon footprint. The price of coffee. The calories in a ready-made sandwich.' I paused. 'Crowds. Clowns. Velvet brushed the wrong way. Rent. Debt. Terrorism. Extinction events.'

'In order to truly live and love, you have to embrace the things that scare you. We live artificially safe lives so our fear is confused, and out of control.'

'What are you scared of, then?' I asked.

'Myself, mostly.' She smiled. 'And I'm scared of bad Wi-Fi and children's presenters and tides and forest fires and ghosts,' she said, 'like the rest of the world. But this isn't about me. Tell me what is so scary that it is keeping you awake tonight?'

Then words flashed on screen: *CREDIT IS ABOUT TO EXPIRE. BUY MORE CREDIT?*

'Your credit's about to run out,' she said. 'And you're scared of your mother.'

'Seriously? I paid twenty pounds. That's insane. Everyone is scared of their mother.'

'Two pounds a minute.'

'Robbery.'

'Most people make better use of the time. I can talk to the dead and see the future, you know?'

I laughed.

CREDIT IS ABOUT TO EXPIRE. BUY MORE CREDIT?

I touched my necklace.

'Butterflies in my stomach, five letters,' she said.

'Crush,' I said.

'Hey maybe this is weird, but do you want to have a drink with me?' Frida said.

'Like, now?'

'No. Come do a crossword puzzle with me in person. I feel a very strong connection to you and I think you do to me. You've been watching me for months. I have a sense that we are meant to meet.'

'Do you say that to everyone?'

'No. I live near a town called Ballards End in Essex. I'm going to be at The Sailor tomorrow afternoon – it's a pub in town. You could come buy me a drink at around three. We'll do a crossword.'

I felt a twist of excitement at this overstepping of boundaries. This was basically the protagonist of a TV drama I'd been binging on all winter, and she'd just looked out through the screen and asked me to buy her a beverage. It was too much. It was breaking the invisible wall between audience and story. It was unsettling.

'I'm busy tomorrow,' I said, palms sweaty. I wanted a pill. 'And I don't know you, and I never really liked my gran when she was alive. I called you because I was drunk and bored and now I feel quite depressingly sober.'

My mouth was dry after all that. I felt flustered, like I was embarrassing myself, even though I told myself it didn't matter. I didn't know this girl. She wasn't a neighbour, or a girl from my school.

'You called me to help you survive. If you don't visit me you are going to hurt yourself.' She smiled, like all of this was very obvious. 'So, you are going to visit me instead. Every day when you wake up you are choosing to be predictable and limited. I reckon we could be friends. I reckon you could stop being scared.'

'I wish my fears were predictable. The other day, out of nowhere, I convinced myself not to get on the underground because of rats. Total meltdown. I'd never given rats a second thought before that moment.'

I was babbling. I babble when nervous.

CREDIT IS ABOUT TO EXPIRE. BUY MORE CREDIT?

'Instinct isn't all it's cracked up to be,' said Frida. 'Your parents construct your instincts. Advertisers and social media manipulate them, allowing you to think you have free will. Society wants to keep you trapped by fear. I will break your fear apart.'

Then my one-to-one chat window flickered and she could no longer see or hear me, but I could see and hear her. I liked what she'd said about instinct though; it expressed something I'd never quite put into words. Like, people in Mum's diet books said 'listen to your body', and my therapist used to tell me to 'trust myself'. But my instinct leaned firmly towards drugs and sugar, and surely I shouldn't trust anyone that was so consistently high, or who had such wildly fluctuating glucose levels. Instinct was shaped and influenced just like anything else – maybe mine was not to be trusted.

At this point Ava came on screen, her wet plait flung over her white t-shirt, and kissed Frida on the shoulder. With her glasses up on the top of her scrappy peroxide hair, her eyes looked smaller and uncertain, like she was an amorphous child. She whispered something into Frida's ear. I guessed it was: *come to bed now, it's late.* Frida nodded and smiled.

It sent a shiver down my spine that they were together. I had never fancied a girl. I considered myself straight, as much as I considered myself as any form of sexual being. Which wasn't much.

'You should write fortune cookies or something,' I wrote in the chat box, wanting to keep Frida's attention for another moment.

'To overcome fear you have to acknowledge the source, and then accomplish the thing that scares you,' she said to me through the camera.

'That one wouldn't fit on a fortune cookie. You want to try something simple like: "No snowflake causes an avalanche." Or: "This cookie contains 117 calories."'

'Okay, funny girl. I have to sign off. Don't hurt yourself. Go to sleep now and come visit me tomorrow.'

I didn't think that I would go, as I fell asleep. In the chemical fug of my dreams I saw the blonde webcam psychic: her eyes closed and the skin on her eyelids nearly translucent so I could see a blue network of blood vessels. In my dream I was watching her sleep. Her skin had a gloss from sweat while my skin pricked. My interest was physical but not exactly sexual. It was intimate though; in my dream I was listening to the dry rhythm of her breathing next to me and this was where I was supposed to be. I felt dread and longing and comfortable familiarity. This spectre was beautiful, tangled in the sheets as if recently washed ashore.

Chapter Two

Seagulls scream in the kicking seafoam of the Yorkshire coastline below. The journalist and I are both parked at the far edge of a car park with five miles of white sand beach to the right and a promontory jutting out into the North Sea in front. Oliver. A gentle name. He is handsome, in a damaged way, with a strong jaw and sad eyes. There is an intensity to his expression that makes my mouth feel dry.

His car is an old blue Peugeot Hatchback with mesh sunshades on the back windows. When he stepped out of his car I saw plastic bags and cardboard boxes on the back seat. Now we are both standing awkwardly in the space between our cars. He holds an iPad and lights a cigarette while I take a sip from a stainless-steel water bottle.

He hands the iPad over, open on a news article. I shade the screen from the sun. He watches me carefully as a red admiral butterfly flutters across the warm air between us. There is a sanctuary at a farm not far away. Painted ladies, small blues, Duke of Burgundies. I took the kids to see the butterfly cocoons a few weeks ago and one landed on my son's nose.

'The remains of two teenage runaways have been found near their homes on the Essex coast, ten years after they went missing,' the article says. Ava's picture is a school photo, taken before the peroxide hair to match Frida's. Grace's photo is of her in a red bikini, smiling coyly.

'The remains were found in the cooling lake of a decommissioned nuclear power station on the Blackwater Estuary. Investigators are working closely with forensic pathologists to determine the circumstances surrounding their deaths.' It does not mention Frida. It does not mention me. There is a photo of the nuclear power plant, its walls covered in graffiti that suggests many years of teenage abandon.

The article reports that Avaline Thomas had gone missing regularly from foster homes and hostels in Essex throughout her childhood. She was a repeat offender with a history of drug abuse, petty theft and solicitation. Although she was reported missing at some point after that summer, nothing came of the search.

'She'd gone missing and turned up too many times for the police to take it seriously,' Oliver says, inhaling his cigarette. 'Nobody really looked.'

I don't reply, just keep reading. Grace Basu was never even reported missing, the article says. From the same town as Avaline, Grace was estranged from her parents, 'a situation that may explain why she was never reported missing'.

The iPad in my hand is old and heavy, in a fake-leather case with worn plastic edges and fraying seams.

'Authorities are asking anyone with information that might shed light on the case to come forward, especially those who may have had contact with these two young women,' the article ends.

Oliver takes the iPad back from me and I am left just holding the physical photograph.

'This photo was the only afternoon I met Ava,' I say, lifting it slightly. I've curled the edges by holding it too hard in my sweaty hands. 'Grace was there for most of the summer, same as me, but left before me – to go and meet Ava somewhere, I think. They were going to go travelling. They were best friends, and troubled, as the newspaper says.'

'What sort of troubled?'

'Anorexia, self-harm, drugs. Frida didn't hurt them, if that's what you're implying. Failed to help, I suppose, but she was a kid too. It's awful that they died, but it's not Frida's fault.'

His green eyes narrow at me and he touches his neck as he inhales. He does this repeatedly throughout our conversation, like he is looking for a collar or a tie. His fingers beat a rhythm on his car, and his upper lip twitches around the filter of his cigarette. He is an unhappy man, with more frown than laugh lines.

'I wish I could be more help, but I don't have anything to add.' I pause. I ought to get in the car, start the engine, drive home.

He leans on the bonnet of his car. When he stretches I can see sweat marks on his shirt, razor burn on his neck. He touches the crook of his arm, like maybe it itches.

'I bet you haven't told your husband much about that summer,' he says.

'I'm not remotely threatened by you or this picture of me and some friends. I can assure you that nobody would care that I spent a summer as a teenager learning to meditate.'

'Why so keen to claim you don't know her, then?'

'It was a weird interlude, and it's not who I am anymore.'

'Doctor's wife in a cute little seaside village, huh?' he says. 'He doesn't know you bat for both teams?'

I cross my arms. Oliver slips his fingers into the front sleeve on his iPad case and pulls out more photos. He holds them out so I can see the top one: me and Frida in profile, smiling, our tongues outstretched and the tips touching.

But when I reach to take the photos in my hand he moves them away, like a flirty schoolboy.

'They're a bunch of the photos she deleted from Instagram,' he says, 'of the summer you were there.'

He flicks through them. I want to see them up close but he doesn't stop. There's a photo of us meditating on the salt marsh, surrounded by puddles of water that look like smashed glass. A photo of Frida stretching, nipples hard, and I want to stop on that photo but he moves on.

'How did you get them?' I say.

Us all wearing long white t-shirts as if they were dresses, limbs intertwined or resting on each other. She is laughing, and I am the one who made her laugh.

'Some perv on Reddit screenshotted them when you guys were starting and later sold them to me when I was sniffing around about Frida,' he says.

'You can't print them,' I said. 'She owns the copyright.'

'I could if there was a crime. That would make it in the public interest.' There are photos of me and Grace climbing trees, me and Grace sunbathing. I desperately want him to stop skipping over them but try not to show it. 'I didn't think I'd be able to print them, they've been in a drawer for a year, then yesterday I saw these dead girls in the paper and recognised them as the girls in these photos.' He smiles, as if this was wonderful. 'Two girls who followed Frida died, most likely while they were living with her.'

'You don't know that. They lived one town over. They were troubled girls, as the article says. In fact, Grace and Ava both left the island before I did.'

He keeps flicking. There are maybe twenty in all. In some of the photos, from later in the summer, I have blonde hair like Frida. Grace, later in the summer, has no hair at all.

He slows down on four photos of the festival we held near the end of the summer, all ridiculous and decadent. They are blurrier than the others – screenshots of a livestream, I know, although he might not. Hundreds of people dancing around a fire in one photo.

Grace in a white bikini with a mask over her eyes in another – the mask resembles the eyes of a discontented seagull and she is lying in the river at medium tide on a unicorn float she bought in town.

Moth sitting up in a tree wearing the same seagull mask with his curly black hair spilling over the top.

Frida standing body to body with me, her arms wrapped around the small of my back, kissing me under our masks – hers a deer and mine a crow.

Grace and I standing in the dark with a fire blazing behind us.

Oliver hands me this last photo. He is watching my reactions carefully now; I can feel his eyes on me. He touches his neck, an increased heat in the air. In the photo, Grace is wearing a white summer dress, with the seagull's mask on top of her head. I am wearing a white t-shirt, jean shorts, and the crow mask over my eyes.

Behind us, two girls are walking towards the camera, holding hands in the darkness. For a moment I don't realise but then I see it. One is Frida with her deer mask. The other is Ava, wearing a golden bird mask on her head and a tight white bandeau dress with bare feet. Ava is tanned and luminous with bangles all up her wrists. I run my fingers over Ava and Grace's pretty faces in this photo.

'You said you only met Ava once,' Oliver says. 'But you're both in this photo dated at the end of the summer as well.'

'She lived nearby. Maybe she came back for this party, I can't remember.'

I close my eyes for a second and see the flecks of grey in the silty blue of Frida's eyes, the freckle under her chin, the way she could make a flower-shape with her tongue. All the hours we spent studying each other over the summer.

'Then, after this party there were no photos at all for a while and soon the whole summer disappeared from her grid,' he says.

'When she started posting again she became much more of a brand, with good clothes and professional lighting. Clean living. Inner peace. No more neo-pagan lesbian animal parties. Why did she delete the whole summer – all the photos of Grace and Ava? Could it be because these photos were the only thing that tied two dead girls to her?'

'Or she just rebranded.' I shrug. 'Neo-pagan lesbian animal parties aren't very *global mass market*.'

A seagull watches us from a tree and ruffles his feathers. It is similar weather to when I first went to the island to see Frida. The same blue sky, and darting swallows, and drought. None of this would ever have happened if it weren't for the heat. It makes people think impossible things.

◆ ◆ ◆

Bay Island is two hours from London, but looks like another planet. Only a quarter of the island is above sea level all the time, and the higher land is surrounded by salt flats stretching out into the Blackwater Estuary and the North Sea. But from the mainland, all you can see is the causeway, then a mirage-flicker of trees, the beach, the shifting water. The Essex coast is made up of around thirty tidal islands similar to Bay. Some are just mudbanks. Some have fancy hotels on them. Others are sinking fast into the water so will soon just be the stuff of folklore and ghost stories.

The heat had a different quality on the island. Less solid than the mainland but also dryer. Not so claustrophobic but also more worrying – trembling and stretching out to the horizon. Once on the island, the track forked, flanked on either side by wildly overgrown hedgerows climbing with dog roses and honeysuckle. These hedges mostly obscured the water on the left but thinned out every so often to reveal sudden flashes of hot mossy shoreline and tidal offerings such as a rotten door, or the rib-like tips of what must once have been the base of a boat.

Coming to meet Frida was out of character. I was not impulsive. When I woke up the morning after speaking to her online, Mum and Roger had already left for the airport. There was a Post-it asking me to water the houseplants, but not to overwater the cacti. Not 'love, mum' or even 'xx, mum'. Mum and I mostly communicated via Post-it note but if she had something more nuanced to express she would put a passive-aggressive *Daily Mail* article on the fridge. Last week this headline had appeared: 'Teens who spend more than three hours a day on their smartphone are "significantly" more likely to be overweight or obese, study warns.'

Thanks, Mum.

In the mirror I saw dark circles around my eyes, and my hair needed a wash. In a photo of Mum and Roger on the wall, my mother's tan skin and ash-blonde hair made her look like a Barbie doll. I wiped snot on my arm and had a shower while my pills went to work on my nervous system. The weekend stretched in front of me, with its promise of Netflix and frozen pizza and mismatched socks; maybe pyjamas all the way to Monday morning. It occurred to me, again, that if I took enough benzos I wouldn't need to worry about anything.

I thought about what Frida had said about instinct not being trustworthy. My instinct said *not* to go and meet her, but maybe I should do the opposite? It wasn't as if following my instinct had currently got me to a great place.

So I left the flat. I took the Northern line to Moorgate. 'Thousands of sun-seekers defy Met Office's warnings to stay indoors and keep their windows shut during heatwave as the "Mediterranean Melt" sends temperatures soaring to 101°F,' said the front of the *Daily Mail,* abandoned on a train seat, covered with pictures of packed beaches in Chichester and Lyme Regis, and attractive tanned women sunbathing in Regent's Park. 'Swedish glamour model determined to achieve the world's BIGGEST bottom reveals how she gorges on six KILOS of Nutella a month to pile on the pounds.' 'Mother's fury at police after son, 13, is charged with ASSAULT after firing a McDonald's chip through a straw and hitting a woman in the face.'

The tube smelled of hot dust and metal mixed with body odour. My jeans were ill-advised and sticky. I walked east from Moorgate to Liverpool Street and found a train heading to Witham via Ballards End.

I scrolled my phone on the train. A fire had started on Winter Hill in Manchester and had joined up with the fire in Saddleworth Moor; the result was like an apocalypse movie. I stared at it for a while, feeling my heart beat faster, then scrolled on. I'd been sent to a school therapist aged ten because I was hyper-focused on the statistical probability of different apocalypse scenarios. Nuclear war: 1–2 per cent per year, rising to maybe 20 per cent over the next decade depending on geopolitical tensions. Maybe 10–20 per cent for total societal collapse from global warming. Pandemic? Asteroid? Robot war? When I told the school therapist, he'd just sighed. Most of the kids he counselled apparently suffered from similar climate anxiety. We ended up having a good chat about it. His money was on alien invasion.

'Homes have been evacuated and schools closed as firefighters prepare to come face-to-face with one of the biggest moorland fires in living memory,' a news site had posted on my feed, but all over the train people were playing Candy Crush on their phones or doing their make-up. I leaned my head against the smudged window. My mouth was dry.

Even with benzos slowing my overactive brain signals, I felt a rising panic. I could almost smell the fires, although it was really just the friction of hot rubber on metal.

I touched my throat. My pulse throbbed there. I took another pill from the pack and swallowed it dry, then closed my eyes. I tried to narrow my attention to one calming sensation, rubbing the edge of my t-shirt between my fingers like I used to do with the silk edge of a blanket as a child. I was heavily sedated so the panic attack could only rise so far under my weighted layer of chemical calm. It bubbled under there, though. *Super-volcanic eruption? Gamma-ray burst? Am I fat? Why have my friends stopped calling me? How will I afford rent?*

The Ballards End stop was outside a church surrounded by little gift shops and flower beds of peonies. Further down the main street the gift shops began to peter out into tattoo parlours and Chinese restaurants until I was pushed towards a promenade looking out on to the River Crouch.

There was no beach, just mudflats full of veiny water. It was low tide and the promenade was lined with huge antique sailboats grounded in the sand at jaunty angles, inelegant as penguins on dry land. The river was pristine and otherworldly. In contrast, the land was grotesquely human with cigarette packets dancing against ketchup-smeared polystyrene and a melted red lolly puddled in the pavement cracks. Seagulls stabbed at crisps, pigeons cowered nearby, and a glossy crow stood on a cardboard sign tied to the railings.

The promenade looked as if it was already exhausted by summer revelry and wasn't sure it could take another weekend of it. Men cleaned rubbish bins overflowing with beer and ice cream wrappers, swept floors, and raised awnings over food shacks. A wedding had obviously taken place on one of the boats recently because there was white confetti everywhere and a banner with a photo of a couple on it that said: 'Step on board to celebrate'. The air smelled of marshy salt, somewhere between sea water and sewage. An adventure playground and splash pool was just opening, along with four little huts offering food, drink, inflatable water animals and plastic buckets.

I bought a bacon sandwich and a cup of coffee from one of the stalls and climbed over the breakers to sit with my feet on the wet sand. I considered going straight home but dug my fingernails into the soft palm of my hand and stayed.

At around three p.m. – the time we had agreed to meet – I doubled back to The Sailor and looked for Frida. She wasn't there, so I ordered a lemonade and a pack of Walkers salt and vinegar crisps. I sat on a picnic table outside, just off the promenade, to flick through my phone. I looked at some of the influencers we worked with at the office, and some of my school friends who had stopped calling. Then I went through the news: fires, factory-worker slavery scandals, famine, despots.

Then, there on the promenade beyond the picnic tables, gesticulating towards the pub, were the boyfriend and girlfriend who had been asleep on the sofa the previous night.

I noticed them before they noticed me. She was a petite but curvy Asian girl, around my age, with shoulder-length black hair, wearing hot pants and a white t-shirt, flip-flops, and huge sunglasses.

She turned to her boyfriend and then pointed at me. He was an uncommonly tall man with tangled hair that jumped off at unlikely angles, as if he had been recently electrocuted. His t-shirt was half tucked and half untucked, his entire body unruly.

She laughed at something he'd said and then turned away from him towards the pub and me.

She looked far too warm in spite of her sparse clothing. Her skin glistened.

A lonely drunk at one of the tables stared longingly at her ass, and an old lady clucked.

'Hey,' the girl said as her red flip-flops stopped at my table. 'Are you Zoe, Frida's friend? I'm Grace. And over there is Moth.'

Grace waited for me to introduce myself.

'Yeah,' I said, and smiled, continuing my lie from last night. 'Zoe.'

'Frida has a migraine and asked me to come pick you up,' Grace said.

Up close, Grace's painted fingernails were bitten down so far that beads of dried blood lined her fingers. She had the raw red bumps of a rash or maybe eczema on her inner arms. She smelled of stale sweat and fresh sunscreen and something oily, which I later discovered was emollient cream for her eczema. I felt disappointed in myself for coming all this way. It was sort of humiliating but I had enough Klonopin in me that the emotion of humiliation was nicely boxed up and detached. It didn't really matter.

'Oh,' I said. 'No, thanks, I'm meeting some friends in London later. I was just going to have a quick drink with Frida, but it doesn't matter.'

'It's a ten-minute drive,' Grace said.

'No, don't worry about it.'

I saw the tattoo of a bird across her leg. I was always amazed by people confident enough in their bodies and identities to get tattoos. How did they know they wouldn't hate the tattoo in a year, in two? I could hardly choose a t-shirt that I still liked a week later. She had a small waist, but big breasts, big teeth, big brown eyes.

'Ah shit,' she said. 'Sorry then. Did you come far?'

'No, honestly, it's not a big deal.'

She sat down opposite me. 'So fucking hot, right? I know it's, like, said about five hundred times a day by every person this week, but I feel like it's a bit of small talk that has to be talked when you meet up with someone, right? It's like you can't get on to any other subject until you've done the weather.'

Over on the boardwalk the tall guy was waving at us.

'I think your, um, is trying to get your attention,' I said.

She didn't look but got up from the table.

'Yeah, we did the supermarket run; need to get it unpacked. We're staying with Frida for a bit. We can drop you at the station and save you the bus though, if you want. It's no bother. If you don't want to come to the house to see Frida.'

'Hurry up!' shouted the guy, walking into the pub garden a few steps and motioning for us to get a move on. 'It's a hundred degrees and there's stuff for the freezer.'

He had a posh voice. A posh vibe, unlike Grace.

'Let us drive you to the station, will you?' Grace said to me. 'I don't like to think you came all this way and we didn't even give you a lift. Frida wouldn't like it.'

She walked off without waiting for me to answer, so I followed her. The guy was in the driver's seat of a white van now, trying to start the engine. He was so tall that he had to bend slightly, and up close his black hair was prematurely streaked with grey even though he couldn't have been much older than me. He gave me a lazy smile through the window.

'The back doors don't work,' Grace said, climbing through the front seat into the back, her hot pants riding up her crotch, then motioning for me to sit in the front.

I hesitated.

'We're dropping her at the station,' Grace said to the guy.

'But *the food*,' he said. So Queen's English, but he had a spiral sun tattoo in the crook of his right arm, radiating tendrils of light. 'Do you mind if we drop the food off, then I'll take you to the station?' he said. 'I promise not to murder you.'

'Moth,' Grace said. 'Frida said look after her.' She splayed out her palms. Her plastic gold hoops swung. 'She wants to go to the station, so take her to the station.'

'You live with Frida?' I said, still not getting in.

'Just visiting,' he said. 'It's her grandfather's house. Come say hi and I'll drive you straight back to the station after.'

'Moth, let's just drop her off at the station. She doesn't want to come.'

'Okay, okay,' Moth said, and smiled at me. 'Sorry.'

I got in. The seat covers were itchy grey material with yellow padding squeezing out in places. They smelled faintly of spilt milk and curry and weed, while the tree-shaped air fresheners hanging off the mirror had long since lost their purpose.

'Moth,' he said, smiling at me.

'Zoe.'

'Nice to meet you.'

'Like the insect?'

'Like TiMOTHy. Moth for short.'

Apart from his greying hair, he was not jolty, or glittery, or in any way moth-like. He had a very solid physical presence, more like a grizzly bear driving a car. His sunglasses were Ray-Bans. Grace's sunglasses looked like the sort you buy in a corner shop.

'How long have you been there?' I said.

'Couple of weeks,' Moth said. 'Not sure what our plans are.'

'I'll just come quickly,' I said.

Moth repeatedly forgot to indicate, and drove too fast, jolting at zebra crossings. We listened to the radio as we headed away from the main drag of town, away from the gift shops and kiosks selling inflatables, through new-build terraced houses with neat front lawns. Near the edge of town, the buildings started to fray and peel. We moved through rows of prefab bungalows, many of them with boarded-up windows and broken bits of furniture scattered in the front garden: mattresses, a rocking chair, parts of a bed. We stopped for a man in a motorised wheelchair with a cigarette in his mouth, who glared at us as he crossed the road extremely slowly.

There was an arcade called Wonderland and a closed-up shop with a peeling sign offering 'Fresh seafood'.

'Would you rather have sex with a merman or a centaur?' said Moth, looking at the seafood sign.

'I hate the smell of fish,' said Grace, as if this was a normal question to ask. 'Has to be a centaur, surely. They're well endowed, I think.'

'Do you think mermaids and centaurs exist, Grace? Tell the truth.'

'I've seen them at the zoo,' she said.

'A centaur is half man, half horse, you muppet,' Moth said. He reached back and touched her knee tenderly.

'Oh,' she said, unperturbed in the way that only beautiful people can be unperturbed by embarrassing mistakes. 'I thought it was one of those half zebra, half horse things. How do mermen even do it? How do fish do it? We need that information to make a decision.'

'I think . . .' I began, then wished I hadn't started. 'Females release eggs into the water, males release sperm, and the eggs get fertilised in the water. No physical contact involved.'

They raised their eyebrows as we turned left on to a long and empty road.

'Want to fiddle with that?' he said, pointing to the radio dial.

I turned the numbers and searched unsuccessfully for a gap between crackles. When I looked up again, the track we were driving along had turned into a half-mile road over the water that I later discovered was called a causeway, with a thin layer of water and ripples of sand on either side. The intricate, undulating shape of the sediment reminded me of a brain. The air smelled burnt now, like wet mud and ripe seaweed.

'Woah,' I said. 'Stop. Are we going to an island?'

Moth stopped the van halfway across the causeway, which was strewn with smashed bricks and samphire; the blue sky reflected in the perfectly still liquid on either side.

'My phone only has sixty-eight per cent battery and I didn't bring my charger.'

He laughed, but then realised I was being serious. 'It belongs to her grandfather. It's beautiful.'

'Like, she has a private island?'

'I mean, it's one fairly decrepit house sinking into some salt marsh. If you're expecting the Seychelles you may want to reset your expectations.'

'Warning to public – this site and its contents are private property', said a sign wedged into the causeway. 'No unauthorised persons allowed on this site', said another, nailed to a tree on the island. 'Danger of death', said the next, bluntly, as we drove over. 'Respect the tides.'

◆ ◆ ◆

The black-cladded cottage with wonky windows sat in the middle of an overgrown jungle of vegetable patches and farm machinery. I followed Moth past plastic rabbits and gnomes, an old washing machine with weeds growing in it, a shower tray and a broken deckchair, until we saw Frida sitting under the shade of a tree with the peroxide blonde from the Tube platform. Ava had Haribo rings on her fingers, and was eating them one by one.

The grass was charred yellow. There were dead rose bushes, and beds of shrubby mud full of browning foliage and rotting leaves. Daisies cooked amongst the burnt lawn, and smashed bricks lay in dead hedges. Eight or nine crows hopped over the raised beds of vegetables, and one sat defiantly on the shoulder of a scarecrow. There wasn't a single cloud in the sky. The house and garden were at the very tip of the island. Above us was an extraordinary expanse of salt marsh.

'Hey.' Frida smiled, languid, from her position under the tree. 'Sorry not to pick you up. My head was painful.'

A butterfly danced at our ankles, unable to decide which buttercup was the most appealing.

Frida's lashes were thick and dark against the white of her eyelids, where the skin was so translucent that the pathway of her blood was visible. She wore a thin white t-shirt, and under it her small breasts stood out from the valley of her breastbone, which led down to visible ribs. Her skin was blotchy with acne and her teeth were yellow. A breeze rustled her hair. I smelled flowers and salt: lilies, rotten, in humid air.

That first sight of her changed me, like looking straight at the sun. There were burnt lights floating on the inside of my eyelids afterwards, in the shape of her. My heart beat fast. I was glad I had come.

Ava had her head in Frida's lap, and she raised her hand idly to Frida's mouth. Frida smiled playfully and bit one of the rings right off Ava's finger. Ava was wearing a bikini and had beautiful breasts. She had a bag of Haribo next to her and a menthol cigarette in her hand. The minty nicotine smell ribboned up in the salty breeze. Ava's purple flip-flops, abandoned on the floor, were Gap Kids.

Ava and Grace both reminded me of a certain type of girl. The sort every school had, stubbing out cigarettes under trainers. The girls who stole, who never did homework but flirted with the teacher, and looked hot even when they hadn't slept or showered. The girls who didn't wear underwear. Those girls were not my friends even in the days that I had friends. Those girls didn't even see me – the geek who used to spend every lunch break in chess or computer club.

I did have friends, in fairness, as a kid. I didn't always seem to understand social interactions, which didn't matter when I was little but became increasingly troublesome over time. I didn't always know if someone was flirty or meanly teasing. I couldn't always read people's body language. I often got the tone of things a bit wrong. People would be discussing a celebrity's outfit and I'd be like: 'Did you know that in 2010 a perfectly round, hundred-foot-wide and sixty-foot-deep sinkhole suddenly appeared in Guatemala City, swallowing an entire three-storey factory? No? Can I tell you about it?'

Now I stared at Ava and Frida and we all heard a low growl and turned. A white Staffordshire Bull Terrier with a black snout was staring out at us from behind a half-smashed greenhouse.

'He's okay,' Moth said, but didn't look convinced by his own words.

'Down, puppy,' Frida said, but the dog didn't move. 'He belongs to the caretaker. Doesn't like strangers.'

Were you meant to stand your ground against an angry dog? Or get down on the floor and act submissive? Or was that bears?

The dog's lips quivered. He barked: a short, hoarse, loud burst of noise that sent birds flying up into the sky from the trees around. What a dumb way to go this would be – attacked by a random dog while visiting a 'psychic' from the internet.

The dog crouched a little, and saliva dripped on to the dry earth.

'Sit, Merlin,' said Frida more sharply. 'Sit,' Frida said. 'This is my friend.'

Merlin whined and then sat down where he was, next to the greenhouse. Even dogs did what she told them to do.

'Sit,' she said to me then in the sunlight, and I did, like a dog. Without the veil of screens, I could see a scattering of freckles on Frida's nose and one slightly crooked tooth at the front of her mouth. Her eyes were blue but with flecks of grey I hadn't seen online or on the tube.

Frida said: 'How'd you get that scar?'

'What scar?' I said, distracted by her sharp collarbones and the very earnest line between her eyes when she frowned. Everyone watched her when she was near them.

Frida's greatest skill was noticing what other people did not.

The real answer was that I'd been on the sofa at a friend's flat and the TV control was on the floor, so I'd leaned down to get it, but my arm gave way and my cheek hit the corner of the coffee table.

Between us in the grass, a dragonfly dodged and weaved.

I shrugged.

Frida smiled at me and I felt like she knew I was lying. Her eyes were intense and I drifted for a second, with the sun on me and the dragonfly buzzing.

'You're so exceptionally beautiful,' she said. 'Do people tell you that?' She put her hand on mine and my body tingled. Ava shifted position on Frida's lap, staring up at me. I glanced at her. Her eyes narrowed but she didn't say anything.

The answer was no. Nobody had ever.

I don't remember a photo being taken but it is this moment that is captured in Oliver Sperling's photograph. A moment before anything had happened. Before I was invested, before those beautiful girls died, before Frida was famous.

Moth must have taken it. I look flirtatious, touching my turtle necklace, smiling a little.

◆ ◆ ◆

The afternoon spread out in front of us. There was lemonade at some point, and we did a crossword puzzle from an old newspaper that someone picked out of the broken greenhouse. Two down, thirteen letters: process of changing shape. Ten across, eight letters: god of the sea.

We went for a walk on the flats and I don't remember a photo being taken but it is this moment that is captured in Oliver Sperling's photograph. A moment before anything had happened. Before I was invested, before those beautiful girls died, before Frida was famous. Moth must have taken it: a group of girls bathed in summer light, white t-shirts glowing against marsh water.

I look flirtatious, touching my turtle necklace, smiling a little, no clue how that particular photo would threaten my world later.

◆ ◆ ◆

'The island won't be here in a few years,' she said. 'Just one bad storm and – poof,' she clicked her fingers, 'the seawall will spill over and it'll disappear. There's a map in the house of all the ghost islands in the world – all the islands that were discovered at some point but then never verified, or that existed but then disappeared like we're going to. Aurora, Thule, Isle of Demons, Nimrod.'

'Nimrod sounds like a playground reproach,' I said. '"You're such a nimrod."'

'*You're* a nimrod,' she said, smiling at me.

Frida had come to the island the previous year to keep her grandpa company. He wasn't well so was asleep upstairs. Before that, Frida and her mum had lived all over the place – Wales, Italy, Spain. Frida said her mum wasn't very reliable, and Frida was the only family willing to live out here. He had stage four cancer and dementia now.

Ava and Grace had grown up in a nearby town. Not Ballards End but a few towns over down the river, called Littlewick. They'd been best friends since they were six years old and had both left school after GCSEs.

Moth had also dropped out of school last year, but intended to go back and do his A levels. His father said he'd cut off his allowance if he didn't finish school. He was, objectively, very attractive. Tall and tanned with big arms. I was surprised to find myself feeling quite calm talking to him, but sort of giddy when watching Frida eating Haribo rings off her own fingers, one by one, slowly.

After about an hour of sunbathing and chatting I went in the cool, higgledy-piggledy cottage to find a toilet.

There was a low-ceilinged living room with a staircase to the left and an arch leading to the kitchen at the back. Beach detritus was scattered amongst books on shelves: rocks, empty gun cartridges, pieces of driftwood, animal skulls and bones, feathers, and replicas of Roman artifacts like little limbless sculptures. Books lay in every spare space. Piled on the floor, jammed into shelves. *Daily Life in Ancient Rome* was next to *The Walker's Guide to Outdoor Clues and Signs*. On a pile by the window there was the *RSPB Handbook of British Birds* on top of *The Mythology of the British Islands* and *The Egyptian Book of the Dead*. But also astronomy and astrophysics textbooks with long titles. There was a drawing on the wall of a cross in a circle, and a snake eating its own tail. A shark skull grinned from on top of the fireplace, next to a British Museum poster of some ancient sculpture and an old map of ancient Europe.

On the windowsill a magazine was open on a questionnaire entitled 'Are you a love addict?' Someone had started filling it in but had only got as far as the third question – there were doodles of hearts and swirls in the borders. The eyes of the 'girl in love' stock photo at the top of the page had been filled in black with biro.

I walked towards a door that must have been the toilet but felt someone staring and turned to the kitchen archway. A middle-aged woman was watching me. She had very long grey hair down to her bum. She wore a green apron that said 'No snacks before dinner' on the front but her face did not match the jaunty graphics.

'Are you staying?' she said without smiling, instead of introducing herself. She had a slight accent, perhaps Eastern European. 'I need to know for dinner.'

'Oh. Hi. Um. No. I mean, Frida invited me for the afternoon. I'm going back.'

'Well, the tide is coming up now, so if you're going you better get started.'

'Right,' I said. 'I didn't realise.'

'Well, now you do,' she said, and turned away, but then Frida appeared behind me. 'For twelve hours each day, Bay Island is cut off from the mainland.'

'Elena,' Frida said. 'This is Zoe. Zoe, Elena is the housekeeper. She's been helping me look after my grandfather.'

I felt tense at the word 'Zoe'. Like maybe she knew it wasn't really my name, although there was no logical way she could have done.

'I'm a trained hospice nurse, Frida. Not a housekeeper. I'm just kind enough to cook for you all so you don't live on baked beans.'

'I should, actually, be going, though,' I said.

'You are not okay,' Frida said to me. 'You're sleepwalking. Stay. You're not going to disturb my grandfather or anything. You can stay as long as you like.'

'I need to get home,' I said quietly. 'But thank you for having me.'

In the cool of the living room, Frida stepped towards me, close enough for me to smell her. I could feel Elena watching and I felt as if Frida was goading the nurse, although I didn't understand the boundaries that were being pushed. Either way, I felt giddy at Frida's closeness to me. That crushed-lily smell but also Ava's cinnamon lip balm and menthol cigarettes. Salt and sweat and

Haribo sweets. I even thought she might kiss me, but she said, very quietly:

'You've scrunched yourself up into a tiny version of yourself in order to get through under the radar, medicating yourself with pills and food. I can feel that erratic energy jangling around you. If you keep growing like this, all tangled, your life will be one of unhappy drudgery – computers, alcoholism, drug addiction, failed relationships. But I can give you the tools for happiness.'

Her breath was in my ear. It wasn't just Elena who was watching us now. Ava was standing at the smudgy window, eyes narrowed.

'I need to get home,' I said to Frida. Breathless at the intimacy.

'Of course,' she said, stepping away. 'Moth will take you.'

◆ ◆ ◆

The tide was already rising as we made our way over the causeway, flooding over sand and rocks. Boats bobbed in the distance as the van struggled, the wheels splashing.

'Will you make it back in time?' I asked. 'I can take a bus.'

'I'll make it just about,' he said. 'I just figured you would want to stay, or I would have taken you earlier. The stars are beautiful.'

'Whenever I see stars I feel like an acne-covered teenage boy might be about to put his arm around my shoulders and mansplain the Milky Way to me,' I said, still feeling all jangly.

'When that light started its journey, humans didn't exist,' Moth said mock-earnestly. 'Frida says an asteroid is going to skim past the Earth next week. Like, woosh, the galaxy equivalent of an inch away from us. Wouldn't that be cool?' He made a *woosh* motion with one hand, then mimed an explosion with his fingers. 'Did you know asteroids skim close to the Earth all the time?'

'Do you really think she's psychic?' I said.

'I know she is.'

'That's ridiculous.'

'Millions of asteroids hurtling towards us and we're just sitting here twiddling our thumbs.'

'Does anyone actually twiddle their thumbs though?' I said, keen to get out of the van now. Bunch of weirdos. 'Why are you staying on the island?'

'Why not? She invited us and it's beautiful,' he said.

'Her grandfather doesn't mind? Elena didn't seem very friendly.'

'Elena disapproves of Frida having friends over while her grandfather is dying upstairs, but what is Frida supposed to do? She can't leave, because he's going to die any day. She wants to be there for him, but she'd go out of her mind with boredom if she didn't have people to talk to.'

'How did you meet her?'

'I was in rehab nearby. Heroin,' he said, but then added quickly: 'Totally clean now, thanks to Frida. I've been to rehab three times but this is the longest I've ever been clean. There was a flyer on the pinboard of the facility with her URL. I started chatting to her online from my room, and she invited me to hang out after I got out. I'd never stayed clean after leaving rehab before, but now I've been clean six months.'

Moth's spiral sun tattoo on his right arm was in fact masking track marks, I could see now.

I'd had a sort of boyfriend at school for a bit, when I was fifteen. He was a spotty, gangly boy who was on the school chess team with me. Mum had flirted with him the only time I brought him home. She got out photo albums of her looking super-hot and me looking fat. My relationship sort of dwindled after that, although it probably would have done anyway.

Just before I got out of the car, Moth cocked his head to the side and said: 'You remind me of Velma in *Scooby-Doo*. The one who wore a polo neck whatever the weather.'

'You remind me of one of the Stone Giants from *The Hobbit*,' I replied.

'That's just the sort of thing that Velma in *Scooby-Doo* would say.'

'It was a weird experience,' I said. 'But thank you for having me.'

'Frida liked you,' he said, and I got out of the car. 'She doesn't like everyone. You should come hang out for longer sometime.'

I laughed. 'No, I'm good, but thanks.'

◆ ◆ ◆

Like others who have entered Frida's orbit since, in many ways I had already disappeared before I met her. I didn't recognise my morose face in photographs. I was so stoned on benzos I barely remembered my days. I didn't play the piano anymore, or laugh much. I hadn't meant to watch an internet psychic, didn't consider myself 'that sort of person'. She was a drug, a sugar lump, a like on an Instagram post, a dopamine surge.

Frida peroxided Ava's roots on a chair in the garden while they listened to pop music on the radio. She tore bits of silver foil from a roll, painting the dye on with a paint brush.

'Will we marry?' someone wrote in the comments on AuraLine. 'How can I learn from my mistakes if he won't tell me what I did wrong or why he left?' 'What hair dye do you use pls share?'

I wondered if Frida was on Instagram but couldn't find her there.

'I loved making jam in the holidays as a child,' Frida said to the camera. 'We lived on a farm for a while. I would pick buckets and buckets of blackberries from bushes and stand on a chair to stir them down with sugar and gelatine. We'd pour the mixture into sterilised jars, wincing as flecks of scalding sugar hit our skin.

I loved the sight of them all lined up, smug as doctors, on the windowsill.'

Roger had proposed to Mum on holiday. I'd received a whole load of text message emoticons from her. I was to be a bridesmaid. She was thinking hot-pink satin dresses.

On the news, pictures of beaches full of girls in bikinis were replaced by more sombre heatwave stories.

'As a crime wave grips the capital,' said a headline, 'a new video shows how FOUR hero bystanders tackled Regent Street moped gang – including a fearless delivery man who came out swinging with his TROLLEY.'

'Mother launches racist tirade against Asian woman on London Underground, after the victim asked her daughter to give up a seat', read another headline.

'Giant 280 ft asteroid will skim past Earth TOMORROW in close flyby travelling at 30,420 miles per hour,' said the news on my phone. 'The asteroid, dubbed 2013 MD8, is expected to skim past Earth at just over 3 million miles away, or about 13 times the distance between Earth and the moon, at 12:55pm (ET) on Tuesday. The huge space rock is expected to make a "close approach" to Earth, but its trajectory should see it soar safely by.'

This was happening, just as Frida had predicted, although I wasn't impressed. Presumably it had been in the press or on social media.

I walked home from work through Camden, where smokers and drinkers were perched under street lights, tearing into kebabs and polystyrene boxes of chips that would never biodegrade, throwing greasy meat into gutters for the rats, laughing. It started to drizzle, and then the hot, fuzzy rain turned into a downpour that sent pedestrians scuttling for cover. Puddles immediately built up around the edges of the streets. A woman in a tight dress ran under a bus stop shelter. She was maybe forty, and even from the other side of the road I could tell she was wearing Spanx. Her leather jacket looked new. She had obviously tried really hard when getting dressed for this evening but now she was all frizzy and melty. As the bus curled towards the pavement, a wave of puddle water looped up over the kerb and drenched her shoes. She stared at the ground, crestfallen. I thought she was going to cry and found the back of my throat aching in solidarity. Tears pricked my eyes. I slipped a Klonopin on to my tongue to quieten the noise of the world.

I watched Frida that week even though I told myself I wouldn't. I took Klonopin even though I said I was going to stop. She ought to be on Instagram. She'd kill on Instagram, with her perky breasts and weird chat.

Sometimes she turned over Tarot cards on her bed. 'The sun shines light on deceit and reveals the truth. Any problems you have been experiencing will melt away with the warmth this card brings.'

Or sometimes she led meditations on camera. 'Clench your jaw and press your tongue to the roof of your mouth,' Frida might say, eyes closed, legs crossed. 'Release, enjoy the relaxed reaction, and go completely limp.'

A lot of it sounded like she'd taken scripts off the internet.

'Hey Zoe,' she said one day when I logged on to AuraLine with my handle, Guest72. 'How's your heatwave going? Want to do a crossword with me?'

'I almost want to go to work just because they have air conditioning,' I wrote. I took one pill, then another.

'You don't go to school?'

'I dropped out.'

'Where do you work?' Frida said.

'A social media advertising company,' I wrote. I didn't say I was a receptionist. 'Lots of women in kitten heels and tan tights. You should be on social media.'

'Tan tights are abhorrent,' she said.

'Every time I see them I think of robbers putting tights over their faces to rob corner shops.'

'Do robbers actually do that? Why would a robber have the hosiery of a middle-class PR woman to hand rather than, say, a balaclava?'

'Does it distort your face? I'm going to try.'

'Oh, so you own tan stockings? Do you wear them to work? Be honest.'

'My mum owns some. Wait a second.' I didn't really go and put a stocking over my head but wrote: 'It's very slimming. Like an early prototype of a filter that blurs away imperfections.'

She laughed on screen.

'Is anyone else watching you right now?' I wrote.

'Couple,' she said. 'Why? You want me to put hosiery over my head? It would not be the weirdest thing someone has asked me to do on here.'

'What's the weirdest?'

'What you would think was weird is just, like, Tuesday on here.' She paused. 'Maybe you can help with this clue. Synonym for "naughty", nine letters, but "debauched" doesn't fit.'

'Audacious?' I wrote. 'Childlike?'

'Nope.'

'Dissolute?'

'Yes.' She looked at the corner of her screen. 'Someone wants to chat so I'd better go,' Frida said. 'But that clue has been sending me crazy, so thanks.'

'Why aren't you on social media?' I typed.

'Social media fuels anxiety,' she said. 'It's not healthy. It's a horrible place.'

'Well yeah, sure. It's full of anxious people. Just like the Northern line, but your message could spread a lot faster on Instagram than it does on the Tube. And on Instagram people are trying to connect.'

She shrugged. 'Better go,' she said.

I sent a waving emoji and the screen went black.

◆ ◆ ◆

'I was all elbows and bones then,' Frida said later online, playing with bits of sea glass. 'Sun-damaged and combustible, surrounded – always – by choirs of grotesque animal children. I have always had the gift. We, the empaths, have been misunderstood through history.'

Four people were watching her. Sometimes it was just one or two. She had this gothic quality but she was so blonde, her clothes always so white.

What did any of that mean? All elbows and bones suggested a gawky, skinny child perhaps. Sun-damaged and combustible, fine. A bit florid, but fine. But surrounded by choirs of grotesque animal children? Did that mean anything at all?

◆ ◆ ◆

The night before I went back to the island I signed in to AuraLine on my phone before falling asleep. Frida had her eyes closed in front of the computer while she was streaming; you could just see her curled hand and the top of her head on the pillow. She had glittery make-up on and flowers in her hair. She was snoring. Not prettily. Like proper, sinusy snores that made me smile. The next day I woke up to a text from Mum.

'Lots to talk about!!! Can we have dinner when we get back from hols and discuss some things?'

I reread the message a few times. They were going to ask me to move out, for sure. That's what 'some things' would turn out to be.

I imagined Mum lounging on a sofa or deckchair, tanned and luminous, painting her toenails pink. Roger would have a niece or an intern or someone who was looking for another housemate in Walthamstow or Nunhead. They might offer to help with my rent for a few weeks. They wouldn't have factored in that at seventeen I didn't even get paid London minimum wage. They certainly wouldn't have factored in my Klonopin habit.

Sometimes when speaking to my mum, my brain would flick on to memories of possessions and television shows from childhood: a cartoon about a talking frog at dinnertime, an American sitcom about a modern Alice in Wonderland who spent her time in malls and at school discos. Trainers with sparkles. An iPhone cover with a hologram of a dragon. My mother's glittery shoes and Slimming World cookbooks.

My brain was so miserably loaded with the world's anxiety before Frida that, even if I knew what I know now, I might still have walked headlong into the wash. I needed to be soaped down; my brain was filthy. I wanted it filled with something better. Cleaner. Calmer.

I picked up a week's supply of Klonopin on my way to work that day. I sat at my desk surrounded by people and their computers and phones, scrolling, blearily optimising their social media traffic, pushing observations or jokes out into the digital ether, chewing sushi, being funny to their small online audiences. In the afternoon I went to pick up coffee and snacks for a client meeting back at the office. While waiting, I signed in to AuraLine, and on the camera Frida was all in white, standing still under the clock of Waterloo station, handing out leaflets while a commuting mire of grey and beige passed by on every side of her. She smiled at people eagerly as they walked straight past her.

I thought about Mum and Roger asking me to move out. Instead of taking the snacks to the office, I went to Waterloo. It was busy with suburban commuters heading home for the weekend. Frida was no longer under the clock and the camera wasn't live now, so it took me half an hour to find her in Boots trying on a bright red lipstick, peering at her distorted reflection in those plastic mirrors that line make-up shelves. I watched her, unsure of my intentions, then stepped closer.

The colour she was holding was called 'Tiger Sun'. In the little mirror I could only see myself in portions: an eye, a curved lip. Mum had taught me how to apply lipstick then blot my lips with loo roll. I felt an urge to tell Frida how when I was a kid I used to find Mum's bright red loo roll kisses in the bathroom after she went out, and I'd store them in a shoebox because it seemed impossible to throw away kisses. Later Mum started wearing a more muted colour, or perhaps she started putting her kisses down the toilet. She stopped wearing bright lipstick when she met Roger, along with sequins and glitter. I've never worn any; it makes my lips feel sticky.

'Does this eyeshadow suit me?' Frida said, wearing a terrible shimmery blue over her bright eyes.

'You look like a psychic,' I said. 'A bad one.'

She laughed, and I was pleased to have made her laugh.

'Come stay for the weekend, or longer, whatever,' she said, talking over her shoulder. 'London is no place for a heatwave.'

'Won't your grandfather mind you inviting randomers you barely know?'

'Not at all,' she said. 'He doesn't think much of anything anymore. He's dying and I could use the company. And Elena is a sweetheart really, and a good cook. So come, honest.'

Moth drove the van round from wherever he'd parked it and picked us up outside the station. The drive out of London that early May afternoon was the gap between scenes – the bustle while furniture and backdrops were swapped. Then the lights came on again, just a moment later, and everything was different.

Chapter Three

My heart is beating fast and my mouth is dry when I leave Oliver on the cliffs. He wants me to go on record telling my side of the story, before it breaks that the missing girls died while living with Frida. I've told him I need to think. For a moment I can feel the panic of the day I escaped Frida, my feet pulsing over the sand towards the water in the dark. Chest aching, salt air thick on my tongue. How I looked back at the house in the dark and saw a curtain twitch, knowing she was watching.

I don't go home after seeing him, in case he follows me, but head to the glass-fronted public library next to the train station. The computers are at the back, far from the windows, and I walk towards them through the aisles of books. I used to bring my laptop here every day to work before I moved in with Ben.

My footsteps are muffled by the worn carpet. People are turning pages, clicking keyboards, whispering. A baby in the kids' section starts to grizzle and I sit down in the furthest corner of the space, in front of one of five computers. The air smells of book dust and air freshener.

I look up Oliver Sperling online. In his LinkedIn profile photo he is much younger and more handsome than now. He studied Film and Media Studies at the University of Chester. He began his career working for a cycling magazine while trying to be a professional cyclist. Then he went on to work for, and later edit, a health and wellness magazine called *WholeLife*, which became digital only under his leadership. 'Strength Training for All Ages'. 'The Best Wearable Devices to Track Your Fitness'. 'How to Build a Healthy Work–Life Balance'. He stopped working for *WholeLife* a year ago.

Frida's face was on the digital cover page of the *WholeLife* website four years ago.

'Stylishly Spiritual', reads the headline. 'Inside the Minds of the Influencers Revolutionising Spirituality.' There is a photograph of Frida, airbrushed and divine, up on a stage.

'This new spiritual elite is not confined to a particular location or segment of society like gurus of the past,' says his article. 'Instead, their church is social media and their influence transcends race, economics and politics. This new spiritual community is right there in your bedroom, your commute, just a click away at any moment.'

The article was syndicated by bigger publications, and Oliver then wrote another article in the *Mail* about how big businesses were hiring spiritual gurus to train their workforce in transcendental meditation, and one about how a Norwegian princess hired Frida to officiate at her wedding. His fourth on Frida was a puff piece about her charity, GreenProject, an organisation dedicated to environmental protection and sustainability.

I scroll back on his Twitter and Instagram feeds. He was into Frida. He reposted plenty of her inspirational quotes, and he ran a marathon to raise money for GreenProject. There are photos he took at one of her seminars – a 'Shadow Work Course' location stamped at the Tobacco Dock in East London. Under all his positive mentions of Frida there are encouraging comments: fire emojis, thumbs-up, agreement, reposts or retweets.

Then, three years ago, the tone changes dramatically.

'Feminism wants equality, but only when it benefits women,' says one of his posts on Instagram. 'Men are hated yet expected to be the providers and protectors. #MensRights #EqualityForAll'.

Another post is words on a black background: 'They say men are toxic, but you do not want a nice man. Stop hating men for being men. #Misandry #ToxicMasculinityMyth'.

There's a handful of question marks and negativity in the comments. Then he's posted a screenshot of Frida with the words: 'These online spiritual gurus like @fridarae are breaking up families and ruining lives but nobody will publish my article about her because she gives money to eco charities #brainwashing #notrust #cult #wokeisbroke'. And there's another screenshot of Frida: 'The #FridaRaeAcademy is a #cult'.

She hated that word.

◆ ◆ ◆

My first night on the island, as the causeway disappeared behind us, Grace showed me to a small and cluttered room with a single bed that smelled as though the sheets had not been changed in a while. There was a pink sink in the room, and piles of boxes.

'This was Ava's room for a bit. She didn't sleep in it much though, if you know what I mean. But she and Frida broke up so she's gone now,' Grace said sadly. The air still smelled of menthol cigarettes. I felt awkward taking the room.

Outside the window, Frida and Elena were arguing in the garden. Elena motioned up to the house. To me, presumably, and I slipped away from the window.

'Elena is annoyed I came back,' I said.

'Just offer to help in the garden,' Grace said. 'Praise her cooking, offer to take a tray up to Jackson, let her tell you about homeopathy. You'll be in her good books soon enough. But Elena is bonkers about Frida really, so it's fine.'

'Was it a bad break-up? Frida and Ava?'

'I don't know. I guess so. She just upped and left. I'm sort of pissed she didn't say goodbye. We came here together. We've been best friends since we were kids. Frida won't talk about it, so I guess it must have been a bad break-up. But Ava's like that, she's always been flighty. She used to run away from her foster homes so often that they stopped looking for her.'

'When did you get together with Moth?'

'Ava and I met Frida when we were on holiday. Like, two months or so ago maybe? There's a caravan park at Jaywick, just down the river. She and Moth went there to play some of the arcades or get fish and chips sometimes. Frida brought Tarot cards and did readings at the fair for a fiver, that sort of thing. We all just started hanging out. Ava and I worked at Topshop but she got fired for shoplifting, and Frida asked her to move in so I came too. He came here in January, I think.'

Grace helped set me up with the internet password and then left me alone. Ava's cinnamon lip balm was in a drawer next to the bed along with a lighter, a tampon wrapper, a nail file, and a stud earring that I spun in my fingers to see little flecks of skin trapped in the butterfly. The sheets smelled of her.

A pair of navy-blue John Lewis school shoes were sticking out from under the bed with stickers inside that said 'Ava Wright'. Her footprint was still pressed into the soles. I googled her name on my phone. There were LinkedIn accounts for account managers and lawyers that were not her. There was a philosophy professor on a faculty website, a gardening enthusiast from Arizona, and a woman who ran a Persian rug business. Only midway down page three of the search did a post come up on a Missing Persons Facebook page, but it was from five years previously.

I opened up the link to a photo of a younger, plumper version of Ava. 'Concern is growing for 12-year-old Avaline Wright, known to friends and family as Ava, who has been missing for three days from her foster placement. Police believe that Ava (pictured) may be living with friends in Chelmsford and have appealed for anyone with information about her to contact them. Ava is 5ft 2in tall and medium build with long dark hair.' This had been shared nine times, and there were four comments. The first: 'mate she doesn't want you to find her she always comes back don't she.' The second: 'she'll be over at the farm, right? Saw a bunch of them down there last week messing it up.' The third: 'will keep a look out.' The fourth comment was a link to a newspaper article announcing her return: 'Missing local girl Ava Wright has been found safe and well, police confirm. The Essex police issued an urgent appeal to trace the 12-year-old girl earlier this week after she left her home at about 4pm on Sunday. In a statement today the police said: "Ava Wright has been found by police at a music festival in Kent. She is now home and safe. We thank everyone who has supported the appeal. We are very grateful for your help."'

A tree in the garden outside rubbed its branches against the walls and made a sound like fingernails rapping a door. Merlin barked desperately. It was too hot with the window closed, but with the window open the room was full of the alien sounds of seagulls and water, so I kept it closed. Pipes in the house clanked.

I listened to the floorboards and doors, the sound of Moth and Grace laughing next door. The creak, creak, creak of the bed, and more laughing, and then faster creaking ending in sudden silence. Then a toilet flushing, taps running, doors closing, pipes groaning, and then when the house fell silent the only sound left was a low wet heartbeat, coming from somewhere through the walls or ceiling, I couldn't quite tell. Like a dragon asleep somewhere nearby. I closed my eyes but my mind had snagged on the noise and couldn't let it go.

Reluctantly I climbed out of bed and opened my door to step into the corridor, hoping that a different angle on the noise would make its origin clear. The rest of the house was quiet but it still had this thud, thud, thudding heartbeat. I ran my fingers over the embossed wallpaper and stepped down the hallway on the edges of the floorboards so they didn't creak so much, then stood at the top of the stairs.

I held my breath. I wanted to find the source of the noise, but then I felt a movement behind me so turned, expecting to see Elena, but there was nobody there. A pipe creaked in the house and I jumped, running back into my room, jamming a chair up under the door handle and leaping into bed.

Thump, thump, thump went the house, until I took a Klonopin. I put the half-full bottle next to my bed.

◆ ◆ ◆

The next morning, the Klonopin bottle wasn't there next to my bed. Figuring I must have left it in my rucksack, I walked over to where the bag sat on the floor by the window.

It wasn't so hot anymore, and the velvet curtain was shifting in a slight breeze. I pulled the curtain – I'd apparently opened the window at some point in the night although I didn't remember doing so. My room looked out on the salt flats and it was breathtaking: low tide, sun rising on the water and reflecting against puddles that looked like a giant smashed mirror. Wader birds that I couldn't yet name searched the newly exposed mud. You couldn't quite tell where the island ended and the sea began. It was neither land nor sea, but somewhere in between.

On the opposite side of the riverbank there were fields, and then further down in the direction of the sea the power plant chimneys raised their fingers to the sky.

I rummaged in my bag with rising anxiety but my pills weren't there. It was almost a brand-new pack and I'd put it by the bed last night, I was certain of it. I looked on the floor, under the bed, in the covers, then thought about Moth. He was an addict, and must have taken them. Panic began to bubble under my skin and my fingernails dug half-moons into my palm. I saw Frida walking away from the house into a cluster of trees in the middle of the island.

I paused outside Moth and Grace's bedroom, considered confronting him directly, but instead I ran down the stairs and out of the house in the direction that she'd gone. He might be dangerous for all I knew, so I decided to ask Frida first. It was difficult walking terrain, with clumps of marsh weed with ankle-breaking holes covered in foliage between them. A stream occasionally came from nowhere and gurgled over rocks like a snake with somewhere important to go. I could see her in the distance on the other side of the island. There was no breeze and the boat masts in the distance were still. A slight smell of sewage hung in the air, and as I got to the edge of the island a nappy was washing up repeatedly in the tide against a yoghurt pot and a beer can. 'DANGER!' a sign said, chained to a buoy currently moored in the sand. 'CHECK THE TIDES!'

She was standing amongst some derelict caravans.

'Moth took my pills,' I said, stomping over towards her. 'I take medication for my anxiety and it was next to my bed last night but now it's gone. Can you get him to give it back, please?'

The caravan next to her had smashed windows and mouldy curtains flapping out, weeds and vines and nettles growing up the metal walls. There was wet pink bunting hung on the inside, and stained cushion covers.

'Grandpa used to run a caravan site on the island,' Frida said. 'It was really cool, way bigger than this. He owned a whole bunch of caravan sites. He used to own the one where I met Grace and Ava.' She paused. 'She left. I guess you know that.'

'They're doctor-prescribed, I need them,' I said.

'Moth wouldn't do that. Shall I help you look for them?'

'I know where I left them and they're not there.'

We walked past a sweet little caravan at the edge of the more derelict ones. It was the furthest caravan from the main house, surrounded by painted wood and bits of boat found on the beaches. A red pickup truck was parked outside. There was a boat full of flowers in the garden; a scarecrow decorated with broken flip-flops and marine rope. On the door was a deflated white football creased into the shape of a creepy smile, to which someone had glued bottle-top eyes and a tangle of fishing-net hair.

It had a garden of roses and herbs behind a miniature white picket fence. Merlin glanced up lazily as we passed, licking his paws.

'That's Stefan's caravan. The groundsman.'

Frida looked at the seagulls hawking and swooping above, fighting over a crisp, a chip – something stolen.

'Is a group of birds called a flock?' she said.

'Or a colony, a fleet, a parcel,' I said. 'A group of crows is a murder, fittingly. Jays are a party. Or a scold. I really need my pills, Frida. Can you ask him to give them back?'

'Geek. What's a group of teenagers?' she said.

'A grunt,' I said. 'Pills. Please, Frida, I need them.'

'Did you make that up? A grunt?'

'No. It's an internet thing,' I said, stepping over a small stream. 'Inventing collective nouns.'

'An "internet thing" is memes about cats and gritty porn, not collective nouns.'

'A group of joggers are a wheeze. Tourists are a flock. You obviously don't spend much time on Reddit. Please just get me my fucking pills. He can't have taken them all.'

'Teenagers ought to be a gaggle,' she said. 'No, that's not right.'

'Fuck. Pills. Frida.'

'Tell me what a group of teenagers should be and we'll go find your pills.'

'A flamboyance?' I said.

'Look. He didn't take your pills, I'm sure of it. Let's go back to the house and look for them before you start throwing around accusations.'

'I'm not an addict. My pills are prescribed.'

'You're very much addicted. I assume you don't get them from an actual doctor?'

'I used to,' I said.

'This is Bay Forest,' Frida said, changing the subject as we walked under the canopy of trees. 'Small from the outside but you'll find it's strangely easy to get lost in here.'

Birds rustled in the trees. The island was a conspiracy of noises: cracks and shrieks and rustles. Then my phone beeped and I took it out. Mum had sent me a photo.

'No,' Frida said, looking over my shoulder at the phone. 'Just no. What is that?'

'I'm a bridesmaid,' I said, then kept walking fast. She jumped to catch up with me, and walked by my side.

'Oh shit.'

'Yeah.'

'Can I come?'

'To the wedding?'

'I'd like to see you in that outfit. Dance to whatever people dance to at weddings – absolutely this wedding will have a fantastically bad cover band. The bride obviously doesn't like you much.'

I walked faster, horrified that tears sprang into my eyes at that comment.

'Sorry,' she said. 'Whose wedding is it?'

'No, it's nothing. I have sand in my eye.'

'Your mother,' she said, keeping pace. Over roots and under branches. We were nearly at the house now. 'I'm sorry, of course she loves you, she just has awful taste in clothes.' Frida laughed. 'It's nice to have you here. Let's go find your pills.'

I managed not to cry, feeling ridiculous, and we continued past an oak tree with gnarled roots above ground and an enormously wide trunk. There was a beech tree that looked like one tree had dived into another and become tangled with its bottom sticking out. There were fallen branches, and desperate tangled vines trying to sip sunlight from the top of hollowed-out trunks. You could see roots of different trees connected under the ground like lovers with their fingers intertwined.

That was the first time I saw what we later called the 'fairy arch', a mossy and contorted trunk that grew up for about five and a half feet before changing course – a storm maybe, or just a sudden loss of ambition. Then it had started growing down again in a slow swoop. At the top the bark was split at the sharpest bit of the bend.

'Don't walk under that,' she said. 'If you find a tree bent into an arch in the forest, it's a door to another dimension.'

'Yeah?' I said. 'Sounds kind of appealing right now. Maybe in other dimensions my mother has better taste in dresses.'

'If you go under a tree arch you'll come out in a parallel dimension, but you can't really tell because it's all just only slightly off, and anyway, she might have worse taste. So don't walk through.' She smiled, half joking.

'Got it,' I said, but put my hands through, then back again. 'Pills, Frida. I need them.'

◆ ◆ ◆

My pills had rolled under the bed. She pulled them out along with a crisp packet and a woollen bobble hat. I swore they hadn't been under the bed earlier, and she just shrugged. I felt embarrassed. We listened to the thud, thud, thud noise in the room above.

'My grandfather's breathing machine. I'll introduce you to him later. He's not very well at all so don't expect scintillating conversation. Come down and meditate with us first?'

'I don't really buy into that sort of thing,' I said.

'Nobody is asking for a *buy-in*,' she said. 'What even is a buy-in? Meditation is scientifically proven to reduce anxiety, sharpen attention and increase resiliency to stress. You have nothing whatsoever to lose by having a go. Take a stupid pill if you need to, but come and meditate with me.'

Ten minutes later I sat, super-awkwardly, on the itchy grass, focusing on relaxing the various body parts as Frida instructed, and imagining walking through clouds or whatever while keeping my mind blank – but memories and thoughts immediately surfaced unbidden and made me flinch. She told me my arms would float but they didn't. I slipped my second Klonopin of the day on my tongue while they all had their eyes closed. She told me my breathing would regulate but it didn't. Instead: social faux pas from years ago, the faces of people I couldn't remember the names of, mean things someone had once said. Frida said some stuff about light and breathing and I thought about the time a friend and I got drunk on alcopops and I farted on the N11 bus and she then got such hysterical giggles that she peed a little bit. Her name was Mei Lan and she was also on the school chess team and also enjoyed a good chat about natural disasters. But a few weeks after the alcopop incident she got a boyfriend and barely spoke to me again. My understanding was that boys liked talking about apocalypse situations more than girls – but boys did not like kissing girls who liked talking about apocalypse events. I still liked her Instagram posts but we never texted or DMed anymore.

I hardly listened to what Frida was saying as she continued. At some point I just opened my eyes and looked at them all. Moth's heavy face and enormous shoulders, still as a boulder. Elena, the nurse, with a dreamcatcher necklace hanging between her wrinkly breasts and long grey hair. Frida in a white t-shirt and bicycle shorts, her bikini visible under her t-shirt, her hair messy around her pretty face. Grace, just in a bikini, one of her bikini straps flopped down to reveal a pale line of winter skin. How was her bikini line so tidy and hairless when mine was either razor-pocked or stubbly and certainly in no fit state for cross-legged bikini-wearing? Why did she shave her pubic hair but not her legs or under her arms? What was the guiding philosophy for her hair growth?

Grace opened her eyes and saw me staring and I blushed, then I walked off to look around the island on my own but felt tired so just sat down under a tree and scrolled on my phone for a bit. I guess I fell asleep because I had a Klonopin dream that my toenails were growing down into the earth like roots and my skin was solidifying into wood, my arms twisting up into the sky. Frida was licking my neck and I felt thirsty, hot, and achy at the back of my throat. A tongue in the palm of my hand. A salty taste of saliva and brine.

'Hey Zo,' came a muffled voice and I opened my eyes to see Frida next to me. I dug my elbows down and pushed my torso up and my legs were bright red. It took me a second to realise 'Zo' was me.

She bent down and put her fingers underneath my chin, proprietorially, as if assessing the worth of a small object.

'The sun moved and you're sunburnt,' she said.

She helped me back into the house. Elena tutted when she saw me and ran a cold bath upstairs. Elena gave Moth and Grace instructions for some concoction to be brewed downstairs while she helped peel my sweaty t-shirt off my body. I felt like a lobster in a pot.

'Let's put some apple cider vinegar in the bath,' Elena said, with Frida standing in the doorway. I could hear my blood pumping and the water lapping at the porcelain tub. A line of ants crawled up the tiled walls into a rotten hole in the far corner of the avocado-tiled bathroom. I didn't want Frida to see me naked.

One time when I went on holiday to Malta with mum aged thirteen or so, I'd got so sunburnt on the first day that I spent the majority of the holiday in the hotel room. I remembered waking up in the night once and realising I hadn't seen her since the previous morning. She'd met some guy.

Frida's blue eyes looked grey in this light. Her smell was intense. I looked at the veins of her wrists, slightly upturned. Purple lines beating blood under her skin.

A tap dripped. I closed my eyes.

Frida put her hands over me like I'd seen her doing to the others during yoga. I didn't feel anything except a strong desire for them all to go away so I could go to my bag and take another Klonopin.

Everyone used to think Mum was my nanny, growing up, partly because she was young but also because we have totally different colouring. Mum was seventeen when she got pregnant. She said it was a one-night thing and she didn't realise she was pregnant until six months after, by which point she had no idea how to contact him. She didn't realise she was pregnant till 'too late' – like missing an eBay auction by a few minutes. She'd felt sick on and off but thought she had food poisoning. She did not feel my heart knit together inside her, the tumble and flutter of toenails and eyelashes forming under her skin. She'd thought she had indigestion, and nobody guessed because she didn't put on an ounce of weight until the end. My mum had the sort of beauty – the bone structure, the lost expression, the gaiety at the back of her eyes – that meant she got seated at the windows of restaurants, and EasyJet employees let her get away with excess baggage. I was born in a hallway in the Royal Free, where Mum abruptly pulled down her leggings and got on all fours to push while the nurses told her she had to wait for a bed to become available, and she told them to fuck off. I fell out of her apparently, the cord still wrapped around my puckered neck for a moment till the nurses could scramble into position. She did not write a father's name down on my birth certificate because she could not remember it.

If I were to guess, and obviously I did a fair bit of guessing growing up, my father was of Asian heritage, with bad eyesight and a less-than-ideal metabolism. I certainly didn't inherit any of these things from my slim blonde mother with 20/20 vision.

'You have rage coiled inside you, Zo,' Frida said to me. 'This knot of despair and loneliness that is escaping in panic attacks and depression but urgently needs to be dealt with, otherwise it will turn into aches and cancers and more bad decisions. You need to address this or you are going to implode.'

'Maybe later,' I said, trying and failing to be funny. 'I have pretty bad sunburn right now and I'm naked in a cold bath with a fake internet psychic staring at me.'

'If you let me, I can heal you.'

'No thanks,' I said. 'I'm busy. I need to get back to London actually, it was dumb to come here. I have a job and I need to find a place to live. You guys are kind of weird.'

'You need help,' Frida said. 'I don't know how you got like this but whatever you're going back to in London is not helping you.'

'Can you leave so I can get out the bath on my own?' I said to them.

They left and I got up and reached for the pills in the back pocket of my shorts, but – again – the packet wasn't where I had left it. Back in my room I looked in drawers, under the bed, under the mattress, anywhere I might have put the packet. My blood started to pump fast as I pulled my t-shirt and knickers on and walked into Moth and Grace's room.

I dragged the sheets off their bed and opened all his drawers, then lifted up the mattress to look underneath. There was dust and sweet wrappers and mouse droppings but no pills. I could hear the sound of my blood and it felt as if the edges were unravelling around me now. One of Moth's sketchbooks fell to the floor on a drawing of Frida's face. Then the door opened behind me and I jumped.

'Where are my pills?' I said, turning as Moth appeared there. 'I don't care that you took them but I need them. I can't breathe.'

'I haven't taken your pills,' he said, picking up the sketchbook and putting it away.

'I flushed them this time,' Frida said from the corridor.

'They're prescribed. I have an anxiety condition.'

'You are conditioned to have anxiety,' she said. 'You don't need chemicals. They don't even stop you from having panic attacks. You wanted me to do this for you. It's why you're here. Because you are broken and need fixing, but you can't do it on your own. Your mother should be doing this but she's not, so we are. You asked me to do this.'

'I absolutely did not.'

'People always say what they need, if you know how to read between the lines. You were expecting me to take your pills, and you were disappointed when I didn't.'

'That's ridiculous. Give them back,' I tried to say, but the words caught in my mouth and I knew the panic attack was about to start. It rose like a creature was going to force itself out of my throat. 'Fuck off,' I managed, but quietly, scared now, as my chest tightened and my heart gained pace.

'You think the pills are solving your fears but they're just masking them. The fears are growing inside you every day, spilling over in strange ways. You need to face your fears. You need to be strong but you don't need to do it alone. We are here for you.'

My hands were shaking, skin sweating, the world was spinning apart like pixels dropping out of a computer image. I was falling into a familiar terror. The terror led down into a spiral of breathless panic that had become almost like a physical place to me over the years. I heard wings flapping, a clawing like mice feet under the floorboards, and blood in my ears. It was the panic of your mother leaving you in the darkness as a baby; of quicksand, endings and disconnection.

◆ ◆ ◆

I woke up in the dark later. My skin and muscles hurt in odd places. Post-panic attack is a particular type of exhaustion.

It was extravagant weather. Hedgehogs bustled across the garden, foxes tiptoed in the busy darkness. Thump, thump, thump went the beat of Jackson's breathing machine.

I fell back to sleep quickly but slept fitfully. I woke up often, sweaty. Or dreamed of waking up. Sticky dreams of Frida standing over me with her hands near but not touching me. Frida didn't ask me to leave.

The next morning I sat up in bed and pressed my thumb into my knees, stretched the skin of my inner thighs in the rising sunlight. I walked to the frosted-edge mirror and looked at my tanned, unblistered skin. I raised my arms and my breasts lifted up. I have a mole on my right armpit. I have another on my pubic line. I have the scar on my right eyebrow that Frida noticed the first day. On my left pinkie toe there's one from a smashed bottle, shiny white in the shape of a hook.

I wasn't sunburnt anymore. My hands were shaking. I threw up in the sink and then crawled back into bed.

◆ ◆ ◆

'The sea gives and the sea takes away,' she said on AuraLine as I watched on my phone in bed. We were in the same house, yet the screen seemed more intimate. 'The first time I drowned I was just four years old, on the cusp between babyhood and childhood. Our worlds are layered and we are all connected. I will save you all.'

Chapter Four

I sit in that hot library for hours after talking to Oliver, too jittery to go home. I reread the article Oliver showed me, but no others have come out about the girls. I look at Frida's socials. Her Instagram profile photo is a professional headshot of her in her white t-shirt. Her face is symmetrical, her teeth white, hair glossy, eyes sparkling.

'Being well adjusted to a depraved society is not a marker of sanity,' Frida says on the library computer, and I lean in to listen so nobody else needs to hear. A homeless man comes and sits at the computer opposite me, smelling of beer. Frida wears a Shanghai Tang-branded collared white t-shirt. A Lancaster watch, Bulgari earrings. I know this because the brands are all tagged. 'Maybe hysteria makes the most sense, in this burning world?'

There are thousands of comments underneath, full of fire emojis and adoration. I start to flick through the pages of her grid: photos of her standing in water with groups of attractive women all wearing white (#bali #selflove #gogirls). Bikini photos. Dancing photos. Waterfall photos. Meditation photos. Videos of the new sauna at the LA retreat, and inspirational text over photographs of Frida looking hot. Five signs of burnout. How to embody your feminine power. The importance of ritual in a secular world.

It looks inviting. There are free online courses in accessing your magic, and finding authenticity, along with competitions to win access to her online and in-person events. On her website there is no mention of money at all, just a photo of her meditating on a beach. 'Join us at one of our three retreats, or on one of our online seminars, to begin your journey and awaken your inner light.' There are also posts about GreenProject, and GoFundMe links.

In the first few years after leaving her, I used to look at her social media, watching her growth and her tactics. She was a drug. I'd give myself little rewards for not looking at her – for a day, a week, a year – but I would fail. I would find my fingers itching to open the little box into her world, aching to know what she was up to. I stopped properly when I met Ben and knew I had to cut away that part of myself entirely.

We think that we control what we look at on social media, but it controls us. These complex algorithms analyse our behaviour – the posts we interact with, share, or linger on – then predict what we're most interested in. And it preys on the tired moments. The weak moments. It knows the subliminal version of our identities, not the version that we present to the world. It knows what we *really* want.

I shiver and look up. More people have turned up in the library while I've been sifting through all this online information. A teenager glances towards me, although he may be looking at the homeless guy who is now asleep on his arms at the computer. I slip down lower in my chair.

So Oliver wants me to go on record talking about that summer. And in return, what? He won't use my name? My photo? Do I trust him?

The glass front of the library gives it a greenhouse effect, and people are sweating. A group of nannies and mothers walk through the door, bringing a smell of milk and nappies. Soon babies are clapping to the sound of a woman in dungarees playing the guitar.

Three blind mice, three blind mice, see how they run! See how they run! Did you ever see such a sight in your life!

Then my phone pings, from an unknown number. The message says: 'Aren't you interested in how I found you? We didn't even talk about that. I was actually going to ask you for an interview before Ava's and Grace's bodies were even found.'

I don't reply, just stare at my screen.

Then a photo arrives and I scoop up the phone to look closer.

It is a photo of me and my two children walking into school. The photo was taken from a distance but my face is in profile and clear.

'She's having you followed. Why?' he writes under the photo. 'Are you scared? Should you be?'

It takes me a moment to decode the origins of the photo. It is a screenshot, taken from Frida's account. No, it's more complicated. It is actually a screenshot of a repost, meaning Frida didn't take the photo or post it originally. She just shared it as a Story, a post that disappears automatically after twenty-four hours.

'You should be scared,' Oliver texts.

The photo is dated six months ago, posted to her two million followers. The hairs on the back of my neck stand on end.

Oliver writes: 'I reckon you two were more than a summer romance. But the question is, what are you risking in order to protect her? You need to tell your side of the story. Control the narrative, or she'll be the one controlling it.'

On Instagram, I quickly skim through Frida's grid with shaking hands, for photos of me. I can't immediately see anything.

In the library, a teenage girl sits at one of the study tables, her head bent over a textbook and earphones visible under her long blonde hair. She is wearing a white hoodie but she does not look up at me. At another table an older man flips through a newspaper, glasses slipping down his nose.

I create an account on the public computer. I deleted mine years ago, and have never created a new one. The person who posted the original photo of me, the one Frida reposted, has the handle @ fumblingjester. I find this account quickly – it has a profile photo of a jester hat just like the one in Oliver's screenshot of me and the kids. The account is private so I can't see other photos they've posted. It has forty-eight followers.

I shiver at the idea that this person – presumably one of her followers – has been following me in the real world. On Instagram, I change my profile photo to a stock-footage pretty girl and post a few random pictures of flowers and shoes, then follow @ fumblingjester from this dummy account in the hope that they return the favour. This person might be right here in the library, watching me.

◆ ◆ ◆

Another mum from Emma's class drops my kids off for me at a café near the library. Emma and her friend play while Leo reads and the adults chat about school league tables and uniform sales. I linger, wanting to stay in this bubble of inane conversation but jumping whenever the milk frother hisses or the door jingles. The other mother thinks maybe I am coming down with a virus. Have I tried echinacea? The clink of mugs and swirl of conversation are too loud. I feel that same prickling sensation at the back of my neck – a lingering pressure.

Eventually Emma's classmate has to go home so we pack up our bookbags and sunhats. The town centre is a mixture of Georgian and Victorian terraces, giving it an old-fashioned seaside feeling. I parked near a farm just outside of town after I left Oliver. So we walk for a bit, the kids moaning. A dilapidated guest house stares down at the end of a row of detached red-brick homes. There's a mother pushing a pram, an old-age pensioner pushing a wheelie bag full of shopping, a man waiting for a bus. When we get to the car Leo sees some kittens at the neck of the dirt track leading to the farm, and we head over to stroke them. The air smells of manure and sheep wool and something thicker, like rot and blood.

I follow the smell with my eyes, away from the kittens. Over by the edge of the barn there is a dead sheep lying on its side with steam coming from its splayed-out innards. There are flies and crows at the body. Caws and buzzing. The crows look on with curiosity. A low, guttural hum, somewhere between a growl and a moan, comes from nearby, and my breath hitches, but I realise it is just a generator in the barn behind. I glance over my shoulder, back to the car. There on the street corner is a young man, partially concealed by the shadow of a brick wall. He is holding a phone, angled up in our direction.

My stomach tightens. 'Excuse me?' I shout across the road. 'Are you taking a photo of my children?'

'Huh?' he says.

'I said, were you taking a photo of my children?' I take their hands and walk over towards him.

He is maybe sixteen on close inspection, with cystic acne.

'Dude, no.' He grimaces.

'Show me,' I say, and he turns his phone towards me.

'I'm playing *The Walking Dead*?' he says, and shows me an augmented-reality game screen with zombies walking down this quaint seaside street. 'You made me die.'

He frowns down at his screen and I usher the kids to the car. We drive off and park outside our double-fronted blue stucco house, with roses climbing over the front. Lavender spills over our front walls, sea thrift waves, geraniums fill the whole garden with colour. It is the sort of house that children draw, like it came right out of a fairy tale or a dream. I find my mind slipping back to a time when I could swallow chemical calm, and all my worries would disappear for a bit.

◆ ◆ ◆

For ten days after I started detoxing, Frida brought me food I barely ate, and strange-smelling teas that Elena made to help with nausea and detoxification. I watched the island through the window and listened to the thud of Jackson's oxygen machine through the ceiling.

The group swam several times a day. They liked the creek to the left of the causeway at high tide the best, where the beach faced the mainland. Behind the house, facing out to sea, was the abandoned nuclear power plant. There was always a layer of yellow scum on the tide there, along with pieces of rusted metal or plastic bottles tangled amongst seaweed.

Stefan, the groundsman, appeared occasionally and then would disappear for days. He had an enormous forehead that created a sort of ledge over his eyes. Merlin followed him around. Stefan picked up rubbish off the beach every day, sorting it into piles while the dog chased the tides. Soap bottles, plant pots, flip-flops, Tesco bags.

The power plant across the river was strangely beautiful, surrounded by barbed wire and fences. A knot of pipes and tracks climbed like brambles around two massive chimneys that were in fact cooling towers, enormous hyperboloid structures that would once have rejected waste heat from the power plant into the atmosphere.

It was built in this remote and sparsely populated place, I read, to minimise the risk to large populations in case of an accident and to reduce public opposition during the planning stages. In my devotion to global catastrophes, I'd read quite a few books on

Chernobyl and Fukushima. I'd pore over them at lunch in the school canteen, wondering why nobody wanted to sit near me.

Seagulls seemed drawn to the area: wheeling around the chimneys, spinning and surfing on currents of North Sea air there. They disintegrated from their packs then swooped up and reconnected.

Towards midday, the water beyond the window would quiver restlessly. Sweat clung to my skin and I lounged in the bubble of heat, dreaming of Klonopin.

Elena cooked and padded up and down the stairs, presumably looking after Jackson, whose breathing machine became almost relaxing to listen to, like the house had a heartbeat. Moth would sit out in the forest with his sketchbook, bent over drawings of seagulls and trees. Sometimes Grace posed topless for him in the garden and I tried not to stare.

At some point I opened my eyes and Frida was lying on the floor with a shaft of sunlight on her back from the window, a pillow under her arms and her big Dell laptop with an external webcam in front of her.

She turned to me. The room was full of her cigarette smoke, and she was ashing into a teacup.

'Hey,' she said. 'You have to go through this or you'll never come out of it.'

'My mouth was fuzzy from vomit and not speaking for days.

'Here's what I know. Fear keeps most people in a box and makes them small. In fact, fear is a compass. It shows you the walls you need to break down and the places you need to grow. Fear is our greatest ally in transformation.'

'Fear is an evolutionary response to threat. It's how we know to run from lions.'

'But there *are no lions.*' She smiled. 'You're scared of clowns and bad Wi-Fi and potential environmental disaster and crowds and the calories in a sandwich.' Good memory, I thought. Maybe that was all being psychic meant – remembering what others forgot. 'You took pills to stop that fear, and then you became so scared of reality that you couldn't stop taking the pills. But here's what you've been missing. Fear is pleasure. Fear is truth. Fear is the path to transformation. What you are scared of is *exactly* what you need to do.'

'Good speech,' I said. 'I feel sick.'

◆ ◆ ◆

I slept, woke up, slept, watched. That week in the dark while she sat on the floor or on the end of the bed, I told her things I'd never told anyone. How I used to imagine that in the moment after a panic attack had subsided, I could walk through walls.

How my first memories were of anxiety: of hating being late, and swimming pools, and being near traffic, and of loud noises. I was *overly sensitive*, people said. I'd regularly cling to my mother when she tried to drop me off at nursery and later school; sobbing, digging my shoes into the pavement and making her drag me as she tried to untangle herself without hurting me, while everyone stared at this fat kid with black ringlets and her perfect blonde mother. Then either the long, defeated playground trudge with burning cheeks, or crying myself into exhaustion while everyone stared. In retrospect these were panic attacks of course; every morning I thought my heart would explode when she left me. It was a daily storm of heart-racing, blood-pounding panic. 'She'll be fine once you're gone,' they'd say, but I wasn't.

Outside the window, the tides shifted the landscape. Stefan tidied the edges of the garden. Grace meditated.

There was a dragging ache inside me as if something was trying to tear itself slowly out of me that week. My limbs felt scrambled.

Ants plodded along my skin. Legs in arm sockets, arms for legs. I woke up to a sugary smell that made me remember making jelly with my grandmother, stirring those glossy cubes into a measuring jug of hot water and watching them dissolve. The light was too bright.

Mum called repeatedly and I didn't pick up.

I bit my tongue and there was blood on the pillow.

I dreamed of Frida, asleep under a tree surrounded by daisies, then about the faceless white matryoshka dolls a boyfriend had bought Mum once, all trapped inside each other, boxes inside boxes. She'd given the dolls away when we moved in with Roger.

I sweated through my sheets as the drugs left potholes and troughs, blank pages, new thoughts about old memories as the chemistry changed. *Mandible. Palatine.* My brain was swollen in my head like it had sucked up the wet marsh air.

As my body began to regulate again, I watched from my window as they lit a bonfire on the beach and played music late into the night, all of them wearing garlands of flowers in their hair. I dreamed that I was standing on a cliff and a wave came and drenched me with water, shells and jellyfish and whalebones, and then the wave shrank back and took me with it.

◆ ◆ ◆

The day after this bonfire party Frida helped me out into the garden. They'd all just come back from a morning swim and were drying in the sun. The air still smelled faintly of their bonfire. Even if I'd been well enough, I wouldn't have swum with them. I didn't swim with them for weeks. I *could* swim, but hated it. The not being able to touch the bottom, the wetness, the oddness. Often when I was about to have a panic attack, it felt just like I imagined drowning would. First, trying to put my feet on solid ground, finding the water deeper than expected, then sinking under into a topsy-turvy place. Just like with a panic attack, I'd read that most people drown silently. Because survival instincts work against you sometimes. When you're about to drown you can't do the one thing that would save you – scream.

I told Frida about the drowning instinct later and she said it was a metaphor for life. When you need help the most, it's the hardest to ask for it.

She used words like metaphor. Like quintessence. Gossamer. Malevolent. Procrastinate. Beautiful words. She said she'd read almost every book in the house since moving here last year – from the astrophysics books to the dense ancient histories that were piled up in corners and on windowsills. She was almost as good at crosswords as me.

She'd travelled a lot growing up, she said, with her mum. Frida would sometimes be sent to school and sometimes 'home-schooled', although that just meant her mum letting her spend time at whatever library they could find. She stopped going to school entirely when she was ten. But she'd had a single-volume encyclopaedia that she must have read, she said, twenty times as a kid.

'Aardvark, Abacus, Abbey, Abdomen, Abel (Niels Henrik, a Norwegian mathematician famous for his contributions to group theory and elliptic functions), Aberration,' she laughed.

Her mum wasn't interested in books or learning. Her mum believed in 'unlearning', apparently. I imagined the mother in saris or Liberty velvet, lounging with pretty men.

'Do you always sleep with your knickers on?' Frida said to me one time. 'I've been meaning to ask.'

'In case of fire or burglars or fake psychics sitting in my room,' I said.

'I'm not fake. There's a huge spectrum of how people read the world. Like, some people have difficulty understanding the most basic human interactions. Some people can't read a face, don't know if they're being impolite and don't care. It's how their brain is wired. But I walk past someone in the street and know what they're feeling. Does that scare you?'

'No.'

'Not so long ago humans thought the world was flat, and that the sun revolved around the Earth. Is it so unimaginable that magic exists?'

'You have a way with words, but the only kind of magic I believe in is sleights of hand. How did you end up on AuraLine?'

'Not much else to do here once I came back to look after my grandfather. But back to the question of your knickers . . .' I felt confused. She was as bony and thin as a child who'd just gone through a growth spurt. 'Do you change your knickers for bed? Do you have, like, separate "bed knickers" at home? I'm genuinely curious.'

I blushed.

Was she flirting with me? I smelled of vomit and the sweats. I didn't remember the last time I'd brushed my hair or teeth.

'You don't wear knickers to bed?' I managed.

'Sane people sleep naked surely,' she said, looking at me with child eyes. 'Born naked. Sleep naked. Die naked.'

'Most people don't die naked. Pervert. I still think you should be on social media, you know. You could have so many more followers.'

◆ ◆ ◆

Grace and Moth had the room next to mine. The door was ajar: a small velvet armchair was covered in a tie-dye throw with a yin–yang symbol, the sort kids buy in Camden Market. A white t-shirt was crumpled on the floor with a frill of yellow sweat at the collar and under the armpits. A condom and a broken biro sat in the bin by the door. On the dresser were Grace's candy-coloured nail polishes, her lipsticks, and some of Moth's sketchbooks. There were bowls of shells everywhere. Bits of driftwood, curls of dried seaweed, shards of sea glass reflecting light from the murky windows.

I stepped in to look at one of the sketchbooks. Inside, there were beautiful sketches of crows and seagulls and eyes and breasts. Then I heard a creak and moved my hands away. I expected to see Elena with her long grey hair and wide eyes. Turning, though, there was no one there. The house was just creaky. The corridors were floored with thin and uneven wood planks, inexpertly nailed down and distorted now, presumably from having swelled and contracted repeatedly. The pictures on the walls clicked as the walls moved with each shift of weight in the house.

The next room on this corridor had two single beds that were covered in piles of cardboard boxes. There was a dressmaker's dummy in one corner, a broken fishing rod, and a box of fake orchids in garish colours along with the top of a cafetière and five forks. A torn wedding veil, a glass-lidded tray of taxidermy butterflies.

In another box there were dress-up masks. There were two novelty latex seagull masks, super-creepy with beady yellow eyes.

The house smelled weird, generally. The hot, dusty, ancient curtains had an odour. The stone fireplace with its gargoyle faces above; the intense and unusual stench of Elena's kitchen. By the next week I hardly thought about it.

The house had been two houses at some point, connected by a door in the living room, next to the stairs. A completely unintuitive place for a door, which was also ever so slightly smaller than normal height.

This door opened with a creak to a thin corridor with a red carpet, where the thump of the oxygen machine was much louder.

The first door must be Elena's room, I thought – there was a crochet dreamcatcher hanging on the doorknob. I turned it, curious, but the door was locked.'

The second door opened on to a thin staircase, through which the sound echoed. I followed the heartbeat up the stairs and straight into the old man's bedroom. He lay asleep on a hospital bed surrounded by machinery and with plastic tubes in his nose. The oxygen machine next to him thump, thump, thumped.

His sun-pocked skin was shrunken against his skull; his ears were full of hair but his head was bald apart from a few spiderwebs near his neck. I stepped inside slightly, looking briefly around at his room.

I wanted to investigate his bookshelves, the replicas of ancient artifacts and figures dotted amongst the books, but I didn't get to because I felt eyes on me and turned, hoping that I wouldn't find Elena standing at the door and staring at me. But it was Jackson, with his eyes open now. He opened his mouth to speak but nothing came out. I turned, panicked, and ran back to my room.

◆ ◆ ◆

The next day Frida introduced me to her grandpa, apologising to him for not doing so before. He stared at us with milky and vacant eyes.

'Was he a historian?' I asked Frida, and picked up a replica of part of some ancient frieze sculpture made of plaster. It was a group of naked men in a queue to get to a tall woman. I turned it over and there was a sticker on the back: 'The goddess Bendis and her followers, maybe athletes taking part in the torch relay race in her honour, or maybe just worshippers. Marble votive relief, made in Athens, *c.* 400–375 bc.'

'Yeah,' she said, and took a book from the nightstand. 'He wrote this.' It was called *The Codex of Shadows: Myth and Mistranslation in Ancient Texts*. 'It was widely discredited for being entirely incomprehensible and wildly off-piste.' She smiled. 'It sold about twenty copies. But you should read it. He was a brilliant mind. The world just wasn't ready.'

She nodded, and motioned for me to touch his hand.

'Say something to your host,' she said.

I told him how beautiful his island was, and how Frida had invited me to stay if it was okay with him, and that I looked forward to reading his book. He didn't nod or shake his head.

I tried to smile at him. There was a photo of him in his younger years in a silver frame on the windowsill. A little chubby, black hair in a ponytail, meditating and holding hands with people. I wondered if he wished he was already dead.

When my grandma was dying, words and phrases fell like bricks out of a wall before her brain tumbled. 'I dead in the wish' was a common phrase of hers after she'd had one or two strokes – I wish I was dead. Her death wish was often followed with 'jammy another' – can I have another jam sandwich. Near the end she would reach out her bony hand to mine and I'd try so hard not to flinch. She would search for ages to try to communicate something and then it would be 'fuss silly bitch' – don't fuss you silly bitch – or 'bring food'. Later, when very close to death, she opened her mouth like Jackson had just done. Expecting words to tumble out. But nothing emerged.

◆ ◆ ◆

That week, wildfires began to erupt across Northern California. Social media filled with burnt-out houses and blazing trees, scorched cars and fire clouds exploding over forests. It had nothing on what has come in the years since, but it seemed dramatic then. Foxes, rabbits, deer and coyotes were either burnt alive, or smoked out of their homes to skulk around towns and cities with savaged fur. The UK had a small taste of this devastation with a haze of smoke forming over Manchester and Liverpool.

An NHS doctor came to see Jackson. He'd had several strokes, apparently, and on top of that he was suffering from stage four liver cancer. The doctor had tea with Elena, discussing Jackson's care, and then he went off again in his little red car.

I texted Mum saying that I was fine, and then emailed work to tell them that I was quitting, but they'd already replaced me when I hadn't turned up. A new chapter was beginning. None of my school friends, or work colleagues, messaged wondering where I was. Not one.

To thank Frida for everything she was doing for me, I gave her the turtle necklace that I always wore around my neck.

Chapter Five

Emma and Leo want to go down to the beach when we get home. We live a few roads back from the beach by the North Sea, the same sea that fed the estuary where Bay Island is located, but further north. Instead of taking them I put on the sprinkler and start dinner. I check my new Instagram account and @fumblingjester hasn't followed me back yet.

I watch my kids out of the window while pulling on an apron and tying my hair back. Emma, my little sprite, is fierce and determined in all enterprises. Leo is more introspective; he likes to read and he wants to be a doctor. He loves our vegetable garden, and while Emma runs in the sprinkler, Leo secures stray tendrils of runner bean plants on their bamboo supports. The long, slender pods are almost ready to pick. In the lean-to glasshouse next to the side wall, the tomato plants are ready and he goes to collect some for me. In the scoop of his school t-shirt he brings in a courgette, some small carrots and five big tomatoes, their glossy skins catching the sunlight. I send him back out for basil and oregano.

The carrots are a deep crimson and are strangely shaped because the earth is too sandy here, and they twist around instead of digging down. I get an onion and some tinned tomatoes out on to the counter, and my sharpest knife. The blade glints. Copper pots and pans hang from a rack above a farmhouse sink. A cookie jar shaped like a lighthouse sits on the windowsill next to some seedlings under plastic covers. Mismatched cutlery fills the drawers. This is my life.

I chop once, twice, and then my phone pings. I look over at it while holding the knife, heart beating fast, but it is only Ben. He is leaving work early and asks if we are still having lasagne.

I wipe my hand on my apron and send a photo of the vegetables that Leo has collected. I chop the rest and add them to the pot.

I get another message from Oliver:

'There's more information every hour. It's only a matter of time before the police find out that they were living on the island with Frida at the time they died. You need to talk to me.'

And there is another news article.

'During scheduled environmental remediation of a decommissioned nuclear power plant in Essex,' it says, 'workers uncovered two human skeletons embedded within a compacted silt layer at the bottom of a cooling lake. The lake, once used to regulate thermal discharge from factory processes, has since become a stagnant body with heavy sedimentation and chemical runoff. Upon excavation, the remains of two adolescent individuals were recovered. Some bones were tangled with lengths of rope, corroded rebar and sheeting. This may have been the cause of the drowning, or potentially an attempt to anchor the bodies or obscure them from view in the event of lake drainage. A forensics team continues to investigate.'

I put the phone down.

I add tinned tomatoes to the saucepan, herbs, and put water on to boil. The lasagne sheets are a little curled from being out in the heat. The air is filling with the scent of tomatoes, garlic and herbs. I glance at my phone. Nothing.

Then Ben comes through the door and the kids yelp while running to him, almost knocking him over in the hallway.

‘Everyone ready for the fair tomorrow?’ he says, kissing me on the cheek. He smells of disinfectant. ‘I’m going for a shower,’ he says, and I put the lasagne in the oven while the kids settle down to watch TV. I head upstairs and lock the bathroom door behind me, slipping into the shower with him. He is surprised and pleased by my urgency.

◆ ◆ ◆

Before I turned up on the island, Frida performed for three or four people a day; by the end she was performing for thousands. As the Klonopin left my system I began to help Frida with researching clients, which is when the business started to grow.

Frida already looked at her clients’ social media accounts if they gave their names, but she just wasn’t very good at it. It’s called ‘hot reading’ in the psychic world, but really it’s just good old research. She said that she’d never owned a phone until the previous year, so it didn’t come naturally to her. Her mother used to reckon that the government was tracking everyone or frying their brains through their phones. So Frida had only ever used computers in public libraries and at school until she came to live on the island to help her grandpa. When I asked where her mum was, and whether her mum minded Frida living here, she just shrugged. She and her mother weren’t talking at the moment, she said.

Frida obviously had no idea how to make dummy accounts or hack privacy settings. I started an Excel spreadsheet on her computer, of the likes and dislikes and salient facts of various regular callers. Some of these notes were gleaned from their social media profiles but some were just ideas from previous calls. People gave away a lot of themselves in the calls as well as online; we just needed a way of keeping track of the facts.

‘Feeling seen is a basic human need,’ Frida said on a video call. ‘It is evolutionary. To be alone, without a tribe, has always been dangerous. Loneliness makes us vulnerable. Now so many of us are alone, in our own little pods with just our phones for regular company, we feel like ghosts. The ping of likes and follows helps to make us less alone. Each ping is someone seeing us, and there’s no shame in that.’

With me keeping track of people’s foibles and ex’s names and dead mothers and jobs, people started to call back more regularly.

Frida said that at the centre of human nature is a desperation to be understood. We hold on tight to our idiosyncrasies and foibles, try to communicate them, and long to feel any sort of connection. That’s why social media is so addictive. We curate ourselves so that we feel seen. And Frida saw.

I am quick online. I found the secret accounts that they kept from their parents. I made up chirpy alias accounts so that people would accept my follow requests. Nothing major, but Frida was impressed by the amount of information I could hoover up. It was one of the reasons I didn’t think she was a con artist. Because this was the con, surely, and she wasn’t any good at it.

‘You like a *project*, don’t you?’ she said as we sat together at the kitchen table.

I do. It can take mere seconds to discover that you try not to worry about your weight, and you want a Labrador, and the names of your cats or your children. You give too much away when you renovate your house. I know where your children sleep. I know where they go to school. I know where your father is buried. I know your local pub.

I started with dummy social media accounts, friended and followed and studied, and Frida laughed at how, within just a few days, she was getting twice as many call backs and referrals. I loved the feeling of impressing her.

I have a logical brain. A coder's brain.

I could clearly see the way to optimise her job, to make it as efficient as possible, although I was pretty sure that the time as computational cost made no sense. She barely made any money from people calling on AuraLine.

Although the client paid two pounds a minute Frida got just one pound, and she was only paid for the one-on-one sessions not for all the time that she chatted to everyone. AuraLine was run by a businessman in Luxembourg who also ran two sex webcam sites using duplicate code, as I found out online. Frida's only interaction with the company who owned the website was small paycheques.

Frida didn't have that many calls in a day so probably barely made minimum wage. She was a cheap online therapist who didn't need to be booked in advance – a transactional friendship for people feeling down. But it didn't seem to matter to her. She genuinely wanted to help people.

'This relationship might have failed but I can sense it has taught you important lessons about your needs,' Frida said, lying on my bedroom floor. 'Think of it as a stepping stone on the path to great success and love.'

'But *will* there be great love?' the client said over the computer. '*Will* I be happy?'

'Only if you create it yourself. If you continue to connect happiness solely with a man, you will never find it. If you find happiness in yourself then love will follow.'

It was odd when she gave quite simple, good advice:

'If he hit you before, he will hit you again. Don't go back to him.'

'Don't trust how you see yourself when you're exhausted. Maybe just treat yourself gently for a bit and remind yourself that pain is temporary.'

'You need to try and understand your son, before you can make yourself understood.'

'Just try this for one conversation. Look for places where you are in agreement, rather than focusing on where you differ? Just try it one time.'

'You should keep your current job while you look for a new one.'

'Don't make permanent decisions in a temporary mood.'

'I can see a man – perhaps he's at your work? Is there a man you work with who has dark hair? Someone with natural authority who has had his own heart broken recently . . . I see him touching your hand.'

'Nigel made a pass at me the other day, sort of, I think,' a client said hesitantly, but then with a little giddy edge to her voice. 'I don't know if he's just had a break-up.'

'Your credit is about to expire,' Frida said.

'I'll call you back next week,' the client said.

Frida would sometimes sit with her legs bent up inside one of her t-shirts, her cheek resting on her knees, and she'd look at me with a quiet smile. It was a smile like she thought I was special.

I wasn't sure what Frida *was*, exactly. She was a teenage internet psychic in a slightly see-through t-shirt designed to confuse me. She was a wealthy someone's granddaughter. A hippy traveller's daughter. She was good at crosswords despite having very little formal education. She was no good with tech but she was a webcam girl. She was increasingly the first person I thought of when I woke up every morning and the last at night.

I wasn't sure what I was either, of course. The daughter of a beautiful woman who men went nuts for. A good student who went AWOL. An addict. A coder. I had liked boys in the past but not with any great intensity, and now I wanted, badly, to touch Frida.

The tides ebbed and flowed. For half of every day, we were trapped on the island.

‘Life is not about becoming,’ she said to her followers. ‘It’s about shrugging off the inauthentic parts of yourself. Stripping away your parents’ expectations, society’s demands, and finding the red tongue in the yellow flame.’

Did that mean anything? Did it matter? Was there anything under the words, or was I just occupied with her red tongue, her flame?

◆ ◆ ◆

During a panic attack sometimes, when I was barrelling down into full disorientation, Mum would lock herself in her bedroom or leave the flat all together. Frida said that there was a bunch about my childhood that I had repressed, and I didn’t know anything about repressed memory, or how memory worked at all, so this seemed a perfectly reasonable statement. After all, there was lots of my childhood I didn’t remember. Small things loomed big, like the horror of the soggy jam sandwiches Mum would make me for lunch, and how I would go hungry rather than touch that sugary wet texture. But things society might consider larger, like being left alone at night a fair bit, were all murky.

Other snapshots were clear as photographs: us dancing in the kitchen, making up dumb routines and giggling. Mum bringing me bags of clothes to try on because I hated shopping. Her brushing my hair a hundred times each night until I was eleven or twelve and cut it off. Had she tried her best? Had she aimed for kindness and fallen short?

I felt a grey blur, a nausea, at the thought of her, though. Mum once let one of her boyfriends put me over his knee and hit me with the buckle of his belt. Mum would ignore me for days, and then when she saw Millie or anyone else from the estate my age she would flirt with them until they said, always, that they wished their mum was cool like that. Mum regularly stayed out all night. As I got older she used to wink at me in this exaggerated humiliating way whenever there was a girl in a short skirt or low-cut top, and maybe she knew I was bi long before I did, and if she knew, why did we never talk about it?

I remembered her telling me to 'just chill the fuck out' when she saw a panic attack brewing in me. Her helping me get ready for a party, choosing the right earrings and lipstick and being so fun and helpful, but then at the last minute feeling jealous or lonely or *something* and telling me that maybe she'd buy me a nose job for my eighteenth birthday or that she'd help me pay for contact lenses or get me on a diet. She knew what I hated about myself, as mothers do. I have such a strong memory of her face in those conflicted moments. Like she hadn't mean to say it. Her lips, hardening around the words.

'You have been conditioned by her to think that you have to live a mediocre life, but you don't,' Frida said to me as I told her things I'd never told anyone. 'You are spectacular. You have had one foot in other worlds your entire life and when you have panic attacks you are standing over the doors into these worlds, into this ultimate knowledge. This uniqueness and vast capacity scared your mother, who is no more than mediocre. She has always been jealous of you.'

This seemed unlikely. My mother had never coveted anything about me.

We meditated, and my desire for Frida seemed so far beyond language. She was a slap in the face, she was the sight of the horizon or a really low moon. She was magnificent.

◆ ◆ ◆

I watched Stefan hold a rabbit down on the floor almost tenderly. Then he put a stick over its neck and wrenched the body up. The carcass jolted and went limp. He looked up and nodded at me before he threw the lifeless bunny on to a wheelbarrow with the others and lifted the handles. There was a shotgun on the wheelbarrow, which made me jump.

Merlin whined. A flock of swallows rose and sank overhead, their sharp little wings slicing up towards the sun and then down towards the water, teasing, then up again. 'Mind yourself on the flats,' he said. I'd just been walking, out on the riverbed at low tide. 'The tide comes up real fast and you don't want to get stuck in black grounds.'

'What are black grounds?' I said. This was the first time he'd spoken to me.

'The incoming tide floods across the sands quicker than a man can run out there, and if you've got your leg caught in a patch of black ground then you're not running nowhere.'

'I've seen you walking out there.'

'We all walk out there. But you've got to have your bearings.'

Oystercatchers and shelducks nested in the large areas of undisturbed salt marsh, according to the book on birdwatching I'd found in my room. Purslane, samphire, sea aster, sea beet: they all had such beautiful names that would forever be connected to the fever of detoxing.

Stefan watched me. My palms were sweaty, and the backs of my knees and insides of my elbows itched.

My phone had messages from Mum on it: 'Where are you? What about work?'

I returned three entirely meaningless emoticon thumbs-ups just as Moth's van pulled up on the causeway to the right of the beach. Seeing me, he got out and shouted.

'Want to come shopping?' he said.

I walked over.

'Get in,' he said. 'You okay?'

'Stefan is killing the rabbits,' I said.

'They have myxomatosis,' he said. 'Slow crappy death so he puts them out of their misery. Some things shouldn't be alive. They don't even feel it. You put your hand over so they think they're about to get dicked and they go all calm.'

'Dicked?' I said, arching one eyebrow.

'Made love to?' he said. 'By Stefan the lonesome groundsman.'

'Shiver,' I said, and then we fell into an awkward silence.

The seagulls careered over the swelling water as we drove over the causeway. Back on the mainland we headed towards the outskirts of Ballards End, past the rundown suburbs of prefab houses, fly-tipped furniture and closed shopfronts.

'How you feeling?' he said.

'Like a dead rabbit.'

'The hardest part is yet to come: you have to *stay off* that shit. Frida will help. I couldn't have done it without her. But it's hard.'

At a roundabout Moth forgot to indicate and several cars beeped as we spun into a Morrisons car park. He parked and we got out of the car. There was something deeply endearing about Moth. He wasn't quite finished somehow, hadn't quite crayoned in all the turns and twists of his personality. But when he laughed it buoyed up everything. Sometimes he would look deeply lost in thought, as if writing sonnets in his head, but if you asked what he was thinking he would say 'Those eggs we had for breakfast were delicious' or something similarly banal.

Inside the supermarket a woman had a disposable barbecue in her trolley with a kid holding a bag of marshmallows the size of his head. A man in tiny shorts was buying a whole salmon from the fishmonger. He had the last of his balding hair caught desperately into a ponytail. Moth was holding a list written in Elena's spidery writing. People stared and I saw us from their perspective: dirt under our nails, salt spray making our hair crispy. We probably smelled of marsh, just as Frida had smelled when I met her on the Northern line. We collected bags of rice, lentils, pasta, filling up the cart, and I found I didn't mind people watching us. I felt, for the first time in ages, like I belonged in my body, my clothes, my self.

Moth paid and I went to get us some drinks from a Starbucks on the other side of the car park. There was a group of four teenagers with heavily lined lips taking selfies on their phones at the window as I sat outside. They would love Frida, I thought. It would be so satisfying to have them follow her.

I opened my own Instagram and location-searched for Starbucks Ballards End and a photo came up under 'recent'. It was of @rubytwoshoes smiling out of the window and holding her drink with long acrylic nails, painted various shades of candy pink that matched her drink. She wrote 'when your nails match your bev #rubyfrappuccino'. 'Saucy little minx,' someone had already written under her picture, moments after she'd posted it. 'Stunning mate,' wrote someone else. 'You are unbelievably beaut.'

I set up an Instagram account for Frida in a couple of clicks, followed the girls tagged in the photo, and posted a screen recording I'd made of one of Frida's AuraLine monologues. I would delete it before anyone on the island saw it. I just wanted those girls to watch Frida. Maybe I wanted to help them, or connect to them. Mostly I just badly wanted them to follow her.

'We ought to be happier and healthier and safer than anyone in human history and yet we're not,' Frida said in that video, smiling slightly at the camera. She was sitting cross-legged, her big white t-shirt pooling around her and hands in her lap. 'Humanity on average has never been richer, healthier or lived longer. But somehow we are all terrified. Our bodies are flushed with cortisol and adrenalin constantly, hyping us up into irrational fear and jealousy. We constantly compare ourselves to others. We are told we can have anything and be anything and so we are standing here like rabbits in the headlights, scared of our shadow.' She paused. 'I can help you break through the cage of your fear.'

I uploaded a profile picture and a little bio. 'My name is Frida Rae. I am a psychic, a visionary, a healer. Welcome,' I wrote, 'to the rest of your life.'

The Starbucks girls followed her.

◆ ◆ ◆

We were always hyper-aware of where Frida was in the house. If someone had been out and walked in, Frida's whereabouts was often the first inquiry. If someone made her laugh, we all wanted to know the joke. Although Moth and Grace were in a relationship, they were still highly focused on Frida. Elena, too, gravitated to her boss's granddaughter. Moth tried to draw Frida in his sketchbook but never got her quite right. He drew Grace perfectly – her big brown eyes and pout. He caught the sweetness and the sadness, with just the right twist of coquettish charm. The one strand of hair that curled slightly at her neck when she put her hair up. Portraits are so much more than shapes and shadows. He caught the little girl in Grace, and the potential grown-up. He caught me perfectly too, always looking down at something, often frowning. It was a studious face. Not pretty, not ugly. But he couldn't capture Frida's mercurial features.

When I showed her the Instagram, she frowned.

'Take it down, Zoe,' she said. 'Elena thinks it isn't a good idea.'

'What's Elena got to do with it? Just look,' I said to her. 'I started this an hour ago and you already have twenty-five people following you. That's twenty-five people who might need your help, and wouldn't have found you on some budget psychic website that looks like it belongs in the nineties. I could make you your own website. It would be so much more efficient to find your own clients and come off AuraLine.'

'She doesn't need more viewers,' Elena snapped from the door.

Frida didn't like being told what to do. Maybe it was just for this reason that she changed the course of our lives and said, casually:

'Let's keep the Instagram.'

She smiled at Elena, whose lips tightened. The tension expanded, then Elena turned abruptly and walked out of the house.

Twenty-five Instagram followers became forty the next week, and forty-five a few days later.

'The portal to the next dimension of reality comes through the parts of your identity that you fear,' Frida said on AuraLine, earnestly. I screen-recorded and put it on Instagram.

'So on point,' someone wrote. 'Love.' 'Keep it cosmic while keeping it grounded.'

On Instagram we posted photos of the sea, of crows, of yoga poses, of our shell collection, of Frida's profile at twilight or her throwing sticks for Merlin outside the window. We all had access to the account and posted photos, but I did so more than the others. People commented with heart emojis, prayer hand emojis, and lots of exclamation marks.

'We transform ourselves in order to change the world,' said the caption.

Out in the forest, Stefan shot a rabbit.

Forty-five, fifty followers watched us.

I coded her a website with video capability. Inputs and outputs. Loops and iterations. I was going to make a success of this: money, a place to live, real friends. My fingers sped across Frida's keyboard, her face on the home screen of her website.

```
if opportunity == 'good':

    take_it ()

else: pass
```

Elena watched us, frowning. Frida started holding my hand sometimes. Stefan threw the dead rabbit on to his wheelbarrow.

Chapter Six

The sun is high over our summer fete, the sea air mixing with candyfloss and charred grass. Rows of brightly coloured stalls fill the field outside of school, each one competing for attention with painted signs. 'Coconut shy', says a sign. 'Sponsor a rabbit!' 'Hook a duck!' The last one is ours, with a hundred numbered ducks floating in our paddling pool. It took us three hours to paint on the numbers and screw in the hooks. Ben and I sat up watching bad TV and trepanning plastic heads.

I wipe sweat from my brow. We ate the lasagne and went to bed early last night, although I couldn't sleep so ended up in my office. My whiteboard was full of notations and quick algorithms for a data processing project I've been working on, and my dual monitors blinked. I turned one of them on. The @fumblingjester account had followed back my phishing account. He or she hadn't posted anything revealing, just the occasional photo of a sunset or a flower. They did indeed follow Frida, and about sixty others – a mixture of male and female profiles, many of them verified accounts with spiritual content, but also fashion brands like Adidas and beauty brands like Glossier.

Now I scan the fair for people holding phones but there are too many. Ben is buying ice cream for the kids and I watch him for a moment, joking with another dad, his hand on Emma's shoulder. He turns towards me as if he knows I'm watching, and smiles.

My mouth is dry and my head is throbbing like I drank a bottle of vodka last night. I reach for Emma's unicorn water bottle, which is a little warm already despite just coming from the fridge.

This is a school fete but a big one, with half the town involved in some way. Leo is talking to some friends now, and Emma is lurking around the teddy-bear stall while licking an ice cream, holding her dad's hand firmly in her little sticky one. I take some money and a kid starts hooking a duck, but I watch my husband and children.

Ben spent his childhood shearing sheep on local farms and you can see it in his body, which is only now turning soft around the edges. He has never and will never live in a city – says he hates being anywhere that you can't smell the weather. He is a doctor at Scarborough Hospital. We met at a medical conference at a dilapidated Victorian hotel on the promenade there, when I was at my first on-staff coding job. It was for a platform that organised survey data and I had been sent to the conference to peddle it to epidemiologists.

For years after leaving Frida I travelled constantly, getting small coding jobs on Upwork and Fiverr. I fixed broken links, slow-loading pages, incorrect formatting, and scraped by. I couldn't exactly put Frida on my CV ('Lead Researcher for online psychic'? 'Chief Marketing Officer to cult leader'?) but much of what I learned on that island proved invaluable. Not just how to grow vegetables and cook, but persistence, confidence, building rapport, adaptability, quick thinking, innovation, persuasion, strategic thinking.

I am a pro at hot reading. And cold reading: looking for clues in body language, and using broad statements that the client feels are specific to them and make them feel seen. I found that small businesses hiring cheap coders on Fiverr weren't so different from people calling Frida on AuraLine: they wanted someone who saw their vision for themselves or their business; they wanted to be mirrored and validated.

I may have used some of Frida's techniques on Ben, too, although my feelings for him are entirely genuine. He is persuading our daughter to give him a reluctant lick of her ice cream, and they both smile at me with Mr Whippy on their noses. I loved him from the moment I saw him at the bar of the medical conference, and if there were small lies or schemes on the road to marrying him, I hope it has been worth it for him. I am a good wife, a very good mother. Arguably there's always a little bit of subterfuge and manipulation to the start of any relationship.

He is fifteen years older than me. I was twenty-two when we met and he was thirty-seven, a fully established and qualified consultant at Scarborough Hospital. The evening I first saw him, his dark hair was sticking up rebelliously in all directions and his shirt was crumpled. He'd had a tough day. He had a strong jaw with a hint of stubble; he'd been too busy to shave that morning.

There were hints of grey already at his temples. There was a tenderness to his face. Not just a kindness, although there was that. A slight vulnerability, a rawness, that spoke of recent damage: a broken heart or the death of a family member. My love for him wasn't starry-eyed or wild. It was a careful love. A thoughtful, attentive love.

I read his name tag and googled him while watching him at the bar. He was a haematologist, specialising in blood disorders. I didn't speak to him that night but he and his friends came over and stood near me at the bar to order a drink. The group were talking about running routes in Scarborough: he ran on the beach at seven a.m. before work whenever he could.

I was not a runner but ran on the beach for seven mornings straight before I bumped into him, and promptly fell over so he would help me. I know how that sounds. Contrived at worst. Vacuous at best. He literally carried me to his car and drove me to the hospital. He wrote me a doctor's note. I was smitten, and soon he was too. We have been happy.

He smiles at me now over the sea of children and the wafting smell of candyfloss. I help another child hook a duck and then turn back to Ben and the kids, but I can't see Leo anymore.

'Ben!' I shout. 'Where's Leo?'

Ben looks around, then shrugs at me quizzically. This is a safe town. I could name half the people in the crowd. Yet my pulse spikes, and I step on a box to scan the crowd. There are people everywhere. Music blaring, bells ringing, people laughing.

'Mummy?' he says, and I turn around. He is standing by the candyfloss stand, unharmed and confused. 'What's wrong?'

'Oh,' I say. 'I couldn't see you.'

He raises his eyebrows, like I am going insane, but then I see Oliver in the crowd, smoking a cigarette near the ice cream van, and my mouth goes dry.

'Could you ask Daddy to man the stall for a bit?' I say to Leo. 'I'm just popping to the toilet.'

I catch Oliver's eye and walk away from the crowd slightly, to the space behind the kiosks, where it is even hotter from the electric cables and generators. There is a smell of burnt sugar and rubbish.

'Someone tried to hide the bodies,' he says. 'I just want to talk to you. We can help each other. I don't want to blow up your pretty life.' He motioned around him. 'I just want to hear about the real Frida Rae.'

'I'm not sure anyone knows the real Frida Rae,' I say.

Then Emma comes rushing over through the heat. She is wearing a Liberty-print smocked dress with a matching bow in her hair, and has ice cream smeared all around her mouth. I flush at the sight of her and pick her up, but regret it because now she and Oliver are face-to-face in the sticky air.

'Daddy says there's an emergency and he has to go into work and can you come back,' she says, then warily: 'Who is this?'

'My name is Oliver Sperling,' he says, shaking her little hand. 'I'm a journalist writing a story about someone your mummy used to be good friends with.'

'I like stories,' she says.

'Yes, aren't they fun? I think your mum is going to help me write a really good one.'

◆ ◆ ◆

We lay in the sun and chatted about possible global catastrophes, and how we might survive them. Would we flee to the basement and duct-tape plastic sheeting to the windows during a nuclear event, or try to run? How would we go about befriending aliens? Would growing our own crops be worth the effort, in case regional destruction from an asteroid or comet impact meant that Morrisons stopped stocking tomatoes from Spain? We decided that only people wearing sensible shoes would survive.

I chatted to the Starbucks girls on Instagram, as if I was Frida. Looking back through their feeds, one of them had posted about raising money for a meningitis charity, and about it being the anniversary of her father's death. The others mostly posted make-up tutorials and selfies.

In the second week of June, a woman and her husband bumped over the causeway in a fancy car, lost on their way to a wedding on a different island called Osea. Their car was a shiny BMW, and it glinted as it struggled over the holes and rocks.

Through the passenger window, this woman was beautiful in a way that suggested lots of money and limited carbs. She was about forty with glossy skin. What must have been naturally afro hair was relaxed into waves and parted at the side. We later discovered she worked for a very high-end clothing brand.

'Um, is this Osea Island?' the man said to Elena, from the driver's seat.

'No, sweetheart,' Elena said in a voice that suggested she liked the look of these people's car, watches, clothes. 'I'm afraid that's the next island over.'

'Fuck,' he said.

Marigolds rustled on the picnic table. They were drying in the sun. Marigolds are a natural antiseptic apparently – good for wounds, burns and rashes.

'I told you we missed the turn,' the woman said from the passenger seat. 'I'm looking at the fucking map.'

Elena smiled at the woman in the car. She opened her palms with a shrug. 'This is Bay. I'm sorry.'

'Bollocks,' the man said. 'I was surprised Tarquin would choose this place. May I use your bathroom though?'

'Of course.' Elena pointed him inside, ignoring his rudeness.

The pretty woman in the car took a deep breath. She opened the car door and swung out her long legs. She was in stilettos, wearing a bright pink dress with a cinched waist. She pulled down her big sunglasses.

'Can I get you a glass of water or anything?' Elena said.

'No, no, I'm fine,' she said, and looked at us all sitting there in the garden. 'What are you doing?'

'Meditation,' Frida smiled.

'Oh,' the woman said. 'Is this some sort of *retreat*?'

She said the word with pleasure, looking around with renewed interest. She clearly liked *retreats*.

'Yes,' I said without hesitation. 'The Bay Island retreat.'

Merlin, who had been lying in the shade of the picnic table, rose lazily from the grass and walked towards the woman. Instead of growling at her like he'd growled at me the first day, he put his nose down and sniffed at her. The woman scratched his head idly. Frida watched Merlin and the woman for a moment. Then we watched Frida walk up to the woman and whisper something in her ear. The woman looked confused for a second, then her husband came out of the front door.

'Let's do it,' the man said. 'We'll still make it for the wedding champagne.'

◆ ◆ ◆

When they were gone I changed the Instagram handle to 'The Bay Island Retreat'.

'It's a good name,' Frida said.

Frida went swimming and I photographed her bobbing in the sun to post. I still didn't swim. I'd wanted to be a marine biologist as a little kid, hence the turtle necklace that Frida now wore around her neck. I used to like reading about the deep ocean, that bit they know less about than outer space. Mum said that I thought about the deep ocean so much – hagfish and vampire squids and giant isopods – that I just went off the water one day. But I reckon I went off swimming because we were on holiday in Magaluf and she drank too much sangria and I nearly drowned, but hey. She never told me about the incident, but Gran did. 'We thought you'd have brain damage after,' Gran said. 'Imagine how clever you might have been if you'd not been left in a pool, huh?'

On our Instagram feed, @RebeccaKing followed us. She had twenty-nine thousand Instagram followers. Posts of sun loungers, spas, handbags, cocktails and fancy interiors.

'What did you say to the woman in the car before?'

'I said she would get pregnant soon.'

'How do you know she wants to? Her Instagram account doesn't look like someone who has or wants kids.' I peered at my phone. 'I doubt kids are allowed in the Dorchester Spa, and she just bought a white sofa.'

'Everything about the car and her outfit said she didn't *have* kids. But that is a car bought with a family in mind. She's in her early forties, so whether she wants a kid or not, kids are on her mind. There was a book on regulating hormones lying on the back seat. Also, cause I'm psychic.' Frida smiled. That smile made my knees weak.

'She just followed the Bay Island account,' I said. 'She has twenty-nine thousand followers. We should talk to her, and some of her followers might spill over.'

'Record me,' Frida said, walking into the water and turning to me. I pointed my camera at her. 'Fear is pleasure, and fear is evolution,' she said. My toes wiggled in the sand. 'Fear is our greatest ally in transformation. If you are waiting for something that you desperately want, if you can hardly breathe because you want it so much, you must explore your fears. It is through fear that we get what we need.'

I posted it to our hundred followers. We walked back towards the house again but slowly, ambling, jumping streams, picking wildflowers for Elena to put in jam jars on windowsills. The island surprised me with a beauty that had something new to show each day. The moss on the trees was fairy-tale green, the scorched earth had lightning cracks teeming with ants and wildflowers.

We passed Stefan's caravan. Through the windows, I could see more beach detritus covered the surfaces. Amongst shells and driftwood and bird beaks were Ava's distinctive, red, thick-lensed glasses.

'Aren't those Ava's glasses?' I said.

Frida squinted.

'She had a few pairs of glasses. Guess he found those ones while beachcombing. I think she lost one pair swimming.'

I didn't think any more of it. Big bits of driftwood were nailed on the wall; a sea-worn children's toy lay in a pile with a man's pipe.

'Do you miss her?' I said.

'She didn't want to develop spiritually, so it was best she left,' Frida said. 'Moth said there are butterfly cocoons in one of the caravans. Shall we look?'

I got out my phone again. Her video had been liked five times. I walked towards her. The caravan wallpaper was curling off in loops and flowery curtains were rotting at the bottom. Saplings and weeds were growing between the floorboards and creepers were crawling over the ceiling. She tapped the Plexiglas. A spider had made its web in one corner of the window and scurried into the shadows.

Frida walked around the back of the caravan, so I couldn't see her for a moment. Then, when she emerged again, she pointed and stretched her bare foot in the sun and I wanted to put my fingers into the pale triangles between her toes.

She pushed open the front door and walked inside the caravan, leaving me standing in the heat videoing her through the blurry window.

'Careful,' I said, 'the floor looks rotten.'

She waved at me through the window.

I loved how she waved with her fingers – always just with her fingers. I still wave with my fingers like that now. I reckon everyone you love leaves parts of themselves on you. I wrinkle up my whole face when I'm embarrassed like my maths teacher used to, and do my mother's coy half-smile in photographs. Little ghosts of them all in my body still.

I stood at the threshold of the caravan, and it absolutely stank. Not just of trapped air and bird shit and mould, but something newer and fetid.

'It stinks,' I said. 'Let's keep the door open.'

The psychedelic eighties swirly yellow carpet was covered in fallen plaster, dead flies and wasps. There were nettles growing all around the kitchen appliances. A surprising amount of stuff was scattered around: a metal kettle, spatulas, spoons, a tray with a painting of a Mediterranean-looking seaside town that Frida picked up and wiped dust off.

There was a Pokémon trading card on the kitchen counter.

'Hey look, Squirtle,' I said, spinning the card, which had a little blue turtle on it. 'When it retracts its long neck into its shell, it squirts out water with vigorous force,' I read.

'Sexy.'

'Gross.' I blushed. 'I loved these as a kid.'

'What is it?'

'Pokémon. Like, the trading cards? The cartoon?'

She shrugged and turned away.

'Moth said there were cocoons in here,' she said, looking around.

'But wait, you really don't know Pokémon?'

Frida's cultural references had been bugging me for a bit. She had read lots of books but she'd not watched *Twilight* or *The Walking Dead* or Kim Kardashian marry Kanye West. She didn't get references to a bunch of famous people – Katy Perry, Miley Cyrus, Beyoncé. I mean, even if she'd travelled around in very counterculture places, surely she would still have some knowledge of the world.

'You look appalled,' she said. 'Why does it matter if I know what a Squirtle is?'

She laughed, but I didn't, and then she turned around to meet my eyes.

'You just have the weirdest lack of cultural references.'

'You seem very hung up on Squirtle,' she said. She said the word like it was dirty. 'Is Squirtle very important to you?'

She came up and stood close to me so I could smell her breath. My lips tingled and I thought she was going to be angry, but she smiled ever so slightly. The air still smelled profoundly of rotten food or flesh.

'Like I said, there wasn't a lot of school. My mum rejected materialism and consumerism.'

'So you travelled around with her. You never met other kids, played games? When I watched you on AuraLine you described kissing Mickey Mouse in a mall.'

'I got in a lot of trouble for that. The kiss was in a Disney store in Rome. We lived in a countercultural, intentional community outside the city. Shared resources, eco-friendly living, organic farms and collective decision-making.'

'Did you enjoy it?'

'Some of it was wonderful. Rome was the best. We'd lived in one in Portugal that was a mess, and one in Wales that was basically an excuse for people to be high all the time, but the one outside Rome was beautiful.'

'But you didn't stay.'

'I wanted to learn about Pokémon cards and Kardashian weddings,' she laughed. 'And I wanted to look after Grandpa.'

'Do you miss your mum? Is she still on a commune somewhere?'

'I don't know,' she said, and looked away. 'Maybe. The Rome commune disbanded so I don't know exactly where she is. I came here, she went somewhere else.'

There was a teddy bear hanging on a string from the caravan roof where Frida was standing. It had bedraggled fur and bulging eyes. The sink was full of mud and bits of broken particleboard.

I felt hyper-alert but not in an unpleasant or panic-attack way. Frida's breath, as always, smelled a little curdled, and her skin of rotten flowers, but none of this – if you can imagine – was remotely unpleasant.

The air around her was much worse.

For a second we were water that was about to boil, stirring under the surface. She put her lips on mine but only for the barest of moments. Just the suggestion of a kiss, really.

'Hey,' she said, pointing. 'Butterfly cocoons.'

She moved away and I remained standing, waiting for the kiss.

She bent down in front of a chest of drawers. I swallowed saliva and ran my nail over some bubbled varnish on a fake wood panel, trying to gather myself again.

I could count the bones of her spine as she bent. I wanted to put my arms around her and protect her.

Hanging from the rim of the chest of drawers were maybe twenty green gems that I wouldn't have known were cocoons if she weren't staring at them. Each was glossy and attached to the drawers by a thread that swayed when she breathed on them. On my haunches next to her, more to be close to her than because of the cocoons, I took off my glasses to see the folds and rivets layered on top of each other like origami.

Then I noticed a mangy rabbit sitting in the corner between the dresser and the wall. The originator of the rotting smell. His eyelids were bloody and swollen. He was half bald, his remaining fur matted with blood or ooze. His ribcage was moving up and down, just about. When something shifted under the rabbit's skin – a maggot rearing from the fur – I lost my balance and toppled backwards.

Frida wasn't in the caravan next to me anymore. I scrambled up from the floor, and tripped over a suitcase, then again over a wonky bit of carpet, and launched myself at the caravan's front door but found it was jammed shut on its rusty hinges. I hadn't even heard it close.

'Frida!' I shouted. My hand was sweaty around my phone.

She was sitting by the tree outside, with a blank expression on her face. She looked as if an hour had passed since we were at the cocoons rather than a few seconds. Moments, like the almost kiss, can be intoxicatingly long. But sometimes days passed before I blinked. Increments of time are not created equal.

'Frida!' I banged on the back window and her expression remained impassive for another beat. 'Frida, the door is stuck!'

Panic rose up in me, the smell of it hitting me above even the stench of warm mould and dying rabbit. Frida got up slowly and walked towards the caravan.

'It's just rusty,' she said.

I took a breath and kicked the door. It clattered off to the side and sunshine poured in on top of me.

'Fuck,' I said, and stepped out. My hands were shaking.

She laughed and put long fingers over her mouth.

'Why didn't you help?'

'I did,' she said. 'You didn't have a panic attack. That's progress.'

'Fuck you. Don't *teachable moment* me.'

'I wasn't aware you were scared of bunny rabbits,' she said, not smiling.

'Just ones that are rotting while alive. Fuck.'

I sat down on the caravan steps and she sat next to me, close but not touching. My breath was shaky as she reached over to tenderly tuck my hair behind one ear. I hadn't washed it for over a week in anything but river water. We both smelled of salt and marsh.

'You have the most beautiful eyes,' she said, and the words lingered like shapes drawn with a sparkler on bonfire night. 'The air is full of spirits today. Can you feel them?'

'No,' I said.

I considered myself to be an independent thinker. All my life people had described me as intelligent. I didn't follow trends. I had a logical mind.

'I don't believe in spirits,' I said.

'Don't say you don't believe in them,' she laughed. 'They don't like it.'

I could still feel her touch in the way my hair was tucked behind my ear. Her heat. Shoulder to shoulder. I could smell her breath. I wouldn't scoff if she were talking about God – and what, really, is the difference between God and ghosts? As she spoke in her rhythmic hushed voice I had a feeling of sunshine spreading through me.

'I'm sorry I scared you,' she said quietly into my ear. 'I don't know why I did it. I don't know why I do things sometimes. Can I tell you something important?'

'Yes.'

'I want to be totally honest with you.'

'Okay.'

She paused for too long.

'Your ears are a funny shape.'

She laughed.

'I have perfect ears,' I said, looking forward.

'No, they're like elf ears.'

'Can I tell you something important? A secret?' I said.

I was looking forward still.

'Yes,' she said.

'You can be a cunt,' I said.

She gave me a quick peck on the lips and walked away, back to the house. For a while, as an act of defiance, I didn't follow.

Sometimes she seemed so young. Like stunted, prepubescent. Then, in other ways, she was almost ageless.

Grace or Moth must have taken a photo of us through the caravan window that day. In the photo we were nearly kissing, framed by the peeling painted windows. Someone posted it on our Instagram with some heart emojis. We all had access, though I used it the most.

Just being followed by Rebecca caused a small landslide of new followers to our account. 150 followers. 250. The number climbed, and we posted pictures.

◆ ◆ ◆

Frida didn't kiss me again for a while, but I spent time in her room now. Being in there was like stepping into the stage set of my favourite show. There was a rumpled, never-made bed. The windowsills were covered in choice tat: shells in jars, dried sea lavender, a sea-sanded bottle of minibar whiskey or rum, a cracked porcelain doll's head with smashed-out eyes.

A pair of white towel shorts often sitting on the floor, abandoned with knickers still inside. Sometimes we sat and did crosswords from this big book of them. *Beguile? Skin on the base of a nail? A fragrant shrub? Lukewarm?* We'd sit there messing around on the camera, until someone wanted to call her.

The windows in her bedroom had been open for so long over this hot summer that fingers of ivy were climbing inside and had made their way an inch or so up one of the walls. It would leave marks on the wall when she eventually peeled it off. A crow often watched through the glass from one of the window ledges. She had two windows. One looking inland, over the garden and forest towards the causeway. One out towards the North Sea.

Sometimes, the crow would come into the room and Frida would gently usher it out again.

There were plenty of books in there too, scooped up from around the house. Books on ancient cultures and mythologies, art books and philosophy books. I picked up a toy replica of an old statue from her chest of drawers, legless and armless.

'Who is this?' I said.

'A lunar goddess called Bendis, spirit of divine ecstasy and passion. Goddess of fertility, protection, good health and good fortune. She was worshipped in Dacia.'

'Where's Dacia?'

'It doesn't exist anymore, but it was part of ancient Rome.'

'Did you come and visit the island a lot as a kid?' I asked.

'Sometimes,' she said.

'But your mum grew up on this island?'

'No, my mum was born in Wales and grew up all over,' she said, but didn't explain further. Looking back, Frida had a way of not explaining the whole truth but not actually lying. She always had a way out, like she had been misunderstood rather than being purposefully misleading.

A copy of Jackson's own book was on her shelf and I picked it up: *The Codex of Shadows: Myth and Mistranslation in Ancient Texts*. The language was so dense that it was almost impossible, but it was basically about little-known ancient religions. There was a chapter on the Dacians, which seemed to be a particular interest of his: the map in the living room, the replica sculptures around. I had to read the first sentence a few times to make head or tail of it. The book had been published forty years ago. The bio said he was a regular presenter at conferences put on by institutions like the European Association of Archaeologists and the Society for Biblical Literature, and a memorable keynote speaker at niche symposia like the International Conference on Ancient Mystery Religions.

Frida sat cross-legged on her bed and I recorded her.

'Around 13.7 billion years ago, everything we know of was an infinitesimal singularity,' she said. 'Then, according to the Big Bang theory, it burst into action, inflating faster than the speed of light in all directions for a tiny fraction of a second. The Earth is resilient. Its history is full of fire and ice and mass extinction. The Earth will heal, and the decaying remains of an extinct humanity will help the plants grow.'

I posted it.

It was mostly not so dramatic. Less hellfire and brimstone. Mostly, young women wanted to know if they should break up with their useless boyfriends. People wondered if it was the right time to sell their homes, or change jobs, or how to deal with mothers-in-law. They wanted someone to tell them to put a plant in the furthest-south corner of their kitchen for better luck, or to give their boyfriends one more chance before breaking it off forever. They wanted to be told that they'd come into money in the new year, or that the person they were with was 'the one'.

Why am I so anxious all the time? How can I be happy? Should I stay or go? Does he love me?

It felt like a not-particularly-funny joke. Frida told an unravelled young woman that someone at work was attracted to her and she should have more confidence in herself. She told a woman in pink yoga clothes that her boyfriend was never going to leave his family. She told a mother that she gave too much time to others and needed to concentrate on herself. She told a middle-aged woman to stop spending money she didn't have, and a young man to take the job in construction while he looked for something better, rather than going on benefits. She took on different personas with different callers. She could be kind or bossy, could listen or scold. She could be startling or comforting, but mostly she kept them on the phone for as long as she could. In so many ways she was what you wanted her to be.

I read somewhere, years later, that brilliant empaths often honed their skills through trauma – if your safety depends on pre-empting another person's emotions, you become good at it.

Of course, there were moments when she got her 'predictions' wrong and backtracked. I liked these gaps and flaws in her performances. She'd be saying she saw a problem with someone's son then suddenly change it to a problem with an animal or a distant family member. When she got something really wrong, she'd say, 'This vision will make sense to you within the next few years,' and catch my eye off-camera, which made me laugh.

People *wanted* to believe her; otherwise why were they wasting their money? They heard what they wanted to hear, and often even told her what they wanted to hear.

Messages pinged as she spoke: 'Is my cat going to survive this? Can we talk privately now, urgently?' 'Prayer for the spirit.' 'Read my mind, bitch. Read my mind.' 'Please, what size are your feet I need to know!'

Between callers, we did crossword puzzles. I downloaded a crossword puzzle app on her phone as well, and so even when we were apart we played. Her old Dell computer had been her grandfather's, but she'd bought the phone herself. It was one of the first things she'd saved up for when she started earning a little money on AuraLine. She'd sit on the floor next to the bed, or later on the bed itself, and we'd chat, or do crosswords.

The hot air released bursts of smells: flowers, marshy bubbles of pollution. Frida held her hands over Stefan, or Elena, or the rest of us.

In the gloom I told Frida things I hadn't told anyone before, about searching through my mother's computer for photos of men with my colouring, of how I became fixated on this one poor Asian man who came to all the chess championship heats at my school when I was ten, convinced he would gather the courage to tell me if I could just win the competition. I used to offer him biscuits and simper around him. He must have thought I was nuts. But he turned out to be a supply teacher supervising the competitions. Frida also had no idea who her father was.

I told her about my panic attacks, Mum's apathy, my loneliness.

Frida had this way of making it feel as if what you were saying was important.

Sometimes when Frida spoke I felt such a debilitating wave of feeling for this scrappy, childlike creature in front of me. I honestly don't think she ever meant for the bad or the big things to happen. With her head tilted, her web of hair swept downwards to show off her profile, talking about the arcs of light and explosion of stars that anticipated her migraines, or stroking Merlin, who sometimes crept into Frida's room, she looked like a strung-out Holly Golightly might look if she home-bleached her hair and shopped at Zara or H&M or Fruit of the Loom.

The sound of the gong exploded, but lightly, covering us and drawing us to the garden for meditation. We closed our eyes and I felt a sense of control developing for the first time in my life. It was as if the whole rest of the world was a labyrinth of traffic jams, social cliques, smog, loneliness, panic and desire, but meditating in that island garden was the beating heart in the centre of it all. Time would stop. Sometimes I would start meditating early in the morning and not emerge for hours.

We streamed the meditations. Twenty, thirty people would join us most days. Grace was becoming more beautiful through those months, and Moth's sketchbooks were full of her. Sometimes I smelled Grace or Moth when I got close to Frida, or Frida on Grace or Moth while we were meditating or eating, but we all sort of smelled of each other at that point. We wore each other's t-shirts, used each other's hairbrushes.

◆ ◆ ◆

'Aged fifteen I weighed nearly five and a half stone,' Grace said quietly on camera, staring out at Frida's followers. 'My parents didn't notice at first when I stopped eating. I have six brothers and a sister. I've had allergies and eczema all my life so food restrictions were nothing new. Gluten and dairy made my eczema flare. I'd always enjoyed the control involved in not eating delicious things. My parents approved. It showed discipline and reserve. But age twelve I started push it further. My best friend Ava and I would fill our pockets with carrots and potatoes, move food around our plates, pretend to have eaten at each other's houses or whatever, triumphantly watching our bones appear. We wanted to be thin as eels, and small as shells. Then Ava found speed. Turns out if you take speed, food stops being interesting. Being an eel was easy.

'Soon I was living with a boyfriend, then when we broke up I slept on couches, took more drugs. My parents said I was wanton and disrespectful and bringing dishonour on the family. I haven't spoken to them at all in two years. Finding Frida saved my life. She taught me to listen to what my body was telling me, not what my father was telling me, or God, or magazines. She is the only person who has ever made me believe that I am worth saving.'

Chapter Seven

'Believe in your infinite potential,' Frida says on my phone screen. The kids are asleep, exhausted from the fair. Ben is at work and the doors are double-bolted, but I know Oliver is going to come. My ears hum. 'Your only limitations are those you set upon yourself.'

What a trite thing to say. Life is full of limitations out of our control. Sometimes she is remarkably average, then sometimes her words are breathtaking in their truth or yearning. I guess if you post once or twice a day for ten years, it can't all be brilliant.

Underneath this nothing quote there are hundreds of comments. Someone saying she has cured them of agoraphobia. Someone else saying that they are trying desperately to find tickets to her next event in LA and are willing to pay above market value. The adoration is somewhere between that accorded a pop star and a religious figure. Someone else has written that Frida touched her hand after an event and she hasn't washed it since.

While reading I hear the crunch of stone outside so walk over to the curtain and peer through the windows, but there is nothing out there. I put the kettle on the Aga, then notice that a window is open in the kitchen. I'm sure I closed everything before putting the kids down. There are fans whirring overtime in everyone's rooms.

I go back to Frida, heart beating fast at the sight of her. There are numerous Reddit pages about her, mostly adoring. On one of these forums I read that Frida allegedly 'predicted' several global events. Like massively raised food prices caused by groundwater depletion in Europe; power outages due to increased energy demand. Nothing she couldn't have read in any number of newspaper articles. But there are a few stranger ones, which have been shared widely on socials. I read through them on a fan chat page. She predicted a white whale surfacing off the coast of Norway, which happened a few days after. She predicted that snow would fall in the desert and a year later it did. She said mass bird migration disruption would cause birds to flock to a single skyscraper and spiral for hours, which happened just a month ago – I watched it on the news. The European starlings danced and danced around the top of the eerie black Willis Tower in Chicago, one of the tallest buildings in the world. Scientists had no idea why.

I read people's descriptions of their sense of awe. Of the sense of purpose Frida has given them. Apparently, she once appeared at a rave in New York and a thousand saucer-eyed dancers dropped to their knees. People want a sense of belonging, but more than that – they want magic. We all want magic.

Several people say that Frida's inner circle knows when the apocalypse will happen, and that believers will be informed.

There are detractors amongst the comments, but oddly few. Some say it's bullshit that she knows when the world will end. 'She took my money and didn't help at all,' someone has written. 'Total batshit,' says someone else. 'Her group is extremely dangerous,' reads another comment. 'Do not trust this group, I gave them everything I own and got nothing in return.' I'm surprised there isn't more negativity, but presumably she deletes it.

I put my phone down again, and notice with a flutter that my cutting knife is in the middle of the kitchen island. I haven't used it since last night's lasagne. I pick it up and slip it back on to the magnetic holder above the counter. On the kitchen table there is a jar of frogspawn from the pond at the end of the garden. It quivers with jellied potential. There's a movement outside. A fox perhaps. A twitch of twigs. It is nothing, I just didn't put the knife back when tidying.

'Power makes the world move,' Frida says to her followers. I didn't mean to keep watching her videos, but I tell myself I am checking if she's posted anything about me. I need to know what I am dealing with. 'Only the unhealed and the backward are threatened by my power. If your parents, your significant others, misjudge my power as arrogance or narcissism, it is because they have not resolved their own issues. Call me. I can save you.'

Outside the window, a warm breeze drifts over the dark grass. It needs a cut.

None of the furniture in this house is mine. Ben already owned the house when we met; I was living in a trailer. Most of our things came from Ben's wealthy grandmother. His family were major landowners around here. There is a gilded mirror above the fireplace, its frame carved with boats. In winter it reflects the flames from the fire and fills the entire room with movement. A mahogany writing desk is decorated with mother-of-pearl; a pair of tufted armchairs upholstered in faded velvet face the fire, their backs adorned with carved swans. It's not furniture I would have chosen, but it is beautiful.

The sadness I noted in him when I saw him the first time was twofold. His mother died when he was five – she fell off a horse on his family's farm. He'd also recently ended a long-term relationship with a tall cardiothoracic surgeon he'd been dating since secondary school. I have met her several times since: she is brilliant and charming and he still has lunch with her regularly.

A photo of me and Ben on our wedding day looks down from the wall. We got married at a registry office and had a party at a local pub on the beach, with the guests eating fish and chips from newspaper. We'd known each other for less than a year.

I pad upstairs. Leo and I made a chandelier out of sea glass and wire – it glints and throws shapes over the ceiling. Just like on Bay Island, there are piles of pebbles and shells on all the windowsills.

The wide-plank oak floors creak underfoot, the surface polished smooth by generations of footsteps. The master bed has a mahogany headboard carved with twisting vines, made for a much larger room than ours. It is neatly made, the pillows stacked just as I left them, and the wardrobe door is closed. I sit on our bed and cradle my phone.

'A supernova is a powerful and luminous stellar explosion,' Frida says. Beautiful Frida. 'This transient astronomical event occurs during the last evolutionary stages of a massive star, or when a white dwarf is triggered into runaway nuclear fusion.'

I go in to look at Leo, fast asleep and topless on his bed. The sheets are twisted around one of his legs and the rest of him is uncovered. His birthmark, a star shape the size of a tennis ball on his shoulder, glints in the moonlight from under his curtains.

In Japan, some believe that if a pregnant woman stares into fire then the child will be burnt with a birthmark. Other cultures believe a birthmark tells of an early death.

Every day, people's lives are destroyed in places that seem just as safe as this. Sometimes it is abrupt: a bomb, a fall. Sometimes slow: a tingle of cancer gathering cells around it; the start of a bad idea.

Outside Leo's window in the darkness, a twig cracks in the undergrowth around the house. I untangle his ankle from the sheet and tuck him in, then there is a knock on the door.

◆ ◆ ◆

'Well, fuck,' Rebecca said from Frida's computer screen when the call began. We were sitting on Frida's bed at the stifling top of the house that hot summer, all the windows open as wide as possible. 'Hello.'

Rebecca was wearing expensive-looking loungewear, her hair perfectly curled. I'd prepped Frida on my Rebecca research before the call. Flat in London, house in Devon. Did a lot of yoga and detoxing. Worked as the brand manager for Fendi.

'Nice to see you again,' Frida said.

'How's the dog?'

'Great.'

'So . . .' Rebecca took a breath. 'I googled you. Saw your Bay Island Retreat Instagram and the link to here. Seems sort of budget, this AuraLine website. You should just Skype clients. And you don't have many followers.'

'Right. We just started.' There was classical music playing on Rebecca's side of the chat, and the tap of computer keys.

'I don't want advice or anything,' Rebecca said. 'I just thought you should know you were right. So, thank you, I suppose? Maybe. I mean, I did a pregnancy test after we came back from our friend's wedding on Osea, while Greg was writing some emails. I had some tests from years ago. I've bought new ones to confirm though, as well. How did you know?'

'Stop typing on your computer while you're talking to me,' Frida said. 'Just concentrate on me for a second.'

'Don't tell me what to do,' Rebecca said. She frowned and looked away. I could imagine her as the boss of a big company.

'I can hear it. It's rude.'

Rebecca laughed. 'You're right. It is rude. My apologies. I'm not really sure why I'm calling. I'm about to leave for the airport. I just thought I should tell you.'

'Your mind and body are whirring so fast, I can help you to—'

'No, sweetheart,' she said. 'Don't tell me to relax, or stop eating gluten, or take a vacation, or calm down or visualise my pregnancy. Don't tell me to melt into a cloud of butterflies – I've done it all. I get pregnant, then I lose the baby a few weeks later. It has happened many times before. Our first miscarriage was ten years ago. I've done it all. So I don't know why I'm calling you.'

'Because you want a baby,' Frida said.

One of the interesting things about listening to Frida work was that most people just wanted to talk – Frida often had to say very little.

'I'd given up on the baby train,' Rebecca said. 'You know? If you hadn't said what you said I would probably have miscarried without even knowing I'd been pregnant and that might have been better. Would it? It would have been better, I think. I'm meant to be drunk at a rooftop charity event tonight but I pushed my flight.'

'Don't get on the flight. It's often when we least expect it that we are given what we most need,' Frida said.

'Fuck off. I'm not sure I can take the disappointment again. I wish you hadn't told me. I thought I was done with that . . . stomach twist, you know, the knicker-checking, the horrible mounting dragging feeling and then . . .' She sighed. 'This was a mistake.'

The computer blinked again.

Frida blinked, then looked at me.

'She closed the private chat,' Frida said. She scratched the arch of her foot. She looked a bit put out, but maybe she was just thinking because then she took a breath and said to the webcam, where Rebecca may or may not have still been watching:

'To be pregnant again after so many miscarriages is to live two lives at the same time. She took a breath. 'Like a Catholic schoolgirl trying not to think about sex, you try not to think about the cells gaining pace inside you, but you think about it *all the time*. Alive or dead? Now? Now? NOW?' Frida leaned forward towards the camera. 'You are forced to exist in each possible future at the same time. Of course you can't concentrate. You can't think of anything except the crossroad that you are standing at. The truth is your child is alive and dead now. Between dimensions. You do not want to be sitting there alone in your apartment sorting through designer handbags and firing off emails. You feel like you might be about to explode. You need to take some action, make this time different from the others. Call me back. Do not get on the plane.'

That was a good speech. Increasingly, Frida was making a strange sort of sense. Outside Frida's window, seagulls surfed in some rare wind that they'd clearly been longing for, allowing themselves to coast up towards the clouds, half merging with them, then freediving towards friends and shrieking at the fun of it.

◆ ◆ ◆

When Frida touched the palm of my hand sometimes I would try to concentrate on keeping my thoughts steady in case she could read them. It no longer seemed crazy to think she could read certain unspoken thoughts. A dilated pupil, a discomfort, fidgeting with the hair at the nape of my neck. Why shouldn't someone be able to read between those lines?

We continued with our crossword. 'Fragrant buttery breakfast offering?'

'Cinnamon toast.'

'Follower?'

'Minion, shadow, client, member.'

'Wish, six letters.'

'Desire.'

I ran my finger along the edge of some cracked pottery on the window ledge and smiled at her, twisting some heart-shaped sea glass and then holding her Dacian moon goddess statue.

'When you are in a state of transition you are vulnerable but desirable,' she said online. 'It is in the space between feeling and craving that the battle will be fought.'

◆ ◆ ◆

She said she'd never told anyone some of the things she told me. She was opening up to me, or so I thought. And some of it was true. The heart of it, I like to think.

How her mum smelled of hyacinths, how her mum had worked as a cleaner sometimes in Wales and Spain and Frida would go with her and sleep through the night shift under office tables, and more about how her mum would change dramatically for every new boyfriend – just like my mum did. One year her mum wouldn't let her go to school because she thought school was brainwashing, the next Frida was at whichever local primary would take her. They didn't eat meat or grains or sugar one year, then the next they lived on McDonald's but her mum still wouldn't let Frida watch TV or read a book meant for her age. Then, when Frida was ten, her mum got another boyfriend, and they joined quite a serious commune that existed in a farm outside Rome. I asked the name of the commune but she said it didn't have a name.

She told me about befriending a mute epileptic ten-year-old boy when she was six or seven, at one of the nastier communes they'd lived in. After a week of laying hands on him, focusing energy on him, he said his first words. She thought she was probably the first person who had ever been nice to the kid, but soon after this the boy stopped having seizures. That couldn't have been because she was nice to him. That's when Frida's mother started boasting that Frida was a healer and a soothsayer. Another time, a baby was born dead on a different commune and Frida's mother brought Frida in to put her hands on the baby. It began to scream. That's when other people, too, started to call her blessed.

'And did you believe it?' I asked.

'I've always wanted urgently to help people,' she said. 'And I think I do have a gift for it.'

I felt more tender than ever towards Frida at these revelations. It seemed clear to me that she was, like all of us, a product of the world where she grew up. She'd been told she had spiritual powers, and so here she was as a teenager believing she had psychic powers. Framed in her room there was a photo of her, her mum and Jackson sitting in a garden, but it didn't look like Bay. Frida said it was the commune outside Rome where she and her mum moved when Frida was ten. Frida's mum looked so much like her in this picture but with short auburn hair framing her pale face. Frida as a little girl had wild blonde hair and the eyes of a sprite, and she was wearing a white dress. They had recently arrived at the commune when this photo was taken. She looked happy in it, and so did Jackson.

Moth had told his dad that he wasn't going back to school in September, and his dad cut off his credit card. Apparently, he had been buying the food and other necessities for the island. We started eating a lot more rice and turning the toothpaste tubes backwards to get the last bits out.

'Doesn't your grandfather have money?' I asked, and Frida shook her head.

'Barely anything anymore. Even this island isn't worth a thing – because it's sinking. No point in building a hotel on it or anything,' she said.

'He must pay Elena,' I said. 'Palliative care can't be cheap.'

She shrugged. 'I guess.'

I would have given Frida anything then, but didn't have much to give. My time, my turtle necklace. Devotion, though: that was the offering Frida liked the most, as it turned out.

Frida showed me a notebook of places she wanted to visit, mostly islands. She'd kept it as a child. She'd loved atlases. There was a cursed island in Italy called Isola della Gaiola, she told me – two rocks linked by a bridge. It was said to bring terrible luck to its owners. Sudden suicides, heart attacks, brutal murders, commitment to mental hospitals, general chaos. She said she couldn't wait for it to be a crossword clue one day.

Maybe some part of me knew Frida was lying about her childhood, or at least not telling the whole truth.

I know she was kind to Jackson, though. She used to read to him every single day. Every day, without fail. Sometimes I'd walk past the door to listen.

'When Croesus, the king of Lydia, was debating about whether to attack the Persian Empire, he decided to seek advice from the gods,' she read to him.

I do think a lot of what she told me during this time was true, although not all of it. Maybe in a way we all do the same when we fall in love – only allowing the other to see the layers of information, letting them 'discover' us but really only showing what we want to.

It wasn't just Frida I got closer with. It felt like a true community. I played cards with Grace. She painted my nails. Did my make-up. Did my hair. We meditated. And when we did, time bled away. People followed. But on the island, it was just us.

Elena taught me and Grace to cook. We made lasagne, and stuffed cabbage rolls from her own grandmother's recipe. She didn't talk much. I'd googled her. She was an accredited hospice nurse, or end-of-life carer, with a relatively big company. The doctor also came over regularly from Queen's Hospital in Romford so I had no reason to think Jackson was being badly treated.

Believing in Frida was like that grey area of childhood where you want to believe in Father Christmas. I didn't believe in ghosts or psychics, but I wanted to believe in Frida. Or maybe it was like frogs in a saucepan – falling in love with her was like being slowly boiled alive.

From my window, I watched Grace dancing outside the forest.

◆ ◆ ◆

'On Midsummer night . . .' – Frida smiled on AuraLine, talking into her phone with the fire licking behind her. We all had wildflowers strung in our hair as we sat around the fire that night. Round pink clusters of thrift. Tiny, bright orange blooms of scarlet pimpernel – 'we wear flower crowns to ward off malevolent spirits.' She touched her flower garland. 'This is a night when the space between dimensions is gossamer-thin and ghosts cross over easily from the afterlife.' Elena had cooked a feast: vegetables, potatoes, and bass that Stefan had caught in the estuary. I breathed in deeply, closing my eyes as Frida droned on in a low, rhythmic voice. We were supposed to be focusing on our breathing, letting thoughts drift by. It felt as if shadows lingered just a second too long at the edges of my vision if I opened my eyes, so I kept them closed.

Frida's voice softened to a murmur, but I couldn't catch the words. I felt myself slipping, my sense of time unravelling, as though I were being pulled away from the present.

Then, when I opened my eyes, I was in bed, tangled in stiff sheets.

I blinked, a headache pulsing. I sat up slowly, scanning the room, half expecting to see someone standing in the corner, but nothing moved. I swung my legs over the side of the bed, a chill against my bare feet. The door to my room was slightly ajar.

Taking a shaky breath, I crossed the room, careful to avoid the floorboard I knew would creak. I looked out into the narrow hallway. There was a dark figure at the far end of the hall and I wondered if I was dreaming.

The man was standing just at the edge of the light, his face hidden. He wasn't moving or speaking, just staring. My breath caught, my pulse racing, then his face moved slightly and I saw that it was Jackson. I'd never seen him out of bed before.

'Help me,' he said, and then Elena appeared next to him. A switch clicked, and dusty light from a naked bulb lit the hallway.

'Oh, love,' Elena said to Jackson. 'Let's get you back to bed.'

◆ ◆ ◆

I went into Jackson's room alone later that afternoon, when the others were outside meditating. Elena said that a period of lucidity often preceded death, and that's why Jackson had suddenly been able to get out of bed: he was going to die soon.

Now he was back in bed and looked only half conscious again. The heart monitor beeped steadily, and he was asleep. An IV dripped slowly into his wrinkled hand. The respirator hissed its dragon breath. The small table next to the bed held an assortment of medications in neat pill bottles, some half used, others unopened, their labels worn. The room felt claustrophobic, the smell of antiseptic mingling with the musty scent of old leather and paper. There were Tarot decks on a shelf, edges frayed from damp and use. Dusty candles, rune stones, amulets, little piles of bones that made me shiver.

The books were predominantly history books with a strong focus on ancient Rome. I touched the spine of *The Twelve Caesars*, a dog-eared *Commentaries on the Gallic War: A New History of Rome and the Barbarians.* I lifted up a book called *Cult Images and Mithraic Reliefs in Roman Dacia* and noted that the front cover was a photograph of the statue that Frida had in her room. The picture attribution said that the photo was of a 'Limestone statue of Artemis Bendis, by a Cypriot artist c. 3rd century bce'.

I picked up a book called *A Course in Miracles.* 'What you think you are is a belief to be undone,' he had underlined. 'Nothing real can be threatened. Nothing unreal exists. Herein lies the peace of God.'

This book and the others were full of lines and notes. 'You are what you believe in. You become that which you believe you can become,' was underlined in a book called *The Bhagavad Gita.*

I opened a drawer, knowing that I shouldn't. The room was a liminal space, Jackson's decrepit physical form meeting what must have been a lifelong interest in the intangible. No wonder he was scared.

There were a couple of reviews for his book in the drawer. One reviewer, in *The Journal of Mythological Studies*, said that the book 'delivers an unconvincing amalgam of speculative leaps, selective interpretations, and tenuous connections'. Another review stated that the book 'cherry-picks evidence from disparate sources with little regard for their distinct cultural contexts'.

These reviews were folded in drawers amongst dusty crystals, trinkets, a flyer for the Bay Island Caravan Site and a pile of photographs. I scooped these out the back and went through them, looking for him and Frida together in happier days, or even Jackson and Frida's mum.

There were photos of the house when it was newer, photos of Jackson when he was young dressed in a tweed suit, photos of the caravan site when he'd rented it out to holidaymakers. Amongst photos of hippies around a fire and sunsets, there was a school photo of a plump, dark-skinned and dark-haired child named Jenny Rae. The sort where the kid looks miserable and the hair is super neat. This Jenny person looked about six in the photo. I put it back. Some relation of Frida's, I supposed.

I sat down on his desk chair. If it weren't for the rhythmic hiss of his breathing machine, I would have thought he was dead.

◆ ◆ ◆

When I found out he wasn't her grandfather we were walking together on the flats, as we often did. I told her I'd gone up to his room to see him and looked at some of his photos. She was silent for a bit. There was a vulnerability to her during this exchange, a rehearsed but imperfect nonchalance that reminded me of seeing stagehands putting out furniture on stage. She must have known we would find out that Jackson wasn't her real grandfather, but her story still wasn't entirely coherent. I liked seeing the cogs move. It gave me the impression that I was peeling back layers to peer in at some version of the 'real' Frida.

We headed out through the suctioning mud, which squelched against our bare feet. It smelled of salt water and decay and something else when we got close to the decommissioned power plant, where she said kids were always going to get high. We could hear the slow rush of distant waves and the occasional call of seabirds. We talked about a bunch of stuff. Nuclear power, the science of rusting metal, the feeling of hubris we both felt at the sight of this power plant. It was so huge, and so much effort had gone into building it, yet it was abandoned.

'There was some girl called Jenny Rae. Is that an aunt or something?'

'Jenny is his biological daughter, but they are totally estranged,' she said casually. 'They haven't seen each other in person since

Jenny was a baby. It was a bad divorce and Jenny's mum moved to New York with the kid.'

It took me a moment before I asked:

'Is your mum not his biological daughter then?'

'No,' she laughed. 'Did I say he was?'

'I mean, yeah. You call him your grandfather all the time. You know you do.'

'I think of him as my grandfather and he thinks of me as his granddaughter. Jackson lived at the Rome commune when Mum and I moved there. He came and went for years while I was there. I showed you the photo of us all, it's framed in my room.'

'But I thought your mum was his daughter. So is your surname Rae?'

'I haven't lied to you,' she said, kicking sand with her feet.

She had, but I didn't say that because she started talking while we walked and I was just pleased for the insight into her past. She described the Rome commune disbanding two years ago, when she was fifteen. It had been the most magical part of her childhood. They grew their own vegetables, raised chicken and goats and cows. Children were raised together, and everyone played a role, but the Italian government got spooked as the commune grew. They declared the buildings unfit for purpose, built on land without proper ownership and zoning permissions. Really they just looked for reasons to shut them down because the group offered a different way of living. When the group disbanded, she moved from Rome back to Wales and ended up in social care. Elena was also an on–off member of the Rome commune. So when Jackson got ill, he hired Elena to look after him, and she asked if Frida could come live with him as well.

Frida scooped up a tiny crab from the mud but didn't meet my eye.

'Don't look at me like that. His family never visit him. He loves me,' she said.

'What's your real surname?'

'Does it matter?'

'I thought you were his granddaughter.'

'He asked me to take his name and live with him. I helped with his pain, and read to him, and laid Tarot for him. I don't know my real grandparents on either side. My mum fucked off somewhere and the social care was worse than the crack dens my mum used to like. Jackson cares about me and I care about him. So I've been with him for a year now.'

'Right,' I said, dubiously.

'The NHS wanted Jackson to go to a hospice because he has no family, but Jackson wanted to die on the island. His grandchildren never even called.'

'Does his daughter know he's sick?'

'I don't know. They've never called.'

She touched my hand with the tips of her fingers.

'I haven't lied to you. He considers me family. I am showing him nothing but kindness. In the commune, we were all family.'

'Do Moth and the others know he isn't your biological family?'

The power plant loomed above us. Crows peeled from the centre and flocked up into the darkening sky. She took my hand in the salt marsh.

'Family isn't just blood,' she said. 'I doubt they'd care.'

'Do they know?'

'I'll tell them,' she said, 'Of course, if it's important to you.'

As we stood there with our toes in the wet sand, I decided she hadn't done anything wrong. She cared about Jackson. She and Elena were there with him when nobody else was willing to be. She had a way of making me seem unreasonable when I caught her in a lie.

◆ ◆ ◆

As promised, Frida told Moth and Grace that she wasn't technically Jackson's granddaughter. They didn't seem to care so I didn't either. In the photo in her room, Jackson clearly does adore Frida. He is looking at her with love.

So, we moved on. Like when we made a mistake during a psychic reading, the best thing was to charmingly move on and hope nobody cared enough to dwell.

Frida said we needed new clothes if we were going to meet Rebecca and get her to come to the island, so we focused on that. But we had no money for new clothes. I'd spent the last of the small amount in my bank account. We really needed to come into some money at this point.

There weren't any good clothes in town anyway, just gift shops selling wooden seagulls on sticks and faux-driftwood signs painted with 'Gone to the beach' and 'What if the Hokey Cokey really is what it's all about?' – and anyway, we didn't have any money.

While Grace distracted the security guards, Frida shoplifted a deep conditioner, a cleanser for acne-prone skin and a tooth-whitening kit from Boots. Frida was an elegant shoplifter. She whispered in my ear, pointing at a sunburnt guy in the toothbrush aisle: 'That guy cries when he's drunk. He's turned on by feet.'

'Feet? You know him?'

'Beige court shoes send him crazy,' she said. 'That woman sucks her thumb.' She pointed to a mother with one kid in the pram and another riding on a buggy board. 'Look how her teeth jut out. She can't sleep unless she's sucking her thumb. She misses her mother every night. Her mother died maybe three or four years ago.' Then, about a young woman in hot pants: 'Compulsive eater. Throws up.'

The four of us walked down towards the promenade past the Chinese restaurants and the tattoo parlours. An old couple crossed the road slowly, a dog barked.

We walked past The Sailor, where I'd first met Grace and Moth, towards the brick wall between the promenade and the estuary. I flicked through a newspaper abandoned on the wall. 'Homes destroyed as wildfires tear through Britain on hottest day in history,' it said on the front. On page three: 'As UK reaches 40°C and fires blaze, scientists warn of such temperatures every three years if emissions are not lowered.'

It was low tide, and a bunch of teenagers were messing around on the riverbed further up, sitting in the empty boats and smoking cigarettes.

'Do you know the white bear game?' Frida asked, as we tracked these girls, watching them giggle.

I shook my head.

'You have to go as long as you can without thinking of a white bear.'

'I lose.'

'Everyone does.'

'Shall we go back to the island then?' I said.

'Not yet,' she said, watching the girls.

She touched my hand slightly, where it rested on the bricks between us. Grace and Moth, behind us, were buying an inflatable swan for floating in the river, haggling over the price. There were maybe three metres of sloped muddy riverbed before the water, scattered with rowboats, rubbish, buoys and driftwood. The teenagers were showing each other stuff on their phones, putting their hair up; a girl and boy were kissing. I saw two of the teenagers pointing at us and then passing around one of their phones, and realised they were the Starbucks girls – our first Instagram followers, who I'd seen messing around in Starbucks when I went shopping with Moth.

They began walking towards us over the riverbed. They were fidgeting and sharing a rollie. One of them inhaling, the other twisting her hair up to let the sea air cool the nape of her neck.

One of them, whose name I knew was Nadia from her socials, had long brown hair down to the middle of her back, and the other I knew was called Bella, with shoulder-length hair held in a messy bun by a gingham scrunchie. They were both wearing jersey shorts and cami-tops with dirty bra straps showing. Bella had a slight limp and dragged her foot.

'She had meningitis as a child,' I whispered in Frida's ear. Bella was the one who had posted about raising money for a meningitis charity, and about it being the anniversary of her father's death. 'Her dad's dead,' I added.

'Hey,' Nadia said to us from the riverbed, shielding her eyes from the sun. 'We follow you on Insta. So can we, like, get a reading IRL or something? We have a fiver.' Bella held a damp note up at us, her cigarette dangling from her mouth.

'Sure,' I said. 'We don't need your money.'

Grace and Moth came and watched from the wall. Frida took off her shoes and jumped down from the wall on to the riverbed so she was standing with them. 'Of course,' she said, and didn't take the money. 'I can feel pain in your lower back even without touching you,' Frida said to Bella.

Bella didn't reply but took a step back, behind Nadia.

'It's been getting worse recently, but you haven't told anyone. May I touch you?'

Bella's eyes widened a little.

'Do it,' Nadia said, nudging her friend.

So Bella nodded and took a step forward and Frida put a hand on the girl's shoulder. I was still sitting on the wall looking down at them, but had taken out my phone to film from above.

'You had an infection as a child, a fever?'

'Meningitis,' Nadia answered for her friend. 'She nearly died. Wow. That's actually impressive. How did you know?'

'The infection has left a wound. May I put my hands on your back?'

'Let her,' said Nadia.

Bella nodded and Frida gently turned the girl around then put her hands on her waist with her thumbs at the base of her spine.

'Close your eyes now and feel the heat of me. Trust me.' Bella closed her eyes. 'You think about dying but it isn't your time. I feel a man's presence is here, an older man. Can you feel it?' Can you feel the heat?'

'Is he here?' Bella said, standing on the riverbed. Her voice caught as she said it.

'Her dad?' Nadia said. 'Fuck.'

Bella and Nadia's friends had made their way over by this point and were smoking and eating crisps while watching us.

'He is here,' Frida said. 'I'm going to start removing the last of the fever from your spine. I'm taking away the pain where your energy has stagnated and is blocking your growth. Can you feel the heat of me?'

'Yes,' Bella said, and she had tears on her cheeks now. Two old ladies were peering over the wall behind me and Nadia was also filming on her phone.

'You are powerful. You are strong. You are free from pain. Your father's spirit is here with you always. I see the letter J.'

'His middle name was James,' Bella said tearfully. Even the boats in the distance stopped making noises. I hadn't told Frida that, but if she'd been wrong it would have slipped away amongst the things she did get right.

'He misses you. Now, when I take my hands away you will open your eyes and your back won't hurt.'

Bella opened her eyes.

'It actually doesn't,' she said. 'This is fucked up.' She walked towards the water through silty mud, putting her feet down carefully, then looked back up at Frida and her friends. 'It actually doesn't hurt. What happened?'

'The spirits are arriving around us now,' Frida said, stepping back. I had the impression of them all standing in a gladiator pit; it was an eerie stage-like setting. The riverbed at low tide, full of grounded boats and glistening water. My unfamiliar friend, a circus animal in a cage, padding over the riverbed. Bella, still splattered with mud and tears, saying she was cured. A darkness in the sky above, a looping grey cloud of fumes.

'Come on, this is bullshit,' one of the teenagers giggled, and Frida turned to her with restrained aggression. The naysayer was tall, and the growth had happened recently – there were stretch marks on her thighs and her jersey shorts were a size too small. She had acne on her cheeks, and her heavy eyebrows were low and angry over her small eyes.

'You have been told you are ordinary so you want everyone else to be ordinary as well,' Frida said to the tall girl. 'You've been told you won't amount to anything, don't deserve love and happiness. But the truth is that life is full of magic.'

'Fuck off,' the tall girl said, balling her fists. She had scabs on her knuckles, like she'd been in a fight recently. Her eyes were older than the rest of her face.

'No,' Frida said, stepping closer to this girl. 'Ordinary people believe only in the possible,' she said. 'Ordinary people are too scared to look up from the pavement. Too scared to break from the safe boundaries of their lives, their parents' expectations, society's plan. But extraordinary people look to the sky. To how the bones of a human hand web together. To immortality.'

'You need to go to a hairdresser,' said the tall girl. 'You look like you dipped your hair in toilet bleach.'

'You are so scared.'

'I'm not fucking scared.'

'I see your worst nightmares,' Frida whispered in this girl's ear, making her shiver. 'I see how you try to impress your friends by not caring about anything. I see your fear of failure that makes you pretend not to try at all. Because if you do try and fail, your mediocrity will be confirmed. I see what you let boys do to you because you need to feel wanted.'

'She's just a bitch, let's go,' said the tall girl with an expression of panic in her eyes, but the rest of the group were rooted to the spot, half horrified and half interested, watching Frida.

'Everyone is afraid,' Frida said. 'Everyone is pretending not to be. You are not alone.'

The tall girl stood there, slack-jawed.

'You have huge untapped potential,' Frida said to the girl, reeling her in now. This girl leaned forward, eyes wet. 'You don't have to be average. You could be spectacular if you let me help you.'

The tall girl stepped forward, towards Frida.

Three of these girls came to the island that evening and slept on the sofas, scattering plastic bangles and glittery lip gloss amongst shells and sea glass on the windowsills: Nadia, Bella and the tall girl, who turned out to be called Ruth. Ruth lived in a group home in Chelmsford. She'd dropped out of school and now made money running errands for a local drug dealer. Frida told them all how beautiful they were, how unique, how their parents and boyfriends and social workers clearly didn't understand. Ruth watched Frida more intently than the others. We overwhelmed them all with affection, and good food. They couldn't believe their luck.

There was a dead bluetit in the field the next day, his eyes closed inside stripes of feather. His head was flung back, his yellow belly exposed and claws stiff. Frida said that meant there was going to be a storm.

Chapter Eight

Ben's grandfather clock strikes midnight. My kids are fast asleep upstairs. Oliver and I sit in the garden looking over the vegetables, the garden wall and out towards the sea. The scent of brine mixes with lavender from the garden and Oliver's cigarette smoke. He has finished one cigarette and is rolling another, the paper laid out on my teak garden table. I adjust my jumper and sip my vodka tonic, my hand trembling slightly. They haven't stopped trembling since unlatching the chain. Oliver walked in as if he had been invited.

Ben is on an overnight shift at the hospital. The slatted chairs are uncomfortable without their matching sage-green cushions. I grip the cool of my drink.

'Why did you give her a fake name?' he asks. 'Your real name, I presume, is Katie?'

'At first, because I met her online. Seemed sensible not to give my real name. But later I just stuck with the lie.'

'Because part of you was scared of her?'

'No, I just stuck with the lie so she didn't know I'd lied,' I say.

With practised hands, Oliver lays tobacco in a neat line, smoothing and shaping the mixture with gentle taps and nudges until it twists into a compact cylinder. 'Does it scare you that she knows where you are? She's had her followers looking for you.

Surely you think that's fucked up. They took a photo of you and your son.'

'Yes,' I concede.

'They ruined me,' he says. 'And you should be more scared than you seem. She has an online army doing her bidding.'

'I looked you up. You were into her. What made you start speaking out against her?'

He bends towards the lighter flame and inhales, then nods. 'Her PR team invited me to one of her big events at Tobacco Dock in East London. It was something called a Shadow Work Course, where we were going to delve into hidden aspects of the self to promote healing and transformation,' he says, and the muscles in his big neck tense around the smoke as he holds it in. Then he blows it out in a tunnel. I see the razor burn on his neck again, like I noticed on the cliffs. Razor burn on a man's neck has always made me feel tender towards them. Men pretend to be so strong but their skin is soft just like ours. 'You ever do that sort of shit?'

'No.' I shook my head.

'I took my girlfriend.' He ashes his cigarette in the grass and touches the crook of his arm. A seagull whirls in the darkness over the garden. 'She wasn't on social media, didn't own yoga pants or crystals or even take vitamins. She ran a building supply company and a year ago would have laughed in my face at the idea she might join a spiritual movement. That was my world.'

He inhales more smoke, and I listen out for any sound of my kids waking up or a car on the drive. Ben shouldn't be home for hours.

'I had thought Frida was really interesting. She seemed so raw, and different from traditional gurus. But I didn't like the seminar. There was this sort of choreographed enthusiasm to it, lots of buzz words and vague promises, testimonials from people claiming miraculous transformations. There was a woman who went up on stage and claimed Frida had cured her of debilitating migraines by forcing her to confront the fact that she had been raped as a child. She cured someone else's infertility. She had allegedly predicted vague shit. Proposals. A sinkhole somewhere. Frida didn't believe in monogamy, or traditional family values. She thought that jealousy was a learned social response, as was greed. Attendees were praised for making stupid life decisions – quitting jobs, severing relationships – on the spot. Despite the message of empowerment, the event felt disempowering. There was a constant assertion that people needed Frida in order to succeed, which reinforced dependence rather than self-reliance.'

His shoulders have dipped. He inhales his cigarette and sips his vodka.

'But Vicky loved it. Vicky suffered from OCD. Like, in a way that sometimes overwhelmed her and stopped her doing her job or living her life. So Frida "cured" this over a session on a video call. One session. Years of therapy and Frida stopped her flicking the lights twenty times and going for a pee twenty times before leaving the house. Frida helped, so I just tried to be positive. Vicky asked me not to write the nasty article about Frida and so of course I didn't. But Vicky started spending more and more of our money on workshops online, and then she started going on retreats. Frida made her feel *saved*, apparently. Frida gave the love of my life a feeling of *wonder* and *delight* that she hadn't felt since she was a child.'

'I'm sorry your girlfriend chose another way of life, but it doesn't make Frida bad.'

'She's making money off people's vulnerability.'

'You could say that of every religion. Your girlfriend left you?'

'Yeah, and left me with a bunch of credit card debt from calling Frida and took a job at the Frida Rae Academy. She sent me the nastiest note about how my toxic masculinity was stopping her from reaching her potential. I was selfish, and backwards. How I didn't understand her "quest for knowing". It was Frida's language.'

He stops and the words linger in the warm air. I pick at a bit of splintering wood on the corner of the table.

'I wrote a horrible email to my mum when I was with Frida,' I say to him. Our ice cubes have melted in our drinks, even though it is the middle of the night. 'Our relationship has never really recovered even ten years later. I didn't really mean it, if it makes you feel any better.'

In front of us, the night is illuminated by the pale glow of the moon. We can hear waves crashing, music from a window nearby, the faint horn of a passing ship.

'I started speaking out against Frida in social media posts, and her followers came at me like locusts.'

He pauses, takes a shaky breath and rolls his shirt a little further up his arm. Just like Moth, there are dots of track marks in the crook of his arm. Small, raised scars or bruises near the veins. Faint, but noticeable even in the moonlight. He can't have been using for long. I remember scars-upon-scars on Moth's arms, a braille of self-harm. Oliver's arms aren't like that.

'Her followers started writing forty, fifty negative comments every day on my archive of journalism, which eventually cost me my job. Nobody would print anything I wrote because it would get hated on so fast. My accounts were hacked, her followers abused me on all the socials. But Frida just kept doing her seminars, saying vacuous things on Instagram while wearing a bikini, and showing her followers the fucking panda bears or indigenous women she was supporting with her enterprises. And my girlfriend was out there in Bali last time I saw her on socials, serving fucking crystal-infused cucumber water to new recruits, and scanning their credit cards for tithes.'

◆ ◆ ◆

We went to meet Rebecca the morning after the Starbucks girls came to the island. The girls were left meditating with Moth, watching him sweat. Online, my video was being watched by hundreds of strangers: Frida standing on the mudflats talking about fear to a dazzled audience of teenagers in hot pants. I'd put it through a pretty, eerie filter. The Starbucks girls had reposted, tagged, commented, and sent it round to their friends.

I kept checking on the views as Moth drove us down to London. Rebecca and her husband had a large house in Devon and a three-bedroom penthouse in a serviced apartment block in Soho, where Moth dropped us off. It had exposed brick across one side of an open-plan kitchen/living room and thick carpet on the floor. The main room spilled out on to the balcony, with three potted lemon trees that turned out to be artificial. Her husband, Gregory, was away on business, as he apparently often was.

Of the nine times Rebecca and Gregory had been pregnant, she always miscarried in the first month, she said. They had done IVF five times. There was nothing technically wrong with either of them, and yet . . .

While Frida and Rebecca meditated and breathed, I took the lift downstairs and looked around the building. There was a pool in the basement. It had a mirror ceiling and azure tiles. An Asian woman wearing a mermaid tail swam back and forth – an actual literal tail. I looked it up, and apparently they were very good for the abs. There was a sauna and a steam room and it was all eerily empty. Later Frida and I went for tea in a fancy restaurant opposite the flats because Rebecca had to send some emails. Rebecca had a tab at the restaurant. We ordered all the most expensive things on the menu – oysters and lobster and soufflé.

'You need to be compassionate towards yourself as your pain bubbles up and heals,' Frida said to the camera, sitting in this fancy restaurant like a proper influencer. 'Be brave. Your pain is valid. Life hurts sometimes.'

I posted on Instagram and we pottered back upstairs to Rebecca's flat. While they meditated on the balcony I messed around on my phone on a green velvet sofa inside, replying to DMs and messages as if I were Frida. At some point, making sure Frida and Rebecca were deeply immersed in each other on the balcony, I walked into Rebecca's bedroom. I ran my fingers over lipsticks, glass jars of vitamins, exfoliants, and hair creams. There was a framed photograph of Rebecca and her parents on the steps of a suburban house. Another photo on the dresser was of Rebecca graduating from Cambridge, standing next to her mother again. Her wedding day. Her and her husband on holiday somewhere hot. I stood in her walk-in wardrobe. YSL shoulder bags, croc-effect totes, leather mules, Jimmy Choo slingback pumps – almost everything in neutral colours. Lots of Fendi. Rows of shoeboxes and bags lined a top shelf. I stood on a little stool to reach for an old scuffed one with teddy bears. It was from White Stuff, the baby department.

I opened the box and there was a cashmere blanket with 'Marcus' embroidered on it. I quickly closed it up and put it back.

That afternoon Frida spoke to Rebecca of the name 'Marcus' coming to her, a soul in limbo waiting for his chance to be born. I'd whispered the name in her ear. I'm not proud of it. It makes me flinch to think of it. Possibly more than anything else we did that summer.

'How did you meet her?' Rebecca said that evening, rolling a suitcase out into the hallway after agreeing to come and stay on the island for a few days until Gregory got home from his business trip. 'She's extraordinary.'

'She cured me of a very serious anxiety problem,' I said. 'I used to be on so much medication that I could hardly get out of bed. But she saved me.'

Rebecca nodded, like that was what she expected.

◆ ◆ ◆

'It is only in staring death in the face that we learn how to live,' Frida said on camera. 'Today, the spirits want me to tell you that it is when we have nothing to lose that we are at our most powerful.'

◆ ◆ ◆

The trees waved gently in the wet hot air. There was a mounting energy that would later become the storm Frida had predicted. A tiny bird was perched on its branch, its throat straining. It flew off into the thickening sky. We only just made it over before the causeway closed behind us. Bread was baking and tomato sauce was bubbling on the stove.

Everyone greeted Rebecca with enthusiasm. Frida took her upstairs, where my room was going to be Rebecca's for now.

Frida stopped smoking that day. Just like that, because Rebecca was sensitive to the smell.

Rebecca unpacked her suitcase upstairs. When I walked past I saw that Elena had put a milk bottle of wildflowers on the window ledge and a pile of folded towels on the bedside table. Rebecca moved carefully, touching her stomach even though there wasn't a bump yet. She was tired and went to bed early the first day, eating the bread and pasta in her room. The night she arrived, Rebecca posted a selfie of her and Frida to her fashionista Instagram followers.

'There is an end in every beginning,' Frida said to our new followers that night. The follower count was climbing. The more people followed us, the more valid we seemed. I watched the livestream from the kitchen. 'The air is thick with spirits tonight and they are all talking to me. I draw a door with my hands like this' – and she drew a door in the air – 'and the air has a different texture on the other side. We could walk right in.'

I heard the bath running through the computer. Also, when I listened, through the pipes of the cottage.

'Can you all feel the intensity rising?' she said. Her hands were shaking and the sound of the water changed tone.

So I wrote her a DM: 'Frida, is the bath overflowing?'

She didn't see.

'FRIDA. BATH!' I wrote.

I headed through the cottage. Water was already dripping down from her bathroom to the corridor, so when she didn't immediately open the door I just walked through into the sodden en suite bathroom to turn off the tap and take the plug out.

I put down a few of her thin towels from the rail. She closed her computer, got up and walked through her messy room, stepping over piles of books and clothes.

'I forgot,' she said, standing in the bathroom doorway.

'It'll dry,' I said, but her eyes were all glossy like she was about to cry. I'd never seen her cry before. I was vaguely mopping up the floor, looking up at her. She was pale.

'I forgot I turned the tap on.'

'Never mind.'

Then she burst into tears. I didn't know what to do, or why she was crying. I thought she would be happy that Rebecca was there. She'd been happy an hour ago. She sat down on the wet bathroom floor, so I sat next to her, both of us with our backs to the bathtub.

'He's going to die tonight,' Frida said. 'Elena says he's near the end.'

'Oh. Jackson. I'm so sorry.'

The bathroom smelled of mould and bubble bath. She wriggled her toes in the thin layer of water over the avocado-coloured tiles.

'He called me his Oracle, because I can see things others don't. Nuances, spirits. I was kind to him.' The bathwater gurgled away behind us. 'I hope you don't think I've done anything wrong. His real family never came to see him, they thought he was a weird, old, isolated man obsessed by old religions and art. But he's intelligent and he cares about me.'

'Of course he does,' I said.

'You won't leave me, will you?'

'No,' I said. 'But we will have to leave the island, right? Unless he has actually left the island to you in his will, it will go to his real family.'

She leaned over the bath and put the plug back in so the water stopped escaping. Then she sat on the edge with her bare legs in the water but her damp, clingy white t-shirt still on.

'Jackson has left me everything in his will. I made sure he put my real name and details on there. There was a lawyer present when he changed it and everything. This was before you guys all came. He wants *me* to have it all. Yes, he thought I was her near the end, but his granddaughter never visited. Never wiped his saliva, fed him, read him stories. That was me. He loves me.'

She began to shave her legs in the bath.

'But Jackson's daughter will find out that her dad is dead.'

'And she'll find out he's left everything to a girl who looked after him.' She paused. 'The island is worthless anyway.'

'You don't have to justify yourself to me,' I said. 'Of course you helped him. And if he's left it to you we can live here, and that's good.'

She nodded, and went back to shaving her legs in the bathwater.

'An infallible authority, six letters. Oracle,' I said then, trying to lighten the tone. 'I'm surprised you don't have an even bigger ego if that's what Jackson called you. My grandmother called me "Smudge".'

'Narcissist's quality, three letters. Ego,' she said.

'Affectionate email closing, four letters,' I said.

'Really? Love? Do you love me?'

I was a little shocked by how the conversation had gone.

'Yes,' I said, and she lifted one of her legs up to get the hair on her knee. I realised she wasn't wearing knickers.

'I love you too,' she said.

I looked away, embarrassed. I felt disorientated in the small hot bathroom, close to her. More than disorientated. Her lack of knickers felt like a slap. Or no, worse than that: a need. Like a pill during a panic attack. I could almost smell the lack of knickers, we were that close.

She had dark pubic hair, much darker than the hair on her head. I'd seen her naked for moments out on the beach when she was about to go in or had just come out of the water, but it was only ever the swift kick of lanky limbs before she jumped.

Now though, she took off her t-shirt but left it with the neck around her forehead as a hairband so she looked like a naked nun. She grinned at me and I felt dizzy.

The soft underside of her breasts was paler than the rest of her body, with a faint maze of blue veins visible. The surface of our skin is only seven cells thick, I remembered from school, but the underside of her breasts must only have had the finest glaze of skin stopping the tangle of bloody pathways from being exposed.

She slipped into the bath, and flicked her cotton white t-shirt habit over the lip of the bath so it didn't get wet, then sunk into the greenish water.

'But will you stay?' she said, turning her cheek to where I was still sitting on the damp floor next to the bath. Our hands were shaking. 'It will be ours soon.'

I nodded. Of course I would.

That night in bed Frida's body felt like the bird that had fallen from the sky earlier: surprisingly bony and fragile. This was soft and urgent.

Windows open, no breeze, the ivy crawling in a little bit every day. Crows and music, coming from somewhere beyond the forest.

I woke up at some point in the night and she wasn't there. The storm was raging outside the window, as she'd predicted. Trees were waving. The wind was trying to snatch open the doors, putting feelers down the chimney and rattling the windows. The lights flickered as the wind shook the electricity wires. She was gone for the rest of the night. I stretched in her bed.

I had never before felt anything like I did with Frida. Certainly not with that fifteen-year-old boy who ended up fancying my mum more than me. And not with some other boy I'd kissed on a house party sofa aged sixteen, who hadn't remembered me the next day at school. Those moments did not fit into the same category of feeling. Not the same universe of sensation.

◆ ◆ ◆

He died that night. Frida was with him when it happened, sitting at his bedside along with Elena, reading to him, her voice soothing him. The next day Elena flung open all the windows to get rid of Jackson's spirit. The house felt different without the heartbeat of the oxygen machine. The doctor came, then later we stood on the wild beach and watched the undertaker take Jackson's body away in a modified van, not a hearse like you'd expect. It was just a normal-looking van with equipment in the back, which staggered over the causeway. The undertaker and his son had to push the van at one point, when the wheel got stuck in a hole. I noticed later that the undertaker's son started to follow us on Instagram.

The wind was still high when the van disappeared from sight. Plastic bags danced in the last of it. There was a scattering of purple-white spheres that might have been plastic but were in fact beached jellyfish, and sticky balls of something that turned out to be congealed fuel.

Oystercatchers and waders dug their beaks into the sand, flipped their catches and then moved in unison up into the sky and vanished into the dune grass and marshes beyond. In a space between a brick and some driftwood, I picked up a sea-sanded, misshapen Lego man wearing a suit, with John-Travolta-in-*Pulp-Fiction* slick black hair, and gave it to Moth. Boats trawled past in the distance. It was hard to differentiate between sand and sea.

I loved the island most when the causeway sank into the estuary each day. It always seemed to happen suddenly. One minute a threat, just a wobble of liquid, then suddenly the causeway had drowned while Frida sat on the grass, easing salt water out of her hair.

◆ ◆ ◆

'Death is not a solitary or incommunicable event,' Frida said in the cool of the forest that afternoon, to the Starbucks girls and Rebecca and her followers online, 'but the most engulfing, communal and intimate moment in the cycle of human life. The smallest sprout shows there is really no death. There is only life.'

Because of Rebecca's selfie with Frida, and her engagement with our posts, the day after Jackson died we had more than a thousand followers, and they were climbing steadily. The Starbucks girls were all wearing white t-shirts now and no make-up. Frida touched Ruth's hand in passing, running fingers over her fight-scarred knuckles, and her old eyes visibly softened. People let down their guard with Frida.

'Nothing collapses, and to die is different from what anyone supposes, and luckier,' Frida said in the forest. I filmed her. 'When a seed is in our hands it does nothing, but when it splits open in the earth and dies, it bears life you would never have imagined. Death is necessary for life. In order to live we must appreciate death.'

I thought of my own grandmother. When she died she still had the camel mohair coat she'd bought in her twenties from a John Lewis sale. She owned beautiful things even though she'd worked most of her life in the library. She would apply lipstick every day till close to the end. She loved her sturdy, warm boots, her charity-shop wool sweaters, the camel-coloured coat. Her small collection of family photos had been in real silver frames with velvet backs and she was appalled by her daughter's costume jewellery and trashy clothes. The last time I saw her alive she was wearing her jumper backwards, which would have incensed her if she'd known.

Gran would have disliked Frida immensely. Mum and Gran both ate margarine on squares of white toast with the crusts cut off, then licked the gloss from their fingers in exactly the same way. Mum said it was a trick Gran taught her 'to make your brain think you'd eaten a piece of toast when all you'd eaten was a crumb'. They were both capable of eating three Maltesers. They wore the same shade of lipstick and had the same colour eyes. I looked so different.

Aged eight, after Grandma went to the hospice without her camel coat or red lipstick, I hit a girl named Brinda in the school toilets. Punched her with a closed fist for pushing in front of me in the queue for the slide. Brinda had gorgeous long hair down to her bum. She got a black eye that swelled and turned various shades of putrid green. They threatened to expel me but nobody really wanted to because my grandmother had just died and I had the reading age of a fourteen-year-old.

◆ ◆ ◆

Two other former members of the Rome commune turned up after Jackson died, one tall and slim, the other stocky. Their names were Nicolae and Alex. Just like all of us, they watched Frida eagerly.

These new guests bunked in the derelict caravans and didn't come up to the main house much, but they seemed as much in Frida's thrall as the rest of us – if not more so. They meditated with Frida. She lay healing hands on them. They did not jostle and square their shoulders in her presence; they bowed their heads and hoped she would look at them.

They started brewing beer, and a rich, malty smell emanated from that part of the island. They played the drums by the fire. More people followed us. We all meditated. Time, again, bled. I was beginning to surrender more fully to Frida's world. When she asked us to detach from the self, surrender to the moment, release all ties to time and place, I no longer had to stop myself rolling my eyes. I felt detached from earlier versions of myself; I was the moment, I felt untethered yet completely sure I belonged.

Nicolae had a crow tattooed on his upper arm, and his face was birdlike. A sharp nose, eyes dark and shiny as marbles. He had a loud laugh. He looked mean but I once saw him crying on Frida's lap, early on after he arrived.

Alex had a kinder face, and he had symbols tattooed on his arms, some of which I recognised from the runes and notations in Jackson's room.

◆ ◆ ◆

Stefan, Elena, Nicolae and Alex were often drinking beer by Stefan's caravan at this point. Elena said Nicolae and Alex were labourers but they were taking the season off because Nicolae was recovering from falling off a ladder at a construction site. Frida had offered to help him heal.

When he was near Frida he bowed his head with something like reverence. A strange sight, this big, tattooed man bowing his head to a petite blonde teenage girl.

'Hey,' Nicolae had introduced himself a few days after he arrived, and shook my hand. I hadn't noticed it from a distance but one of the reasons that he looked like a crow was that he had scars that elongated the crease of his smile – on both sides. They were faint, like maybe a childhood scar, but also deliberate. These two identical cuts on either side of his face were like the long openings of a crow's beak. Once I saw those scars I couldn't unsee them.

'Zoe, correct?' he said to me.

I nodded. Alex also shook my hand. They both smelled of woodsmoke from the bonfires they made outside the caravans at night. They had not acknowledged me until that point.

'You're the social media mastermind then?' Nicolae said. His hands were always drumming something. His knees, a tree stump. He was never still. I wasn't sure how to reply. Nicolae's crow-smile glinted. 'Very pretty shop window. But don't ever get me or Alex on camera, okay? We are very shy people.' Then he smiled, like he wasn't shy at all. I nodded. 'Say it, please.'

'I won't photograph you or Alex, or put you online,' I said.

'Then we can be good friends,' he said, fingers drumming on his knees.

◆ ◆ ◆

'We are all connected,' she said to her expanding audience, all commenting and liking online and breathlessly adoring on the island, 'I am communicating with you like a tree or flower or mushroom sharing distress signals through the air or under the soil. There are energy lines moving through the earth, veins that spread lifeforce and information. Just as plants speak to each other through their roots, places are connected by these invisible fingers. Some call them fairy paths, or ley lines, or magnetic fields. In China they call them "dragon lines", South America "spirit lines" and Australia "dream lines". All it means is that there should be no loneliness. Just reach out and touch me. You are me and I am you. We are all connected.'

◆ ◆ ◆

Frida felt the tension in Ruth's jaw, and sensed that she'd been having intrusive thoughts. Frida promised to help her deal with them. Bella's limp came back but Frida helped keep the pain down. Frida felt that Nadia was struggling even though she was smiling. She could see that Rebecca's disordered eating still troubled her, and that she had lost contact with nature through too many years in the city. Frida told Rebecca she must not wear shoes for a month, she needed to ground herself. She needed to eat with her eyes closed to taste every morsel. She needed to meditate for at least an hour after her morning swim and visualisation exercises.

Rebecca was smitten. She poured her heart out to Frida, bare toes wriggling in the sand. Later, Frida reported back to me. Frida reported everything back to me, curled up in bed, me resting my forehead in the space under her shoulder.

Rebecca's first miscarriage was age seventeen, Frida told me. She'd grown up with her mother, father and two brothers in Chelsea. As a teenager, when the wetness and the heaviness came two weeks after she missed her period, she was hugely relieved not to have to go through the drama of an abortion. She was a straight-A student at a good state school, aiming for Cambridge, and had no intention of disappointing anyone. She'd not wasted much thought on the incident, but she remembered looking up the word 'embryo' in her father's dictionary and discovering that, as well as being an 'unborn or unhatched offspring', it meant 'a thing at a rudimentary stage'. Later, when she started having regular miscarriages, she thought of them all as seeds of ideas that wouldn't go anywhere, as stories that wouldn't be told.

Cambridge, then jobs in the fashion industry for ten years, during which time she married Gregory, they bought a flat and started trying to have a baby. They wanted three children. She didn't mention the first miscarriage to him; she hardly remembered it. The second time she got pregnant, she allowed a celebration. He signed the baby up for schools. He bought a giant bear with a ribbon around its neck. She had a miscarriage at eight weeks and the look on his face was crushing, like she had personally murdered the child. He'd lived an enormously privileged life. Private school, white, rich, trust fund; he was not a man accustomed to failure. He discarded the giant bear on the street and she had to walk past it for a week before someone put it in the boot of their car.

Over the next ten years she had repeated miscarriages. They bought a house in the countryside. They travelled. She saw all the best doctors, then worked her way through the best acupuncturists, nutritionists, healers, reiki masters, herbalists, shamans, and eventually ended up sitting on a salt marsh in Essex with a webcam girl.

I noticed that Rebecca kept a wide berth from Nicolae and Alex, which reinforced my own wariness of these men. They were not savoury characters. A person like Rebecca would not want to associate with people like Nicolae and Alex for long, surely. One or the other would have to go. I told Frida this, but she said Nicolae and Alex were part of the community where she'd spent years, and they needed help as much as Rebecca did.

But for the moment everyone was in Frida's thrall. Frida told Rebecca that she would have a son with big brown eyes. Rebecca glowed.

◆ ◆ ◆

'At first when I saw spirits they were just flashes of reflected light, or dust in the air.' I videoed Frida talking. 'First a hiss in my ear and then the hairs of my neck would rise from being watched. The hiss rises until the outline of another world is superimposed on to our own.'

◆ ◆ ◆

Three thousand followers. Four thousand. Five. Frida's followers kept growing. Frida and I shared a room now and slept curled together.

'Over half of Elena's patients experience visitations from spiritual beings, synchronicities or strange behaviours by animals, birds, insects, that sort of thing,' Frida said online to her followers. 'Even those who never gave the spirit world a second thought before. It's the norm rather than an oddity in her line of work. If you work with the dying on a regular basis there is no debate about a spiritual dimension existing. It just does.'

Off screen but listening, Elena nodded in agreement, always taciturn.

We stopped AuraLine altogether then, since we were bringing in so many clients ourselves – the AuraLine clientele were fuzzy, often low-income. Frida now spoke on YouTube and Instagram, and we billed privately for her calls.

Ten thousand followers. Twelve thousand.

In the house we all wore crew-neck white t-shirts from a brand called Toteme, chosen from Liberty by Rebecca. There were Celine and Yves Saint Laurent glasses, Max Mara and Chloé shorts that arrived in the post to a PO box in town, either bought on Rebecca's credit card or sent to us directly by brands Rebecca had contacted. She wanted us to be cooler. Her own aesthetic was valuable – her Instagram was super high-end – so she didn't want to be slumming it. Clearly she was disappointed at the level of luxury on the island, although grateful that Frida's magic was working when all manner of luxury retreats and potions had not. I knew from my former day job that Frida was just a nano-influencer at this point. At best we might have got small brands to send stuff in exchange for posts or mentions, but nothing like the mainstream brands Rebecca got.

She wanted us to be implausibly beautiful. It wasn't enough to be spiritually enlightened.

She reposted Moth, muscles damp with sweat, meditating topless in new £400 trainers. She posted Frida's face, very close up, in thousand-pound sunglasses. Silver cracked-leather Louboutin sneakers. Real gold hoops, not the plastic crap she was wearing when I first saw her on the Tube.

Someone played the guitar down at the caravans – Nicolae, perhaps – and the sound carried along with the drums. The Starbucks girls sang. Ruth, who had doubted Frida during the performance in town, was particularly devoted. She spoke online to her seventy followers about how she had changed the course of her life in the last weeks with Frida's help. She meditated first thing instead of reaching for a spliff or pill; she swam and exercised instead of eating McDonald's and throwing it up. 'Frida Rae has changed my life,' she wrote in the caption, and we reposted the video.

Frida bought me contact lenses because she said she always wanted to see my beautiful eyes, and I was flattered. She touched me in public. I never wore any glasses but sunglasses in front of her again.

She was so charismatic. She told us to sink underwater and scream, releasing the trauma we all had pent up inside of us. A strange gang: three burly men, one middle-aged woman, a posh public school boy, and a bunch of teenage girls, all sinking underwater and screaming at the tops of our lungs for no one to hear.

A few days later, Frida dyed my nondescript black hair peroxide-blonde to match her natural blonde, and cut mine short because she said it framed my face better. With freckles and bright eyes now, I looked and felt brand new. Sometimes when I saw myself in a photo on her grid, all filtered and strange, I barely recognised myself. And I felt thankful.

Chapter Nine

Oliver fills up his drink from the vodka bottle I brought out into the garden at his request. I'm sipping San Pellegrino. He covers the track marks with his shirt and relights his cigarette. A metallic click sounds out in the quiet. I take a sip of my water while he sits back against the wall and inhales.

'Tell me about Jackson,' he says. A flag outside our neighbour's house flaps in the slight wind. I am pretty sure now that Oliver is sleeping in his car. He's shaved without a proper mirror. He has puffy eyes and the smell of weed sits on top of an older version of the same scent, mixed with a tang of fast food. I know the signs; I lived in a van for years after leaving Frida. It is rarely a restful night's sleep in a town or city: car parks, lay-bys, back streets.

'Jackson was a historian of sorts,' I say. 'He'd not published anything for about forty years before he died. He had cancer and dementia when I knew him that summer.'

'She conned her way into his will but I'm not sure how they knew each other. I can't work out who Frida's real family was, or much about where she grew up. I've spoken to Jackson's real daughter and granddaughter though, who tried to bring legal action against Frida, and they were threatened by some lowlifes who worked for her. They dropped the case.'

'I know that the real daughter never visited her father,' I say. 'Frida used to read to him for hours. She talked to him, she cared about him. He adored her and wanted her to inherit the island.'

'But her real surname isn't Rae,' he says.

'I don't know her real name.'

'The granddaughter spoke to me at length, saying that she was sure Frida was a con artist. She was happy to go on record for my article. But then she retracted everything, said it was all off the record and she'd sue if I used her in my article. Obviously she had been threatened again, but wouldn't say.'

The grandfather clock behind me strikes one a.m. The house creaks slightly in the falling heat. I glance casually around the garden. I didn't do much to the house when I moved in, but I did transform the garden. I took down sagging fences, twisting brambles, and dug up cracked soil. There are birdfeeders hanging on all the trees.

'Someone tied the bodies down so they wouldn't be found,' Oliver says. 'You read the second article?'

'The article said *maybe* the bodies were tied down. The girls were drug addicts and that power plant was a notorious hangout for heroin addicts. I guess they drowned, maybe got tangled in stuff while high.'

'They died the night you guys had a big party though,' he says. 'They found jewellery that matches jewellery they were wearing in the Instagram photos she deleted from her grid.'

My eye twitches. I can feel it, a little software malfunction. Twitch, twitch. I don't think he'll be able to see it, though. He's not really looking at me. He thinks that he wants my information but really he wants to hear himself talk, and the tug-of-war bothers him. He can't bear to keep his cards close. He wants me to know his hand.

'Show me?' I say, careful. He and I both have a lot to lose here. I wish I was at my computer, tiptoeing through code rather than conversation.

'Forensics found plastic feathers and glitter and bangles. The bangles Ava is wearing here.' He fumbles out the photo of us all by the fire on the night of the party, the ones he didn't properly let me look at up on the cliffs. He holds one out, hands shaking, and I take it. It is a photo with me and Grace in the foreground, hundreds of people in the background. Grace is wearing a white summer dress, with the seagull mask on top of her head. I am wearing a white t-shirt, jean shorts, and the crow mask over my eyes.

Walking towards us out of the crowd behind are two girls holding hands in the darkness. One is Frida with her deer mask. The other is Ava, wearing a golden bird mask on her head and a tight white bandeau dress with bare feet. Ava is tanned and luminous with bangles all up her wrists.

'Forensics found bangles in the lake,' he says, taking out another screenshot of our livestream that night, this time an image just of Ava dancing, bangles jumping.

'But she might have worn them for years,' I say. 'Before and after the party.'

'But Ava wasn't seen after the party. And they found this turtle necklace,' he says. 'That Frida wears through much of the summer's photos, and you also wore at the start of the summer. I think that puts you or Frida at the scene. The police will certainly be interested. I think the whole summer was taken from her grid because these two girls died the night of this big Instagram party.'

His words hang in the warm air. My eye twitches. He looks so pleased with himself, puffing out his chest. I lean over and take his pack of cigarette papers and tobacco.

'I want to interview you on record later today. All legit, not in your garden in the middle of the night. We'll meet at an office and I'll record it.'

I begin to roll a cigarette, hands shaking.

'You understand?' he says. 'I want you to start at the beginning and tell me who Frida was, what her childhood was like, who she conned, and why these girls died the night of your festival. Tell your side of the story.'

Just then his phone rings through the silence and we both jump. He frowns, looks at it, then picks it up. He listens for a moment while I lick the cigarette paper and put it in my mouth.

'Now?' he says into the phone, then puts it down and turns to me. 'I have to go, something happened to my car, but is that agreed?' he says to me. 'I'll send you the address where we'll meet later.'

He lights my cigarette, and I inhale. It's not as good as a benzo. I blow smoke out of the side of my mouth, eye twitching. How long would Ben stick around? He'd try to, however bad the revelations, however many photos of me in the paper, but he'd leave me in the end. He'd take the kids.

'Don't look so worried. We're going to bring her down. You'll be free.'

I hug my arms around my body, cold now.

'I'll see you later,' he says.

I nod, and don't show him out. I just sit there in my beautiful garden. When the front door closes, I realise my whole body is shaking.

◆ ◆ ◆

Mum had stopped calling. I'm not sure when. Sometime in July. I let Frida teach me to swim. I swam as the rain turned the sky and the river upside down so it felt as if I was flying. For the first time in a long time, certainly since adolescence, my body felt connected to my brain. That's not to say that swimming didn't scare me. The water was cloying around me. Often when I was swimming the idea of letting myself sink would make me flinch and I'd have to hum a tune or turn over on to my back or say something to one of the others in order to knock the thought out of my head. But I liked the sense of crossing a boundary. I liked that my instinct said that the water was scary but I wasn't obeying it.

'Authenticity is the next great frontier,' Frida said to my camera, while people drummed in the background. 'Our world is more and more dominated by technology. We must hold on to our humanity, the essence and connectivity of us that lives beyond the precise and brilliant artificial minds of the machines that are coming.'

Sometimes Nicolae and Alex would leave the island for a few days, but they always came back. They sat with Elena and Stefan in a tight circle most nights, their silhouettes jagged against the flicker of a dying bonfire. Each of them held a drum, their hands thrumming out an unnatural rhythm. The sound was deep and resonant, like a heartbeat. Occasionally, one of the men would glance upward, his eyes reflecting the firelight. The tempo would quicken, growing more urgent. It filled the island. Whatever they were calling to – or calling forth – it felt as though it was already watching.

◆ ◆ ◆

I was only on the island for five months. Such a short time, although it didn't seem that way at the time.

The Starbucks girls were always laughing and whispering, wearing old swimsuits tucked into shorts, peasant skirts and plastic earrings. They had smelled of fake tan and cheap body spray when they arrived, but now they smelled of river water and mud like us.

They all said that Frida told them 'things she couldn't possibly know' about their dead parents, or their dreams for the future. She told them about the boys they would love and the places they would travel.

Frida spent hours with Rebecca, in 'healing ceremonies'. Rebecca's husband thought she was on a spa holiday, apparently. Clearly he didn't look at her credit card bill, or maybe this was normal spending for her. Liberty Ianthe Cotton Sateen duvet sets. Five-hundred-thread-count sheets for the island.

We were still waiting for the probate to come through, but Frida was confident, and until then, Rebecca was paying for everything. She was two months pregnant.

I would often come across Rebecca and Frida looking dreamy and paralysed in the midday sun. The sky so bright that it hurt, crows strutting over the sand. Rebecca lying down with her head in Frida's lap, or sitting in the lotus position face-to-face with Frida. Rebecca began to look so much happier in a short time. Her hair returned to its natural afro, and she ate dinner with us quietly, touching her tummy often.

She also floated with Frida in the river. We screamed underwater. Little bubbles would rise up silently and melt with the other foam and agitation. We breathed in strength, then went underwater and breathed out our limitations. Frida spoke of spirits and parallel dimensions and we nodded along.

Her audience – online and on the island – wanted to believe her. That's the central trick of all this. If you call a psychic or visit a healer you are rooting for them to have special abilities.

Frida relied on people's own minds betraying them. I *knew* this. But soon my investment in her was so huge that I, too, began to believe her. We wanted her to be magic. For all of us to be spectacular.

It's amazing how often followers would claim Frida predicted shit she'd never even mentioned, or knew things about them that would never have occurred to her. I saw this happening. And yet, later on, my own memory developed holes and inconsistencies.

I can't tell you when exactly I started to feel the presence of spirits and to believe Frida when she said they were speaking to her. She said I wasn't starting to believe, my mind was just opening so I could see.

Frida declared that we were going to have a huge party on the first of August. Lughnasadh, pronounced Loo-nas-ah. Lugh was the Celtic sun god and his festival marked the midway point between summer solstice and autumn equinox, when the moon was closest to Earth. It had been a big deal in one of the communes she lived in. There would be a bonfire. A burning man. Costumes and dancing. Old friends and new.

We'd been instructed to get the island ready for this party. Nicolae, Alex and Stefan renovated the caravans so more people could come and stay. The caravans were all covered in peeling paint, marred by cracked windows and creeping rust. Alex was stocky with a sawdust-flecked beard. His hands sanded away layers of faded paint to reveal the bare aluminium beneath. A small radio played tinny spiritual music near him – gongs and chimes and flutes. Occasionally, he paused to wipe his brow with the back of his glove, squinting critically at his progress. Nicolae, taller and wiry, would be perched on another caravan fixing the roof.

We tidied up all the junk in the garden and Elena planted vegetables, the scent of freshly turned soil mingling with the herbal tang of incense drifting from a stick wedged into the ground nearby. I learned a lot from Elena. We turned soil, organised the rows with markers. We planted leafy greens, root vegetables, rhubarb and herbs. The sun cast long shadows across the garden.

Ruth had hair woven with flowers, and she hummed a tune that seemed to sync with the breeze. Stefan's sunburnt shoulders moved as he gently set down seedlings.

Elena taught us all to cook. Everyone took an evening; she said she wasn't cooking for this growing gang. There was a rota for who woke up to knead the bread, who fed the sourdough starter, who made the chickpea curry, the vegetarian chilli, the lasagne, the salads.

Some of the photos I took of Frida went on social media, some didn't. I posted photos of all of us out in the clearing, sun on our freckled faces, mud on our tanned knees. Others I did not post: Frida's smiling face over the covers, the ridges of her body like a snowy landscape underneath. Unshaved armpits, unshaved cunt. The bow of her mouth blowing me a kiss over her shoulder.

Merlin padded around the island, nose in the water. Frida spent time with everyone individually. She made everyone feel special. Grace and Moth spent time with her together, and some time with her on their own.

'Over a thousand years ago, a Viking force landed on our island and defeated a Saxon army,' Frida said on camera, lying with her eyes closed in the grass while I filmed her. Off camera, her hand was on my foot. 'The Vikings brought their water spirits to the island. Their Nøkken, Nøkk, Neck, Nixy, Nix, Nykur or Nixie. Their shape-shifting ghosts were left here – at least that's what my grandfather reckoned. I never met Nixy, but the power of water has always overwhelmed me. We have an aquatic past; we even have gills in the womb. Water bears life. Water takes it.'

Moth and Grace were lying next to Frida – there was an ankle, a wrist – dismantled and hot and blissed out in the sunshine. Rebecca and Elena were behind me.

'I am immortal,' Frida said, still with her eyes closed. 'I am every gender. The whole universe, animate and inanimate, past, present and future, is within me.'

Then, off camera, I laughed.

'What?' she said, opening her eyes.

'You can't say that.' I laughed again. '*The whole universe, animate and inanimate, past, present and future, is within you?*'

She sat up and frowned at me, irritated.

'You sound like Yoda again,' I said.

Behind her, the others opened their eyes too.

'Put the camera down.' I did. She got up on to her knees so her face was an inch from mine. I thought for a moment that she was going to hit me.

Then she laughed.

'You're right. Cut the last line and post the rest.'

We all exhaled, but she was still staring intently at me. It could have gone either way.

'Please don't undermine me in public like that,' she said that night.

'Sorry.' I came up to her, flirting. 'Can I undermine you in private?'

'Don't do it again,' she said. 'You hear me?'

'I'm sorry, Frida.'

'Just never undermine me again.'

We lay in bed, not touching, but as the dawn broke her hands found their way over to me and I was glad. Her hands around my wrists, my waist.

It was a house where you closed doors and they were open again ten minutes later. Or where footsteps couldn't quite be traced. Someone left one room and you thought their footsteps would move in one direction but they sounded somewhere else. A house where the walls sweated. There were radiators, but an empty space where the boiler had once been. It was the sort of house, and island landscape, that lent itself to the idea of spirits and thin lines between dimensions. Those thoughts seeped from the island, from Frida's mouth, into our heads.

◆ ◆ ◆

Jackson's daughter, Jenny, turned up with a lawyer a fortnight after he died. She had an austere black bob of hair and thick eyebrows, but was recognisably the child from the photo I'd found. Her accent was American.

'It's not my fault you never visited your father,' Frida said to her and the lawyer. 'I looked after him. Elena looked after him. You didn't.'

'Whatever. You and I know both know he was a piece of shit,' the daughter said. 'He just was. He never gave me or my mum a cent. Never called. He cared more about spiritual planes of reality and ancient religions than he did actual reality. But he was still my father. You didn't call so I could say goodbye, but then you might not have got your hands on his money.'

'We didn't know where to find you,' Elena said. 'And he doesn't have any money.'

'He has an island.'

'It's not worth much. Maybe he knew you'd just sell it but I would use it for good, and community.'

'Why didn't you use Jackson's lawyer then, for the new will, if it was so legit?' the daughter said, motioning towards the dour lawyer standing next to her. 'Why some lawyer from another town? The family lawyer knew where to find us.'

'How were we meant to know who the family lawyer was?' Elena said, all innocent, wiping her hands on her apron. 'It's not like you were visiting the poor old man. We have been here for over a year and you never called or visited. He never mentioned you.'

'How come there wasn't an autopsy?'

'He'd been dying for years,' Elena said, exasperated. 'He had cancer and dementia. I'm sorry you didn't get to say goodbye but it is not my fault or Frida's fault. Jackson was looked after by a local doctor who prescribed the medication, and who came over regularly. I will give you his details. I am a qualified end-of-life nurse with twenty years' experience. His care was exemplary. His will reflected his desires, I promise you.'

The daughter did not seem convinced, but in the end she never came back so the doctor must have corroborated these facts.

'I'm not going to let you get away with this,' she said before she left.

'Hey,' Frida said, and put her hand on the daughter's arm. The woman looked up in shock, feeling Frida's strange warmth. 'He loved you very much. He may not have said it, but I felt it.'

'I doubt it. My mum hated him. But I wish we could have spoken before he died,' she said, and for a horrible moment I thought that Frida was going to tell her that she could speak to ghosts or that her grandfather was there right now.

But Frida could read a room like a book and this woman in her grey suit and helmet of hair was not the sort to engage with such things. So instead she said: 'He loved you and I am so sorry that we couldn't find you.'

'Was there even a funeral?' his daughter said.

'He didn't really have many friends around here,' Frida said. 'His remains are at the crematorium outside town for you. We're having a party in three weeks, on August first, for Lughnasadh. We'd love you to come.'

◆ ◆ ◆

'I had everything money could buy as a kid,' Moth said to the camera, to fifteen thousand followers. 'Luxury holidays, all the gadgets, the finest education. But I lacked the warmth, attention and emotional connection of being loved. As I got older, the emptiness seemed consuming. I was surrounded by other wealthy children but the relationships were superficial, based on status. My dad never even wanted me home for the holidays and I started going to friends' houses or just couch surfing, doing a little of this and a little of that. It was heroin that filled the void in the end, the nagging emptiness. I've been an addict since the age of fifteen, and now I'm twenty. I've been to the best rehabs in the world, paid for by my dad. I've had the best therapists. But nobody has ever managed to help me apart from Frida Rae. If you feel like you can't fill the void, like you are slipping away, give her a call. She has changed my life and she can do the same for you.'

◆ ◆ ◆

Elena made Rebecca fertility teas, and specially blended smoothies. Work on the house, gardens and caravans continued as we prepared for the Lughnasadh festival. We made bunting, and strung up fairy lights in the trees. I slept curled up in Frida's bed. During the day Grace and I scrubbed and scraped Jackson's house, using a knife to get in between the floorboards. Every sponge came away filthy and we worked until our knuckles were raw. Then we started to paint. Tearing off wallpaper with little rabbits jumping over mushrooms while fairies played lutes. The paper curled at the corners, faded in rectangular shapes from the window across the wall. We smelled of paint and turpentine. We chipped the filth off the grouting, scooped it from under furniture.

Rebecca did several treatments with Frida every day, both out in the river and meditating in the forest or on the flats, and

Rebecca paid Frida well for all this. Elena made her homeopathic remedies: calcarea phosphorica, ferrum metallicum. Rebecca wore the same white t-shirts as the rest of us, with cotton harem pants or jean shorts. She took deep breaths, swam, ate well, and the lack of make-up made her look older but prettier.

Rebecca told Grace that Frida had 'saved her life' and was 'fixing what many thousands of pounds in doctor's appointments didn't come close to fixing'. She described how extraordinary the heat of Frida's touch was. She could feel the energy healing her. She wanted to find a way to help Frida spread her healing powers. She reckoned that we should hold events and she showed us pictures of conference halls and hotels that Frida could be booked to speak at.

'The importance of ritual cannot be underestimated,' Frida said to her audience online. 'Rituals safeguard the chaos of grief, absence and the supernatural, but most rituals have been stripped from modern life. It is no surprise that sometimes we cannot process these big occurrences.'

Merlin barked and chased rabbits.

'The idea that we live in better times now is insane,' she said, 'we are literally inhaling plastic, and vast amounts of toxic information is dumped on us daily: famines, wars, corruption, the private lives of celebrities, the private lives of our friends. It is all too much.'

Grace and I painted ceilings, arms aching. We tried cleaning the carpets but they were so appalling, almost more so once clean, that we ripped them out. Instead we sanded and varnished the floors. We chipped paint from the windowsills and watched YouTube videos about Polyfilla.

We grew lithe and strong and saw muscles we never knew we had.

'Does it hurt?' I said of Grace's eczema one day on a break from sanding the front door. We were sitting on the branches of an alder tree in the forest. Alders are swamp-dwellers, water lovers, and were Frida's favourite type of tree. Water doesn't rot an alder tree but makes it stronger.

The wood is beige but turns blood-red when cut, making people superstitious about it. It was an alder that formed the fairy arch, which Frida said was at the exact spot where several ley lines passed each other. The energy of this intersection had formed a door to a new dimension. Elena told us not to climb the alders, that they had hidden pockets of rot, and mostly we took this advice.

In the forest hush near the fairy arch, Grace's fingers found a raw patch on the inside of her elbow. Frida had taught her to tap the skin instead of scratching but today she scratched absent-mindedly while we sat on the branch. In the tense quiet of the moment: scratch, scratch, scratch. It was one of those shivery noises. A mouse clawing behind built-in furniture or under floorboards, that sort of thing. It made me want to take her fingers in mine to stop her. There was eczema on her navel, the concave dip of her stomach. Her nail circled, circled, circled around the patch of eczema on her arm.

'Maybe you should see a doctor,' I said.

'No, I just need to stop getting distracted during healing. She thinks maybe I've sort of plateaued, spiritually. I don't feel as connected. My dad used to wrap me in Vaseline and cellophane as a child,' she said, dangling her feet. 'I made a boy try to asphyxiate me with plastic wrap once. Frida thinks maybe there's a connection.' She laughed glumly. 'If I gave up caring what other people think, the eczema would go. I am still too tied to my childhood and my looks and all this fragmented identity stuff. I've been at war with my body all my life. I wanted to be a dancer. There were brief periods when my skin would be good, and I would take dance classes. There's this moment, right? Do you know what I mean? When you dance or fuck or when swimming or meditating, often when listening to Frida, when it feels as if everything is combining. You are water or movement or love.'

'You *grok*,' I said.

'Grok?' she laughed. 'That doesn't sound right at all.'

'It's a geeky techy word for what you just described. It means to understand so clearly that you merge with something – whether it's a person or a crowd or a concept.'

'Exactly. Yes. But "grok" is not the right word for that meaning. Everything I do, every drug, every guy, it's just a desire to get back to those tiny moments in my childhood when I danced.'

'Bless,' I said.

'Fuck you,' she said, offering a small smile.

I watched her, dangling her legs just like a little girl. She looked delicate and yet too-worldly, itching the inside of her arm.

'Grok,' she said quietly. 'What an ugly word.'

'It's from some 1960s sci-fi book, and the word is from a Martian language. Humans do not grok. We all live our sad little isolated lives. But now it has moved into the tech world. You grok when something – a code or program – becomes part of your identity.'

'I just want to merge with the world,' she laughed, throwing her hands wide and jumping off the branch we'd been sitting on so she could face me. 'I want to be the light!'

'Be the rain!' I said, and I jumped off the alder branch to be next to her.

'Be the sea!' she laughed, and walked over to the fairy arch. 'Maybe I should go through the fairy arch.'

'Naa,' I said. 'Let's go make a sandwich instead.'

◆ ◆ ◆

Grace shaved all her hair off a few nights after we sat on the alder tree. Frida did it for her, I think, although I was asleep at the time so missed it. There were before and after photos for me to put on Instagram though. It symbolised her letting go of possessions, ego and vanity.

She looked monastic but still, for sure, sexy – an odd combination. This was a new beginning, and the embracing of simplicity. She really had such a beautiful face. Without her hair she looked younger and more raw. Moth and Frida kept running their hands over her head. I felt a little jealous. I used words like 'humility', 'surrender' and 'cleansing' in my posts, and people posted fire emojis and expressed their own desire to shave their heads.

Grace left the hair outside for birds to use in their nests. There was a creeping layer of eczema on her neck now, and a little on her right eyelid. Grace said she had never felt happier, but there was a hesitation. I caught her touching the space where her hair used to be, sometimes.

Like one of Frida's shells, or her obsession with infinite universes, it's hard to see the turning points while you're spinning in them.

On Instagram, we invited our followers to the Lughnasadh festival.

◆ ◆ ◆

The probate ended and Frida officially inherited the island. We celebrated by lighting a fire in the field, a practice for Lughnasadh. The men drummed, drummed, drummed, and we danced. We filmed it, enticing people to come to the party. I videoed Frida sitting on one of the caravans with her tanned bare feet dangling over the edge, seagulls dancing behind her.

'One of the first times I scared anyone was when I brought an owl back to life,' Frida said to her increasing number of followers on and off the island. Two more followers had turned up in person at this point, both women around the same age as Elena. They were sharing one of the caravans. Online, we'd made it to twenty thousand people watching her.

'The owl had his wings spread out as if he had crashed while drunk-flying, and his head was resting on the side with his eyes closed. We all kneeled down to get a better look. One of the kids poked him with a stick and the creature didn't move. Something made me put my hand forward towards the bird though, and I felt heat, and a quiver in my throat, and yearning. So I picked the creature up in my arms while the group made disgusted noises. Twigs cracked and sunlight fell on my neck through gaps in the trees. My energy built up in the way I imagine a seed feels like before it grows roots, or a cancer cell before it divides. The animal was totally still but I could feel its potential. I didn't let my concentration slip even though the kids were walking away now. One boy stayed, crouched with me on the forest floor. I felt the owl's heart, and the murky energy of poison dissipating from a dying mouse. When the owl flinched, then raised his head with a jerk and a flap, the little boy who had stayed to watch then screamed so loudly that people stumbled out of their caravans, away from their card games and their barbecues and their movies, to watch that owl fly up into the daylight. I've always felt an affinity with owls and bats and crows, creatures of the night who pass most easily between dimensions.'

Twenty-thousand followers became twenty-five thousand.

◆ ◆ ◆

We posted Grace meditating in a bikini, Frida holding her hands over her and flicking away bad energy. We posted the sea. Swimming. Sunbathing. I can't say exactly when it became a bit more fire and brimstone. At some point there were comments like this one, which ended up going viral the following year because she allegedly predicted Covid.

'The Earth will stand still one day soon,' she said, with a heavenly smile. People will hide from an invisible enemy. Birds and wildlife will re-emerge. Waterways and oceans will briefly clear. The Earth will start repairing herself. Foxes will walk in the urban streets. Many people will die during this time. It will be a crossroads. We will think that life must improve afterwards. That we will look after the environment, and our nurses, and our children. But we won't.

'As artificial intelligence becomes more advanced, there will be growing debate over whether machines can experience consciousness, or even spirituality. But that is missing the point. We will *be* consciousness. We will *be* the spiritual experience, as all our previously isolated and lonely minds come together into a single spiritual being. We will not just talk to each other; we will merge like trees and animals. Join me. We are the collective consciousness. We are the spiritual future.'

But the more theatrical stuff was mitigated by monologues that bordered on life coaching, which is what it was in many ways.

'The things you hope might distract you from depression – they will in fact make you worse,' she'd say to people online, wise way beyond her years. Or, 'Wear factor thirty even when you don't think it's sunny, and on your lips too because people forget that.' Or, 'If she's gossiping about your mutual friend to you, she's gossiping about you.' Or, 'Never be afraid to be afraid – what you are scared of will help you grow.'

But then, also, hidden in the good sense, she snuck in some crazy: 'The first trauma is our birth, and our bodies remember even if our minds have learned to forget. Once the negative memories of birth are released through water meditation and breathwork, the relationship between your body, mind and spirit becomes lighter.'

I was working hard researching each client, keeping notes, updating her website, plodding on with growing her social media. I trained the Starbucks girls to help, and we had a little office in the living room most days, with them taking notes on everything they could find out about clients. Frida's praise was addictive.

People need help managing life. It would have been the Bible, once. There was a Christian girl at school who I was sort of friends with in the year before I left. We didn't have much in common apart from that we were both unpopular. She had this book where you'd look up 'guilt' or 'lust' or 'depression' and it would give you Bible quotes to help you with the problem. A perceived absolute truth source, telling you not to be a shit person, to love your neighbour, all of that. There's something to be said for it.

Social media, replying to her messages, keeping notes on her clients. I plucked her eyebrows and the black hair around her nipples.

The smell of her would hit me sometimes when I was meditating or working. A trace left on my fingers, my hair.

'This isn't heat,' Frida told her audience. 'Not in the way you will one day know heat. One day you will have to put aluminium foil on your windows to keep the heat out. One day the birds will fall from the sky, and water will be scarce. Acceptance is radical. It makes you stronger. Reject yourself, and you will waste your life in a civil war.'

We felt as if we were floating.

'We are releasing, letting go, dissolving elements of our minds and bodies, releasing them into space.'

Rebecca reposted and liked our videos, and soon her friends did too. Adults with real money and connections started calling us. The hourly rate was up to £500 a session, with sessions booked weeks in advance.

◆ ◆ ◆

Mum called me sometimes and I texted back saying I was good. Happier than ever. She texted me saying they were making my room into an office and I needed to come and box up my stuff. It could go into her storage crate in Brent Cross for a bit, although she was going to get rid of that soon as well.

As I texted Mum, a fox's head peeked out from behind a tree and nuzzled the ground for a second, then pricked its ears attentively. Two sparrows exploded out of a tree and landed, squabbling, on the gravel, then darted up into the air chasing each other. I couldn't think of a single possession that I needed.

'Throw it away,' I wrote, stretching my toes in the sunlight. 'I'll pick up my computer sometime, but you can bin the rest.'

'What do you mean?'

'I don't want any of it.'

'What about the Abercrombie hoodie?'

'I shoplifted that from Selfridges.'

'Are you okay?' she wrote.

'Yeah. I'm good. I'm actually really good.'

'If you're sure,' she wrote. 'Hey, look. We're thinking we might get married at the registry office, then do the big thing next summer. We're each going to bring a witness. You'll be mine, right?'

'Course,' I wrote.

'I'll send you the date. It's in two weeks.'

That would be a few days before Lughnasadh. I figured I'd slip off and go to the wedding, and pick up my stuff, and be back for the festival.

◆ ◆ ◆

Rebecca had grown fatter and so much happier through July.

I liked how Rebecca laughed with her mouth wide open and how she didn't dissemble or mince words. Although I didn't like the snobbish comments she made about Essex girls or the merits of various London postcodes.

In the middle of the day we stood in the tiny puddles of our own shadows.

I spent hours with Frida's direct messages, replying to people who poured their hearts out to her. In moments of extreme vulnerability – after being fired, during a divorce, coming off prescription drugs – people would go online looking for spiritual solace, and they were guided towards us by the invisible hand of social media recommendation algorithms.

'It is crisis that changes our physiology,' Frida said online. 'The ten-car pile-up, the adrenalin surge of love, the bad trip. These things change the structure of our minds. The basis of our identities. These days most of us are surrounded by moments of crisis. Industrial toxins, pollutants, heavy metals, chronic stress, addictions, highly processed or high-fat diets, widespread pathogen load, polluted water. This constant crisis is causing our identities to shift underneath us and this is what makes you feel you are running on quicksand, unable to find your footing in the landslide. And you're told to "be yourself", but which self? Yesterday's? Before he hurt you? Before the fall?'

'I squandered my teens and twenties in the rubble of ignorance,' someone commented, 'but I always felt your salvation was around the corner. I worship you.'

'I am ready for the coming evacuation of this ruined and forsaken planet,' said someone else.

But others wrote, 'What brand is your hair dye? Looks fab' or 'I'll pay you to suck my toes'.

◆ ◆ ◆

One night I woke up because it was too hot and looked out of the window to gauge the time but saw a boat floating in Southey Creek, a tidal inlet to the west of the island. At first I thought the boat had broken its mooring and was just floating on its own, but then I saw the oars moving, and there was a dense area of shadow in the middle – figures were on the boat, all dressed in black. I woke Frida up and she kneeled on the bed next to me, breathing hotly into my ear. The tide was high. The boat would have snuck past the town where Grace and Ava were from, the nature reserve, then the power plant, maybe all the way from the North Sea. It approached the eastern shore of the island and became shielded by overgrown reeds and low-hanging branches. We lost sight of it. A faint light flickered somewhere: low voices, then the boat started off again in the other direction. Someone had come in the dark to hand something over to – presumably – Alex and Nicolae. Maybe Stefan. I couldn't see their faces.

'Don't jump to conclusions,' she said in my ear.

'What, you think they're exchanging . . . crafts? Cupcakes? Gossip?'

She laughed.

'Maybe they have an Etsy shop,' she said. 'Bongos?'

'Fuck, Frida. They're criminals, right? Proper criminals.'

'You're so cute. Proper criminals. Improper, I imagine. But minor. Yes, I think we can assume they don't have nine-to-fives. But they're not bad people. Just . . .'

'People like Rebecca aren't going to stay if people like Nicolae and Alex are hanging around,' I said.

'Zo-Zo,' she said seriously. 'Just relax. You can be very disapproving.'

'Oh,' I said.

'They're free thinkers. The government likes to call free thinkers criminals. Every time I think that you are becoming more spiritually aligned, you surprise me with some socially constructed, conservative thought process. Only blood is family. Love is monogamy. But we're all fine. We're better than fine. We're on a roll. Everyone who comes to us may not be part of conventional society, but we accept free thinkers. We are liberators. Are you a free thinker?'

'I mean, probably not?' I said. 'I'm a strategic thinker? And people like Rebecca with legit money, the sort of people we could start attracting, and helping. People like that don't like being near people like Nicolae and Alex.'

'People like this and people like that. We're all the same. We're all energy.' She put her hand on the inside of my thigh and moved it further up. 'We're just bodies.' Her fingers were high now, climbing under the elastic of my knickers.

She was a slow erosion of limits. She broke my boundaries so delicately, nibbling away at my sense of self. I had offered myself up to her at first – I was the one who looked people up online, who found Rebecca's baby name in her bedroom. I tiptoed into the murk and then she took my hand in hers and led me further in. I accepted more and more. I loved her.

'You look so cute when you're worried,' she said, fingers in my knickers now. 'I love you.'

'I love you too.'

'We're the same, you and I. We are stronger than anyone imagines, but you need to trust me. Your instincts are trying to keep you on some mundane path, like the drudgery of your life before you met me. Remember how sad you were before?'

'Yes.'

'That is the danger. That devastating mundanity is the danger. The prescription drugs, nobody touching you. Now you are star seed. You are beyond all that. You belong to me and we are going to take over the world. We're in this together, right? Us against the world.'

'Of course,' I said, taking a deep breath. She looked at me, wide-eyed, her fingers inside me.

◆ ◆ ◆

I spun sea glass around in my hands, my ankles wrapped around hers in the unmade bed, our sheets now crisp and newly white. 'I'd like to have a veranda and sit on it with you during thunderstorms one day,' Frida said to me as I replied to her direct messages in her bedroom. 'I'm so glad we found each other.'

I laughed, although even then I was scared of her. 'Rocking chairs maybe?'

'I want to sigh, say that the vegetable patch really needed this rain.'

'I'll build you a veranda and wash the peas.'

'Record this?' she said, and I took out my phone. In the video she was reclining in bed – white hair, white sheets, white vest top with her breasts and hard nipples visible underneath.

'We're scared of childbirth and death, the beginning and the end,' Frida said to the camera as I held it up to record her, taking it all in. 'We drug people to get through it because we are scared to see transformation or acknowledge other realities. When the lights go out, when the hospitals burn, we will have forgotten how to take a shit on our own. My name is Frida Rae. I am not here to relax you. If you are looking for relaxation, then go and watch Netflix or take a bath. No judgement at all. The world is stressful. But I have no intention of relaxing you.' She did not smile. 'I am here to liberate you. I am here to help you travel to new dimensions. Welcome,' she said, 'To the rest of your life.'

Eighty thousand. A hundred thousand.

'I love this! #Truth even if your voice shakes or cracks, speak the truth,' wrote someone. 'Fuckin right babes. mine be like>> clear AF.'

'Do you ever miss Ava?' I said to Frida.

'You jealous?' she said, leaning on my chest. I could feel her smile as her fingers drew shapes around my belly button. 'Don't be jealous. We cannot limit ourselves to single connections. We are trees in a forest and our survival – our power – relies on multiple energy lines and roots.'

I sat up so she was forced to sit up too, her hand no longer spinning around my belly button.

'You are my only "energy line",' I said, doing air quotes like that was a euphemism when I knew it was only a euphemism for me. 'You will always be my only energy line. There's nobody else for me. Not ever.'

'That's not true,' she said, earnest. 'You have helped me connect to thousands of people and that is just the beginning. We are about to snowball. I am THE connection. I will help everyone transform as I have helped you to transform. That is my purpose.'

'Nicolae and Alex need to leave, Frida,' I said. 'You said you were going to talk to them.'

'They're going to knock it off,' Frida said. 'They're wheeler dealers and an opportunity came up.'

'An opportunity?'

'But it's done now. So can we drop the subject?'

◆ ◆ ◆

Behavioural patterns are contagious. Families and friendship groups absorb each other's mannerisms and inflections: an accent, a stutter, a twitch. When we find someone attractive, we echo their body language.

Freud believed that being part of a crowd is a way of unlocking our unconscious minds. A crowd has three stages: submergence, contagion, suggestion. During submergence, we lose our sense of individual self and personal responsibility. Contagion: we begin to unquestioningly follow the dominant beliefs and feelings of the crowd. Beliefs can spread like a disease.

Examples of collective consciousness are everywhere – any shared belief, idea, experience or moral attitude that unifies a society. Religion, musical preference, politics, even hysteria. We all began to see a shimmery line between our world and the next world. Frida's belief was contagious.

We floated in the water as the heat exploded across us for the day. We gardened and cooked and meditated. We did not sleep much. We told the camera things that we had never told anyone. The more we shared with her, the more 'authentic' we were being and the more we were 'healing'.

Merlin trotted along next to us, then veered off to meet Stefan. Nicolae and Alex drummed and fixed the caravans. The Starbucks girls came and went, but increasingly stayed.

Grace and I started going scavenging with Elena over on the mainland forest or just walked quietly out there alone for hours every day. I liked watching Elena pour boiling water into a jar full of linden, rose and chamomile, the steam leaving beads on her nose. It was dark in the forest, even in blazing sunshine. The branches weaved together, letting pillars of light in through tears in the roof without any warmth, allowing the odd brave foxglove or wood sage to grow there.

One time we found the rarest mushroom Elena had ever seen – a devil's finger. It looked like a starfish with five blood-red curving arms erupting from a small egg of jelly. The black gobbets are the spores waiting to attract flies to carry them off. The egg is quite small, about the size of a cherry. Flies were dotted around it and it smelled of rotting meat.

'Is it dying?' I asked.

'They mimic the smell of rotting meat so flies disperse the spores,' she said. 'They are all connected.'

Everyone meditated and swam together – Stefan, Elena, Alex and Nicolae too. We were all becoming increasingly devoted.

◆ ◆ ◆

'The electricity went out in our house the moment I was born,' Frida said online. 'It was the worst flooding in twenty years, with seventy millimetres of rain falling in six hours, and I was premature. Nature knows what it wants, and so does technology. It is all connected.'

The new recruits sat around the bonfire. The Starbucks girls had hung bunting on the newly renovated caravans where they now slept; they brought their make-up and teddies and ring lamps for evenly distributed light in their social media posts. They reposted, they took selfies, they adored, and they helped me with my research.

◆ ◆ ◆

Frida had become progressively successful online in the weeks before the festival, and people were asking more of her. It wasn't like how it had been at the beginning of the summer after I came off Klonopin and everything seemed sort of funny, and we would often laugh together when she came off calls. Now that we charged £500 for a half-hour call, her clients were more demanding. People weren't just calling on a lonely or tipsy whim for £2 a minute. People had serious concerns. When Frida messed up it wasn't cute anymore.

Over the last few weeks there had been the wife of a wealthy businessman with cancer who called all the time. She was seventy, full of Botox and hair extensions and sadness. She'd called the first time around when Jackson died. She and her husband were the first people I researched in a way that went beyond just googling, and I did it because this woman was irascible and hard to please and – I told myself – we needed more ways to help her. She wanted proof that Frida was psychic, specific details such as the name of her son, the colour of his eyes. Her son no longer spoke to her or her husband and she wanted to know that he was safe – but more than that she wanted to know where he was and whether he would forgive them one day. I had sent her an email from a dummy account that included a link to a site for a ground-breaking weight-loss pill. When she opened the link I had access to her computer. Photos, search history, it was all there, and this woman never got angry at Frida or called her a fraud again. A couple of social media DMs, following the trail of her son's friends, and I found his alias account. He was living in Joshua Tree in California with a stripper named Lucy. The client wired Frida more money than we asked for, after every phone call. Maybe this sounds underhand, but we made her happier. A week before the festival she apologised to her son for aspects of his childhood, and he apologised for other things, and they reunited. We spent it on food for the festival. It was a success all round.

'We are born into lives we don't control,' Frida said to us and her followers a few days before the festival. 'We find ourselves in a civilisation that puts us into little boxes from the time we are born. From birth to the cot to the classroom to the rented room we can only barely afford, we are expected to stay in our prescribed boxes and follow the path of least resistance set up by the wealthy and the powerful elites. Don't you wish to be truly free? Free of the shackles of this constrained and controlled life that each of us experiences right now?'

Later, in her bedroom, Frida said to me, 'Zo-Zo, come over here.' She smelled of shea butter and of me, from spending the last hour in bed. 'Tell me a secret.'

'Like what?'

'Something you've never told anyone. I'm bored. Tell me a secret.'

'My best friend in primary school was imaginary. My mum wanted me to be popular so much, but I just wasn't. So aged eight I invented a friend who lived a few floors up in our building. Mum never found out.'

'What was her name?'

'Stacey. Her existence was so convenient that she became a protagonist in my life for years, allowing me to spend days on my own without Mum asking questions.'

'Your mum never wondered why she never came over? Never wanted to meet the girl's mother?'

'Mum was pleased I always went to Stacey's flat instead of her coming to ours. Mum wasn't very present those years. The trick with lying is to keep it simple and tell people what they want to hear.'

'Good advice.'

'Poor Stacey was forever mediocre and unworthy of much discussion. She liked My Little Pony and was always the dog in Monopoly games, then she was into glitter pens and going to ballet classes even though she had flat feet. Her mum didn't mind me spending time over there. Stacey was terrible at spelling, allergic to dairy, and I feel like if Mum were to be listening to this, Stacey being invented would be the most shocking thing.'

'More shocking than what?'

'More shocking than you.'

'Am I shocking?'

'A bit.'

'I wish I could have been your friend.'

'Me too.'

She told me about finding her mum blue and choking on vomit one day when she was a kid, and calling an ambulance just in time. About how they used to find food in restaurant dumpsters, and beg on the streets.

How her mum would go to prison and leave her with strangers for a while. How she used to read fortunes to tourists on European street markets as a child. She was so hurt and huge and beautiful. I was insane to think someone so spectacular and traumatised could belong just to me.

In the days before the festival it rained, although it would remain warm and humid into August. In pauses between downpours we collected chestnut-brown bay bolete mushrooms, and ox tongue fungus that stuck rudely out from the low trunks of oak trees.

'You own me,' I said to Frida.

'I know.' She drew a line up my thigh and kissed me behind the ear.

She would draw the outline of a door in the darkness and the light would remain, like ink on paper. Crows watched us.

We were all meditating in the forest and on the flats three times a day. Crows and gulls wheeled and dipped, and behind their noise was the primal tide over sand and mud, making new patterns for the new island we would wake up to later. The sound felt as if it were a part of our bodies: our nerves, blood, mouths. The air smelled of rose verbena and burning wood.

Moth had grown in stature but also in presence. He almost seemed like one of the adults, and Nicolae and Alex taught him to drum with them. When he bowed to Frida before and after meditation he looked like a yielding Goliath. He could drum for hours without pause.

◆ ◆ ◆

On the first of August, the morning of the festival, Rebecca lost a pair of diamond earrings that she'd arrived with. They were worth thousands of pounds. Even before the earrings went missing, Rebecca had visibly recoiled in Nicolae and Alex's presence. Now she looked angry and I was worried she would leave, ruining Frida's mood.

That morning Nicolae and Stefan were building an enormous scarecrow to burn on Lughnasadh. It had stopped raining just in time. The air was wet and warm. Stefan had nailed together some wood into the shape of a star, twice the size of himself, then everyone helped wrap hazel, willow and vines around this frame until a human form emerged. I found myself standing by Nicolae's caravan. He always locked his caravan, even when he was just going to the fire or the main house.

I watched them. Moth and Stefan were drumming now while Nicolae, Alex and the rest of the group were working on the wicker man. The caravans were bright and newly painted in blues and greys. Moonlight glinted on the aluminium roof, bunting and fairy lights hung between them.

I walked over to his caravan and walked around the back. I'm not sure what I expected to see through the window; it's not like he would have the earrings displayed on his kitchen table. They had a plastic fermentation box outside near a generator which smelled sour and fruity. I went up on my toes to look through the windows. Inside Nicolae's caravan I saw sanitizing solution, strainers, enormous brew pots for boiling the wort from the malt extract. The sound of drumming mingled with my heart pounding in my chest.

His windows were locked as well. Through the dated curtains I could see piles of books, some of which I recognised as Jackson's. *A Course in Miracles*, *The Bhagavad Gita*, *The Kybalion*, *The Secret Teachings of All Ages*, a *History of the Dacian Kingdom*. I wouldn't have taken him for much of a reader.

I moved over to Alex's caravan, but his curtains were closed. This caravan had another door at the back and, to my surprise, I found that it opened. But as I began to open it, the hinge creaked so loud that I froze, grimacing. I peeked through the one-inch crack. The dim interior was lit only by a small, flickering LED clock on the counter. The wind rustled the bushes behind me and the drumming continued. Nobody had heard.

I had some lip balm in my pocket. The sun had made my lips crack so Elena had made me some with coconut oil, beeswax and shea butter. I smoothed it on the two rusty hinges, working it into the crevices, then tried again and the door opened smoothly.

Inside, it smelled of stale cigarettes and damp wood and fermentation. My eyes adjusted. There was a beaded curtain cutting the sleeping space off from what must be the kitchen space beyond. A thin bed was crammed into the corner of the bedroom, its sheets rumpled. There was a table cluttered with papers and an empty coffee mug. Overflowing ashtrays. Then, as my eyes adjusted to the dark, I noticed the gun on his bed. My breath caught; I'd never seen one before in real life. It had a theatrical quality: compact and sleek, glinting in the LED light. Stepping closer, I saw that the grip was slightly worn at the edges. Beside it a small box of ammunition lay open. A cleaning brush and a little bottle of gun oil were out on the bed covers. The air smelled intimately of Alex: his cigarettes, his sweat.

Merlin barked in the distance, followed by the low murmur of voices. Still distant. Not him. I exhaled and walked over to a chest of drawers, where one drawer was open. On top was a calendar with naked women on it, a pack of Tarot cards, a goat skull and, most oddly, a photograph of six children ranging in age from maybe six to thirteen, all dressed in white with flower-garlands. I touched Frida in the middle of the group, staring sadly out. It gave me a deeply uneasy feeling, although on the surface I supposed it was a flower girl photo from a wedding.

I lingered a little longer on the photo. She was thin in it, almost malnourished, and her eyes were very deep set. She did not strike me as looking happy. The photo was unsettling. Ceremonial, certainly.

I opened the drawers. Socks, underwear, nothing else interesting. No earrings. I opened the drawer in the table by his bed: condoms, weed, cigarettes, and a pile of credit cards with different names on them. No earrings. But there were also three passports. They were all from different nations: Britain, Romania, Italy.

I opened the British passport. It was Alex's photo but the name was different: Paul Jones. I opened all three and they all had his photo but different names. Then came the faint creak of the caravan door opening and I froze in his bedroom with my hand in his bedside drawer.

Heavy boots thudded into the kitchen, but thankfully there was the beaded curtain in between. His shadow skittered through the beads. If I moved at all he would he hear me, so I just stayed very still and hoped he didn't need anything from the bedroom.

He opened the fridge, clinked the tops off some beers, and I held my breath. I heard the front door open and smash closed again, then the key turn in the lock. Flushing with panic, I pushed my way through the beaded curtain and out of the still-open back door. I rested my back on the side of the caravan and caught my breath in the cooler fresh air. My chest was tight and the air felt difficult to swallow, just like in my panic attacks. I hadn't had one since quitting the benzos. My heart was pounding and erratic. My vision narrowed and I thought I was going to faint. The feeling is temporary, I told myself, hearing Frida's voice in my ear.

Then I heard a twig snap and turned to see Merlin staring at me from behind a nearby tree, salivating. I stayed very still. Footsteps crunched over dried mud and twigs, louder and louder. Stefan appeared right in front of me, maybe five steps from where I was standing.

'You see a rabbit, boy?' Stefan said, bending tenderly to Merlin. 'Good boy.'

Stefan looked right in my direction. I'm still not sure if he saw me or not. Sometimes when I replay this moment in my mind I am sure he saw me and just decided not to get involved, because he led Merlin away from me.

I exhaled and sat down on the ground, heart still throbbing. Every sound around me was amplified and jumpy: insects and birds and the sucking tides. I don't know how long I sat there but eventually my body stopped throbbing and I managed to stand. I walked around the back of the island to avoid my friends drumming and making the wicker man. My sweat still felt cool on my neck and I needed time to think.

◆ ◆ ◆

The photo was the thing that niggled at me the most. The passports, credit cards and gun weren't such a surprise. But that beautiful photo of Frida as a child, all dressed in regal white, her face somehow imperious but so sad – that made me itch.

I walked in a giant loop past the causeway and then ducked into the forest from the west. The soil soft and spongy, the forest swallowing the sounds of my footsteps. The smell of damp earth and decaying leaves filled the air, and the trees were wrapped in twisting vines.

Chapter Ten

When Oliver leaves my house to get his car, I lie back on the grass in our garden and concentrate on not having a panic attack. I still use Frida's techniques. 'Here's what I know.' I can hear her voice in my head. 'Fear is our greatest ally in transformation.'

I focus on my breathing, on physical sensations. Dew is beginning to settle on the courgette leaves in the raised beds – little gems in the moonlight. Tendrils curl and the garden feels alive but tranquil. I take a deep breath. I'm okay. I love the smell of the night-time.

I take my phone out of my pocket and dig my toes into the dark grass. Then I open up Instagram and change the photo on my new account to a real photo of me, and the handle to @Guest72, the handle I had when we started. Then, for the first time in ten years, I write Frida a message.

'Five- and seven-letter words that together answer the clue "theoretical boundary from which nothing can escape",' I write in her DMs.

A cricket chirps and a seagull screams. That is the first clue we ever solved together. I remember sitting at my desk in that tiny room above The Queen in Kentish Town, surrounded by coding books and pills.

I sit up, then stand. I feel shaky. I don't know what I'm going to do tomorrow. Have I already said too much?

I put the phone in my hoodie pocket and go check on the kids again, locking the back door behind me and double-bolting everything. Ben thought I was crazy when I got the bolts put on all the doors after moving in.

There is a faint scraping sound coming from somewhere in the house. Maybe it is the building stretching in the heat, the groans of the old wood. My bare feet pad up the stairs, leaving dew prints that disappear in the warmth almost as they are left.

Leo's door is ajar, when I am sure I closed it. Maybe he went to the toilet. I push the door open slowly, my hand trembling. Moonlight spreads across his bed, and the window is open. It was definitely closed earlier. The fan whirrs. His bed is empty.

My vision blurs for a second.

'Leo?' I whisper into the room, heart beating fast, then run to the window. It is too high for anyone to climb in without a ladder, but why is it open? 'Leo!' I shout, and I run into Emma's room, but she is asleep all curled up under her robot duvet cover. Then I hear a noise in the master bedroom.

I stand outside it for a second, heart beating in my ears, then open the door with a creak.

He is sitting up in bed, his skin flushed. I step forward to put my hand on his forehead and he is burning up.

'Baby,' I say, nearly collapsing with the relief of him being there. I go for the Calpol. I refresh his water bottle with cold and give him the medicine, then he crawls back into my bed. His body is shaking with fever.

'Where were you?' he says. 'Who were you talking to?'

'I couldn't sleep,' I say, trying not to lie. 'You're burning up.' I pull up the covers and get in next to him. It doesn't take long for him to fall fitfully asleep in the crook of my arm.

I take out my phone again. The blue light spreads around.

'Event horizon,' she's written under my message. 'Hello Zo-Zo.'

◆ ◆ ◆

In the afternoon, when we were all crazily preparing for the festival, Ruth came forward saying she'd taken the earrings Rebecca had reported stolen and she was sorry. Frida told the girl to scrub the whole cottage until it was spotless, and she did so, down on her hands and knees, only stopping to eat and sleep a few hours. Her knuckles bled. I didn't tell Frida about the strange photo of her in the caravan. I felt odd at the thought of those solemn children all dressed in white.

A large fire pit was being set up in the field, stones arranged in a circle and kindling in the centre. The air smelled of freshly cut herbs, woodsmoke, and the damp scent of earth. We were all out collecting wildflowers for garlands. I'd been speaking to one of Elena's friends outside the forest. She had untamed hair and a necklace of moonstones. As this woman walked, she whispered words of blessing under her breath. She was also an 'end-of-life practitioner' and worked for the same company as Elena. She'd been on the island for about a week.

I veered off from this woman at some point, following a crop of dog violets into the darkness. Frida knew I was in the forest; she'd asked us all to go in and get the flowers. Hundreds of people were set to turn up on the island. Most were coming in groups. There were people from all walks of life. A management consultant and his law school fiancée; students from the University of Essex; travellers. There ended up being more than double the number of people we'd expected.

The sound of bass reverberated from speakers that Alex and Nicolae had brought over. I heard a laugh that sounded like Frida's in the forest somewhere, so I walked towards it. Then I heard a groan and stopped in my tracks.

Another groan, louder this time, and movement. A rustle. I saw a flash of colour beyond some undergrowth in the gap between two trees, a flash of pink moving back and forth just behind.

I tilted my head. From this new angle I realised that the pink was Grace's bra. She was naked apart from it, her thighs on either side of Moth, who lay on the forest floor with one hand on Grace's right breast as it bobbed from over the top of her bra. Coupled with her monkish bald head, the pink bra and the breasts looked strange. I blushed and turned away, but in doing so I stopped still at the sight of something far stranger.

It wasn't just them in the forest. Frida was there too, entirely naked and illuminated by shards of sunlight spiking in between the trees. She looked like a marble sculpture, standing there with Grace and Moth. While Grace moved on top of Moth, his hand was wrapped around Frida's ankle. She was standing over them, legs slightly parted, touching herself.

It was a bit like when you learn the meaning of a new word, as a kid. Fabricate or feral. Intrepid, insular, maverick or meticulous. And then hearing that word all the time and realising you just didn't understand. The love of my life, the person who had ignited pretty much everything, leaned down and kissed Moth while Grace rode him. I could hear my heartbeat and my breathing became rapid and shallow. I leaned on a tree, feeling dizzy, but wondered how a person was meant to react to something like that. There was no rulebook for this. No collection of instructions and procedures that could help me handle this particular operational task. I could almost feel Moth's hand wrapped around my own ankle, feel her lips, and my knees felt weak. I ought to have seen this coming.

In coding, every action or decision is an input that becomes an output via a function. It's great. Code can be debugged. So your mother is going to chuck you out of your accommodation; you debug by finding somewhere else to live. Hate your job; find a new way to make money. But this scene in the forest, the bare skin and the panting, this was a runtime exception I did not know how to fix. I didn't even know what to think.

◆ ◆ ◆

Grace was the one who found me, later in the day. I was reading in the forest, a streak of sunlight coming down through the trees like a nightlight. I'd considered leaving but hadn't acted on it. I ought to have been replying to DMs about party logistics.

'You dare me to walk through the fairy arch?' Grace said casually, coming over to me. Her head was growing a bit of fuzz. She touched the upward bend of the arched tree, with its wrinkled skin. Her eczema was looking bad that day. 'What are you doing out here on your own? There's a lot of party prep to do.'

She ducked under the fairy arch with a smile. The space was leafy and dotted with wildflowers and she knocked a few of them sideways. From this angle the arch looked like it was a creature taking a low, obsequious bow.

Afterwards she looked around, as if disorientated. She looked raw and unformed for a moment. Her cells had shattered from their places and then hurried back to formation. She tried to smile but the smile didn't fit anymore, it was someone else's smile, and then it was hers again as quick as a blink.

'It's just a tree,' she said, to herself, but she sounded unsure.

'I know that.'

'Nothing is going to happen.'

'I know that.'

'You have a gecko face. Fuck,' she said, joking.

'Rarrr,' I pretend-roared, not smiling.

'Just my luck to jump into the multiverse and come out in lizard land. Fuck this. Fuck you.' She paused. 'You could have joined us,' she said softly, coming over to me now and sitting down on some tree roots next to me. So they had seen me standing there. My cheeks flushed. 'You were a virgin before Frida, weren't you?'

'I just feel stupid. Like, I always miss the nuances of social things. I didn't know.'

'You thought you were, like, going steady?'

'I thought she loved me.'

'She does.' Grace laughed. 'Love doesn't have to have the boundaries society defines.'

'But I didn't know.'

'I thought it was obvious.'

'Well, it wasn't. How did she grow up?'

'In communes.'

I wasn't sure how to put the picture I'd found into words, or explain why it troubled me.

'Everyone goes at their own pace,' she said. 'Just know that there's nothing to be jealous of. She loves you. She just doesn't believe in ownership, and that's okay.'

I picked up a bird egg that I'd found earlier and had laid down in the mulch next to me. I turned it around in my hands. It wasn't cracked open like the baby had hatched but had a hole like the goodness had been sucked out. Then I looked up at the shapes of light spilling down the branches.

'Sex is such an easy way to find connection. You turn your head off and you don't think about video games, or funny lines in TV sitcoms, or Toblerone bars.' Her trainers were toe-to-toe with mine.

'Toblerone bars?' I said.

'Those giant ones that you can only get at airports. Confectionery for a giant.'

'I've never liked Toblerones.'

'What do you think about during sex?' she asked me.

'Nothing. Just her.' I paused. 'Come away, O human child. To the waters and the wild with a fairy, hand in hand, For the world's more full of weeping than you can understand.'

'Did you write that?' Grace said.

'An Irish poet called Yeats,' I said, pointing to one of a few books from Jackson's shelves that I had out there in the forest: *W. B. Yeats: The Last Romantic*.

'Stay in school, kids,' Grace said in a funny old-man voice. She was quiet again, and said: 'I actually feel different. Do I look different? Do I have a gecko face? Is this another dimension now?'

She turned on her side so she was close to my face suddenly.

'What if I'm in a different universe and don't know it?'

'I think it's the same universe. Don't stress.'

'Maybe I'll be better in this one. Content, happy, less itchy. Maybe I won't fuck people for a moment of unity. People my friends love. I'm sorry. I've hurt you, haven't I?'

'Maybe,' I said, unsure. It felt like if I reached out, she would easily move her head down and kiss me. There would be a connection. An urgent and thrilling reciprocity.

'You're so up yourself,' she said, and I was surprised by the change in tone. 'You think you're better than everyone because you're bright. But you're the same. Why should you have her? All of her?'

'You're not in gecko land,' I said blankly. Then I paused, with the threat of a kiss no longer hovering in the forest.

'Fucking her is grok,' she said.

'How many times have you?'

'A lot. Too many to count.' Grace laughed, and itched her arm. The sound of nails on skin merged with the forest sounds: birds and breeze and music in the distance. 'This afternoon, fucking him in front of her, I forgot my name,' she said. 'It was odd. I couldn't remember anything before Frida. I liked it.'

◆ ◆ ◆

'You did not arrive into this universe,' Frida said to thirty thousand followers while Merlin nosed at her hand in the garden. Seagulls cawed above, almost sounding like laughter. People were beginning to arrive for the party. 'You emerged, like trees emerge from mud and sunlight. And you too will have many phases of consciousness. You have been mud and you will be mud. You have been sunlight and you will be sunlight. A fear of death is the invention of human ego. The spirits want you to know that we are all just different shades of light.'

Nicolae and Alex watched us. Watched her.

'And soon, we will be technology,' she said. 'Just as now, all the trees are speaking to each other. The dead bodies of ants and Vikings and fish are all merged and growing together. Soon we will all be one mind, bound by a supreme and almighty technological reality.'

Her advice often belied her years.

The connection between pleasure and pain is deeply rooted in our biology. All pain makes our nervous system release endorphins, which act to block out that pain. It's not so different from how opiates work, ironically.

Later, I became an obsessive long-distance runner. When you run there is a moment when it starts to hurt. Your body responds by releasing the body's own narcotics – endorphins.

I still only wanted her. But the pain of sharing her went beyond jealousy into something intoxicating.

◆ ◆ ◆

Hundreds of people poured over the causeway for Lughnasadh. Couples, groups, single people came over the causeway towards the soft thrum of music from the speakers. Some had backpacks with tents, others had blankets draped over their arms, ready to claim a spot on the grassy field. Welly boots and short skirts, mud already splattered on bare legs. Flags and banners. Cans of beer and spliffs. We'd hung cheap animal masks on trees, and left them in buckets on the paths, so people chose one as they arrived. They became rabbits, foxes, owls, seagulls, wolves.

'By exploring the ways you connect with your own subconscious death urge, you give yourself the opportunity to start unravelling the metaphorical and literal mindset that creates a lack of vitality in your life,' Frida said online. 'You will be a spirit one day. You already belong to them. You must do as they say, because their anger will break you.

'It is so important to appreciate death. I have died many times. Often the effect of this subconscious death urge colours relationships, creates "no exit" situations as well as generates trapped feelings and difficult or stuck emotions. When we can sit with our fears, it allows the soul the time to find a path that will lead us home. This path is ours to travel and ours alone. The only help we can hope for externally is the renewed faith that this path does exist – and, if we trust in ourselves, that we will find it.'

◆ ◆ ◆

Grace, Frida and I got ready together as people arrived, posting selfies. Frida wanted her hair curled so we borrowed tongs from the Starbucks girls. Grace's brow furrowed as she wrapped strands around the heated tongs. I didn't say that I'd seen Frida with Moth and Grace in the forest. We were all dancing around each other. The fact of it was sitting low in my stomach like food that didn't agree with me. But her fingers touched my knee, her toes touched mine, and Grace's fingers touched her, and that distracted me. She painted her fingernails while I did her hair. She slipped rings on our fingers; a follower had sent us them last week. Amethyst for spiritual protection. Citrine for wealth. Hematite for grounding. Selenite for balance and harmony. Grace danced to music on the radio.

I wanted to get her on her own and ask about the photo of the people bowing to her, and about the forest, but Grace lingered. We didn't usually do these vain things, but she said that rituals like this had a place. It was a synchronisation. Then my phone rang and she looked at it with an annoyed frown. It was Mum. She'd called me a few times the day before as well. Then, with a shudder, I realised that I'd missed her wedding: I was supposed to have been at Camden Town Hall a few days ago.

The phone rang off and I called back. Fuck.

'I don't want to talk to you,' she said, breathing heavily down the phone. I turned away towards the window, where people were setting up tents near the caravans.

'You called me.'

'You missed it.'

'I'm sorry. I totally forgot. Why didn't you call to remind me?'

'I did. You are so selfish.'

'I'm so sorry, Mum. Honestly.'

And I was, genuinely. I'd meant to slip off for it. Mum used to let me sleep in her bed as a kid. She'd said it was because if I saw her next to me on waking then I'd fall right back to sleep rather than crying. Closing my eyes for a second, I could smell her warm pillowcases, never washed enough, with their little half-circles of mascara on them. I was almost glad when she said: 'Selfish little cunt.'

The words punctured the guilt, giving righteous indignation room to expand.

I didn't reply for a moment.

'Well, you are,' she said. 'That's what you are. You've always been in your own world.'

'Maybe I didn't want to come and wear some figure-hugging pink satin dress that made me look like Barbie's fat friend. I've been in my own world because you didn't want me in yours. I was a mistake and I've known it every moment of every day.'

'I gave up my life for you. You ruined my body, my opportunities. I worked myself to the bone putting food on the table.'

'What?' I was half laughing, half spitting. My cheeks were flushed. 'Did you read that line in a magazine? You never worked. You fucked men for pocket money while getting child benefit—'

She put down the phone on me.

Frida, listening from the bed, raised an eyebrow. My ears rang. I was standing in the room, but felt as if I were floating.

'Come back here,' Frida said. A flock of golden plover glowed in the sunlight, reflected in the glistening mudflats. 'Don't worry about your mother. That was healthy.'

Grace brushed my hair and Frida held my hand.

Frida told me to write Mum an email saying I never wanted to see her again. Frida said it wasn't fair that my mum had put the phone down before I was allowed to 'speak my truth'. Another nudge, Grace now tonged my hair and put glitter in the roots. Frida put perfume behind my ears while I smashed my fingers against the phone keyboard, typing my thoughts to Mum. Grace gave me perfect flicky eyeliner and very red lips while I thought about the next paragraph I would write.

That evening, waiting for the party to start, I tapped out things to Mum that I would never be able to take back. 'I don't blame you for how our relationship turned out,' I read to Frida, dry-mouthed, 'I know you have your own struggles. But I can't keep giving pieces of myself to a relationship that drains me and doesn't allow me to be the person I am.'

'I don't make this decision lightly,' Frida suggested. 'For my own well-being, for my own mental health, I can't continue to allow this dynamic to control my life. I need space to heal, to find who I am.'

'Please understand this isn't a decision made out of anger or hatred,' I read out as I typed. 'It's out of a deep need to take care of myself. I hope one day you can understand why I've made this choice. I need to find peace, and I can't do that while remaining in this cycle.'

Send.

Mum never wrote back to the email.

I get that Frida used me, and controlled me. But she also loved me and gave me a great deal. It's not black and white. Even after everything, I truly think she loved me. I certainly loved her. That letter haunts me, though. The things I wrote could never be taken back. I know exactly how people disappear into Frida's orbit.

'Take a photo,' she said, and I turned to her, all made up and spectacular. She was glowing, hair glossy and curled with wildflowers pinned in, glitter on her lips and eyelids. She was going to be social media gold tonight. *Click*. In the photo she is standing by the open window looking at a crow perched on the window ledge. My beautiful friend, leaning her forehead against the glass, wearing a white t-shirt like a dress. She had never looked so extraordinary.

She was wearing my turtle necklace.

◆ ◆ ◆

A moment after taking that photo, out of her bedroom window we saw a fancy car driving over the causeway. I was bent over my phone posting the photo when Frida said my name and pointed at the BMW disappearing behind hedges then reappearing.

'Maybe a party guest,' I said, but we both recognised the car from the day Rebecca came to the island by mistake. I could see the vein between Frida's eyes throbbing as the car rounded into the driveway. Frida was already on her way downstairs when Rebecca's husband got out of the car. I was right. She was leaving.

I followed Frida down two stairs at a time, our curled hair bobbing with each step. Out on the driveway Rebecca had emerged from the cottage into her husband's arms. She smiled at Frida like it was all just normal, like her exit wasn't a big deal.

Gregory was wearing a cotton-pique polo shirt, linen cargo shorts, blue boat shoes, and sunglasses, as if he were going to a golf weekend rather than rescuing his wife from a teenage psychic on a marsh. Not that there's a socially acceptable outfit for the latter occasion, I suppose.

Gregory stepped forward, in front of his wife, when Frida emerged.

'I am so thrilled that I'm finally going to be a dad,' he said to Frida. 'I honestly can't thank you enough.'

It was so casual. Like he was picking his wife up from a spa weekend.

'I'll continue to follow and help with everything, of course,' Rebecca said to Frida, still standing slightly behind her husband. 'I hope you will continue to support the pregnancy?'

Frida paused. Birds chirped. The tides shifted and Gregory's car engine vibrated. He hadn't turned it off. There was a theatrical politeness to the moment, but the little things – their body language, the idling car – suggested that everyone was aware the scene could get nasty.

'Of course,' Frida said, also theatrically calm. 'But why are you leaving? You didn't mention it. I would have advised you not to, for the sake of your baby.'

Others had heard the car and were watching us. Elena was wiping her hands on her gardening apron; Ruth was behind her.

'Well.' Rebecca laughed with her mouth but not her eyes. 'I have to set up the nursery. I have a career. A husband. I am so grateful to you, but I'm not going to *stay here*.' She laughed and I saw Frida flinch. 'My hair needs a deep clean. I think maybe your mattress has mites.'

Rebecca laughed again with her mouth. Her eyes looked hard and worried. Stefan now appeared and held Merlin by the collar at the edge of the garden.

'But we're renovating things,' Frida said, and she sounded sort of pouty and lame. Too little, too late. The golden goose was flying away.

'Look,' Rebecca said, and I saw the businesswoman we'd first spoken to, although she was standing behind her husband's big shoulders. 'You have the potential for a powerful brand but if you want to be mainstream you have to clean up your act.'

Frida flushed. This is what I'd said.

'It's all a bit skanky around the edges, isn't it?' Rebecca said, her hand on the car door. She wanted to be gone. 'Some of your friends are not people I want to associate with. I've spent a decade working on my brand.'

Rebecca turned towards Gregory, who opened the car door for her. Frida's hands were balled together and her cheeks were flushed.

'You shouldn't leave,' Frida said. 'I promise. You know I have the gift, and I'm telling you – for your own good – not to leave.'

'I'm afraid we have an appointment,' Gregory said, and Frida stepped over to Rebecca. He stood in front of his wife, his hand protectively over her shoulder.

'I need to tell Rebecca one thing, please,' Frida said.

'We're done here,' Gregory said. 'Rebecca, get in the car.'

'I have a gift for you,' Frida said with a smile, and took off one of her rings. 'It is obsidian stone to absorb negative energy, purge toxic thought patterns and protect your energy.'

Gregory looked sceptically at Rebecca, who nodded slightly and took a small step away from her husband in order to receive her gift. Frida slipped the ring into Rebecca's hand and said something into her ear that we couldn't hear.

Rebecca frowned and flushed a little. Frida's face was also set in a stony frown. Rebecca kept the ring in her hand but didn't put it on. She slipped into the car and Gregory shut the door then got into the driver's seat.

Then they drove off, the car jumping through potholes.

'What did you say to her?' I asked as the fumes dissipated into the salty air.

'I told her the baby would only survive on the island,' Frida said, walking into the cottage and sitting down on the sofa in the living room. She reached under the sofa and took out a pack of cigarettes – she'd not smoked since Rebecca arrived. Now she lit one and ashed directly on the wood floor.

'Don't look at me like that,' Frida said. 'It's true. I'm only trying to help her.'

It felt as if the light had a hard time getting into the low-ceilinged space, full of books and ancient bits and pieces, sculptures and maps. She picked up a book of crosswords on the top of a pile. She opened it.

'She shouldn't have gone,' Frida said. 'That's all.'

'Or you should have asked Nicolae and Alex to leave instead.'

'Don't tell me what I should and shouldn't do,' she snapped. 'If Rebecca is that ego-driven, it's best she's gone. But her growth and her child's growth depended on her staying here. Never tell me what to do. You do not see the layers that I see.'

She looked down at the crossword on her knee. She exhaled a column of grey smoke.

'Distress at sea?' she said to me. 'Three letters.'

'SOS,' I said quietly.

'Stage of growth?'

'Phase.'

'Small bit of laughter, ends with two Es.'

'No idea.'

'Teehee?'

'Teehee? Teehee is not a word.'

'This isn't Scrabble. But google it.'

'A giggle or titter, especially a derisive one.'

'Titter,' she said. 'Titter. That's as bad as teehee.'

'Stop tittering.'

'Teehee,' she said, but she wasn't smiling and certainly not laughing. She inhaled. 'Turn the camera on, please. I have something to say. I bet she's watching me right now in the car. She knows what she just did.'

I took my phone out of my pocket. Frida took a deep breath. She was sitting on the sofa, hair glossy and glittery, eyes and lips defined. She held the cigarette off camera so nobody could see. I almost asked her to go outside because this light made her look a bit witchy, a bit sinister, but maybe that's what she was going for.

'Alone we are fragile, just a single spark fading into the dark. Alone we control nothing, not even our own decisions and desires. But together we are a force, a collective will, a synchronicity that can bend time and substance. Together we are ancient and unstoppable. You think I'm just a kid.' She stared into the camera for a beat there, and I shivered. 'Maybe you think I'm a criminal. Poor. Ugly. But I am the only person who can save you from yourself.'

She paused.

'You need me.'

She got up, leaving me on the sofa. The air in the room was still and soupy. I posted it while she paced the room.

'If I could rearrange the alphabet I'd put U and I together.' someone wrote underneath the video, and I considered reading it out to break the tension, but her face was so set that I decided against it.

'Rebecca will come back,' I said. 'Let's just enjoy the evening.'

Frida's lip quivered slightly.

Comments flashed underneath the video: 'What a f*cking crackhead', 'GREAT STUFF. Please like my videos too and follow', 'HAHA I'D LIKE TO LICK HER ASS', 'Am having trouble with my sexuality but have no money can I have free reading?'

I put the phone away.

'The baby's soul stayed on the island,' Frida said. 'It can't survive without her here.' She lit another cigarette, inhaled, and ashed. 'Rebecca will be back. She'll lose the baby and come back. I've promised her a baby and she will get a baby. Tonight the door between different dimensions is open, and magic is possible. She'll come because her baby is here,' Frida said. She was still speaking quietly, looking off to the side.

'That doesn't make sense.'

'It will make sense soon. Let's go to the party,' she said.

The air was beginning to darken outside the windows. People were arriving, tramping over the causeway in small groups from the bus stop, or pouring out of taxis using their phone lights as torches. Bunting and twinkling lights hung from the trees in the forest and around the caravans. The wicker man was ready to burn in the middle of the field. Music was playing. We'd bought hundreds of animal masks off the internet and we had them lying around in baskets.

By the time darkness fell on the island, the tide was high and the only way to escape was to swim.

◆ ◆ ◆

Maybe a wedding in a fancy hall, a rave in a loft, a Mad Hatter's Tea Party. Everyone has one party that defines them.

The night was thick and hot. It pressed on our skin, and the full moon cast a glittery sheen over the island.

At the heart of the field, the bonfire started to blaze, although the wicker man would be put on later. Sparks burst in the sky in time with the music. There were flutes and synths over a sound system, creating a trance-like, ethereal mood. Nicolae's home-brewed beer sat in kegs, and people poured it for themselves. Frida wore a deer mask with papier mâché antlers. Grace and Moth both had matching seagull masks. All of them were achingly beautiful.

'We long to come apart at the seams and scatter,' Frida said in a video, filmed by me as we walked over. 'To split open and explode.'

We had thirty-five thousand followers at the start of the night. The next morning, we had a hundred thousand.

I decided to try something new and began a livestream, geotagging the location and using the hashtag #fridaraefestival, messaging the Starbucks girls to do the same in their own videos. I hoped it would catch on.

I livestreamed Grace in a bikini reclining on the unicorn inflatable she'd bought in town, laughing as she tried to get her balance.

Moth in a tree wearing a seagull mask. The Starbucks girls dancing. They'd invited a bunch of their friends, everyone clutching their phones. We were racking up the likes and our follower count was growing in front of my eyes. Forty thousand. Fifty thousand. A photo of me and Frida kissing got us thousands of likes.

The hypnotic rhythm of drums was like a combined heartbeat. We danced. The fire rose, the guests spun. There were hand drums, frame drums, bongos and timbales from Nicolae and Alex's collection.

I was bent over my phone commenting and replying to people on the other side of the field to me, but also people all over the world. People quoted Frida, reposting her on TikTok and Snapchat, sharing her videos on WhatsApp.

'We are standing on ley lines here at the island,' Frida said on camera, sweaty from dancing and almost metallic from the moonlight, while the drum beat more quietly. 'Can you feel it?'

Fifty thousand. Sixty thousand.

She was standing on a tree stump over the crowd of dancers, who had stopped to watch her. She had taken off her t-shirt and was just wearing her white bikini, but the moonlight made her appear burnished. She really did look like a deity from a temple. A lion-headed Egyptian goddess, carved in marble. Sexy as Ishtar, the ancient Mesopotamian god of sex and war. Strange as Hecate, the Greek goddess of crossroads, entrances and witchcraft.

Crows sat in tree branches above her, watching.

Sixty thousand. Sixty-five.

I filmed. 'Even at home, if you concentrate on me, feel me, you will feel the energy of these veins that spread energy and information. Just as plants speak to each other through their roots, mushrooms through spores, us through the internet, places are connected by these invisible fingers of energy. They are places where dimensions split open. These are the places where it is possible to cross between worlds. Light is pouring down on us. Fifty thousand people thinking of healing light. If you are hurting we are here for you. If you ache. If you are sad or lonely, know that our light surrounds you.'

The music and drumming had stopped. More than a hundred guests were watching Frida on the island, but many thousands were watching online.

'There is no barrier. I love you. You are me and I am you. We are all connected. I am the moment when the beat drops. I am our heartbeat. I am your dragon line, your spirit line, your fairy path and dream line. I am uncontrollable and irreversible. I am you and you are me. We are the singularity. Fear is pleasure. Fear is truth. Fear is the path to transformation, so what you are scared of is exactly what you need to do.'

She raised her hands and the crowd cheered. On the Instagram livestream, comments poured in underneath. People reposted, and sent videos of themselves quoting Frida.

Seventy thousand. Seventy-five thousand.

'By pinning our fears on the dying sun, we are giving him the energy he needs to make the journey into darkness,' Frida said. 'This is the turning point. This is the beginning.'

Stefan put the wicker man on the fire and it began to burn. Eighty thousand followers.

◆ ◆ ◆

That livestream went viral. People joined it around the world. We had people commenting in Japanese, Russian, Kurdish. People were posting pictures and videos of themselves dancing in their bedrooms or shared dorm rooms, or burning their own garden wicker men.

None of us usually drank, but we all had a few beers that night. I'm not sure how long the party had been going on when I saw Frida dancing with another girl. They weren't touching or anything and I walked closer, still livestreaming from my phone. The girl was wearing a golden bird mask on her head and a tight white bandeau dress with bare feet. She was tanned and luminous with bangles all up her wrists. Backlit by the fire, Frida and the girl cast long shadows on the grass that seemed to grow and shrink, twisting unnaturally.

Then the girl with the golden bird mask on her head lifted it up and I saw Ava. Ava, the girl who'd shared Frida's bed before me. The girl who had smelled of menthol cigarettes and cinnamon lip gloss; who'd left her school shoes in my bedroom. Ava, who had been in a relationship with Frida before me. Behind us, teenagers in white with animal masks danced in the field. Ava's hair was no longer peroxide blonde like Frida's. I turned the livestream off as Ava kissed Frida on the lips, just a peck, but my brain felt too big for my head, full of revulsion and longing.

It wasn't the same as a panic attack, but more as if a puppeteer had let go of my strings. It felt as if I had fallen to the floor, but on inspection, I was standing stock-still and staring. I put my phone in my pocket.

It wasn't anger exactly, either. I felt my stress response kick in: blood pumping hard in my ears, blurred vision, dry mouth. My lips itched, imagining their lips touching. Jealousy is just fear with a different name, I told myself. A baseless, socially constructed fear generated from the idea that love is finite.

They were holding hands as they danced now. I could feel their touch. It itched to the point of pain, like chickenpox. I watched as Ava dragged Frida towards the fire. This wasn't just bodies. Ava had slept in Frida's bed. They'd shared lip gloss and cigarettes. Ava had done Frida's hair in the garden and whispered in her ear. Frida had eaten Haribo rings off Ava's fingers. Their feet were pounding the earth, bare feet digging into the soft ground, spinning wide arcs as they circled each other with hair twisting behind. I'd never felt so still in my life. Every so often they stopped dancing. One would whisper something and the other would reply with a laugh. They glowed with an intensity that bordered on the unnatural.

'You okay?' a voice said next to me. I jumped. It was Moth. He took my hand and led me away from the fire. 'You look like you're about to faint.'

'No.' I shook my head, but was grateful to be led away from the light of the fire. Frida hadn't even looked up and seen me watching her.

The forest smelled of decay and earth. Moth's eyes were wide and unfocused.

'When did Ava come back?' I said.

'Just this evening,' he said, leaning into me. 'You're shaking. Hey, they're just dancing.'

Moth reached out and held my hand, which I hadn't realised was shaking.

'Frida wouldn't agree with this, but maybe just try not to think about it? You being jealous of that is not going to go well. She was here first.'

'Do they love each other?'

My words were quiet. He had to lean even closer to hear me over the drums.

'She loves you too. Just don't think about it. I come from a long line of successful rich men who squash their emotions. Aristocratic white men have used the stiff upper lip to keep themselves in power for many generations. Maybe there's a time and place.'

'I'm not sure the aristocratic white man would know what to do with this particular situation,' I said.

'Hey,' he smiled. 'Aristocrats love a bit of debauchery.'

'Oh?' I said.

'Absolutely. Can I ask you something?' he said. Big mouth. Wide shoulders. White teeth. I caught him in bits; my real focus was the lithe and fluid bodies of the women in front of the fire.

I nodded.

'Just girls? Any nuance?'

I turned my face up at him. He was so tall. Beyond his body, I looked over at Frida. She was kissing Ava now. Properly kissing, bodies together.

He shrugged his big shoulders. I could feel his pulse in time with the drum. 'Frida's right, you know. Sex is energy. Not ownership. Maybe you could just . . . enjoy it? The freedom?'

I rolled my eyes but he leaned towards me. I could taste Frida in my mouth as Moth's fingers found their way around my waist and his breath into my mouth. Kissing Moth was so different from kissing Frida.

I felt angry with Frida but also giddy. I knew I wasn't doing this for the right reasons. I was hurt and angry. I needed some place for these emotions to go and Moth's body seemed as good a place as any.

'I'm going home tomorrow,' I said, and he didn't reply.

It was rough and inelegant but I was in the wave and there was no stopping it. His tongue on my neck and my wrists, places that belonged to Frida. I was keen for the oblivion, particularly when I suddenly couldn't see Frida and Ava by the fire. I imagined them in the shadows somewhere, two halves of the same being, untethered and heavy against each other on the sand or the mud. When I closed my eyes under Moth's hands it felt as if we were changing state there on the edge of the forest. The air was thick. Ava and Frida in my head, bodies sweaty. Me and Moth, also beyond the realm of thought suddenly. Guttural, reaching, all of us combined by the island's drumbeat.

◆ ◆ ◆

He was tender but insistent. When we were done my insides throbbed, so different to with Frida. More painful. A different pleasure. Not equal exactly, but still good. But angrier. Much, much angrier. Tears sprang into my eyes.

The party was still going. Fire spitting, people dancing, filming and posting. Frida and Ava weren't there. Moth and I emerged back into the party and warmed ourselves by the fire. On my phone I checked Instagram, and although I'd stopped posting, photos were still being shared and liked at pace. We had ninety thousand followers.

Grace came over and started chatting to Moth, and then they started kissing. I felt numb, neither irritated nor interested. I wanted another drink so grabbed one, but I didn't want to talk to the Starbucks girls, or their friends, or anyone else. I wandered off and sat near the fairy arch for a while to drink my beer, putting my hand in and out. There was blood in my knickers and jean shorts from Moth. I went back to the cottage on my own but couldn't sit still.

It was low tide. The full moon reflected off the puddles. It gave off a strong light and I saw two silhouetted figures walking right through the centre of the river. They were holding hands and their white clothes glinted: Ava and Frida.

Jealousy is worse than fear. There's a clarity to fear. Fear says run, hide, survive. Jealousy says negotiate, beg, deceive. It was hot and fierce in me that night as I left the cottage, through the dewy vegetable garden, over the garden wall and out towards the flats to the sound of ethereal music drifting in the dark air. The moon felt higher than ever.

'Great social media tonight,' came a voice as I was about to step in the river after Frida and Ava. Grace was sitting under a tree looking at her phone. Moonlight reflected on her bald head. 'Was it okay, with Moth? I didn't think you bent both ways.' She winked.

'Sorry,' I said. 'Do I have to say sorry?'

'No.' She shook her head. 'I'm all for sharing, but I'm guessing you're not feeling so generous. You should just leave them for a bit, you know? They have history. It doesn't mean she feels any less for you.'

'I just need to talk to her,' I said.

'She loves you. The grid is full of you and her looking at each other with crazy eyes. Just chill, it will all be fine.'

I started walking through the water and Grace followed, idly, splashing her heels. Waterfowl called to each other in the distance, and insects buzzed. Water sucked at the mud. A fox barked somewhere on the bank and we walked over the partially exposed mudflats towards the looming power plant beyond. The ground was uneven and slippery and it was difficult to gauge distance, but I knew from other days that the power plant was a twenty- or thirty-minute walk over the mud. Laughter drifted from the bank in the dark. A flock of crows flew out from behind the tall fence at the edge of the river. They looked like scraps of sky disintegrating off and twisting around in the moonlight. Behind the fence was the power plant.

'Radiation Area. Keep Out', said a sign attached to the fence.

'What are they doing in there?' I said.

Grace shrugged. 'Ava and I used to go there to get buzzed all the time. You can go inside those cooling towers, it's one of Ava's favourite places.'

The two huge industrial towers reached up into the sky – the cooling towers. A motion-activated spotlight flicked on while Grace and I squinted through at knotted metal and concrete, and we saw a shadow disappear out of the puddle of light, into the dark beyond. Breeze blocks and piping and rubble and a bad smell, like old eggs. Then the light went off and we were left in the moonlight again.

'Like, what were you expecting from her? Matching wedding dresses and a white picket fence?' Grace said. 'A pet pit bull sleeping at your feet? She did not grow up being taught that monogamy was somehow morally superior, and maybe it's not. You can't really be mad that she is who she is.'

'She said she loved me.'

'She does. She just loves a bit different.'

'How do you get into this place?'

'Let's just go. Leave Ava and Frida alone.'

'Please tell me how to get in?'

Grace reluctantly pointed at a break in the fence around the side, hidden by some shrubs. I ducked through the fence. For a moment the only sounds were liquid: the hush of lapping water, the occasional drip hitting metal somewhere in the shadows. But then I heard them laughing again. It was a disorientating sound, difficult to trace.

My phone flashlight cut a thin, trembling line through the blackness and I braced myself for the spotlight to come on with our movement. Grace came after me, through the fence. We stared around in the moonlit darkness of this hinterland. Amongst the dirt-etched concrete pathways and rusty pipes were occasional bright pink or yellow graffiti slashes, remnants of kids like Ava and Grace getting high or drunk here.

And then I heard laughter again. Voices, light and playful, muffled by something. The flashlight's beam caught glimpses of abandoned machinery – massive generators, rusted pipes looping along the walls, and then the curved wall of the first enormous cooling tower.

Then the motion sensor activated and we were bathed in yolky yellow light. Metal stairs zigzagged all the way up the outside of the tower like corset strings, and underneath the stairs an arched door led through thick concrete into the middle of the tower.

I thought the voices were coming from the other side of the arch, inside the tower. We stepped out of the light into darkness again. I could see why people might want to explore this; it had an apocalyptic grandeur.

The massive chimney was wet and cool. Algae made the concrete slippery under our trainers. The moon threw a perfect circle of light down from the chimney hole at the top, right into the rubble-strewn middle of the space: metal walkways, dirty pools of water, and some greenery where the sun must have penetrated most. This alive area was a perfect circle. One tree was trying to climb up and out. Primroses spiked up from the undergrowth. Bubbles popped in water.

'Up here,' Frida's voice came, and we jumped as the sound echoed against the concrete walls. We looked up and saw two figures standing all the way at the top, on the rim of the tower.

The air smelled of rot and water. My heart beat fast and loud. It's hard to even explain how huge this tower was up close, or to understand the perfect engineering that meant that it curved like it did.

A moment later I was following Grace out of the chimney to the bottom of the external stair-corset, then up it. The stairs shook with every step. The first small flight of stairs led to the area above the stilts. There, a rusty metal door was kept open by a breeze block.

We began to walk up, drawn to the sound of laughter and conversation above. It felt as if we were walking directly up towards the fat bright moon. Each wet step creaked under us. Occasionally I saw glimpses of white above – a flicker, like flashes of light. About halfway up I made the mistake of looking down and had to stop, pressing myself against the wall, barely daring to breathe. There was an eerie hum in the air, and wind whistled through the gaps in the stairs.

'You okay?' Grace said, a few steps above me. 'You want to go back?'

I shook my head, hearing movement up at the top and spurred on by the question of what they were doing. She pressed on and I followed. Step after damp, slippery step, one hand gripping the railing and the other balled up into a fist. The dark machinery below spread out: a field of slain buildings. Thanks to the full moon we could see the island, the town, even the tributaries of the river snaking out to the North Sea. We could see the fire still burning on our island. The waves hushed against the mud.

I took a deep breath before stepping on to the platform at the top, a moment after Grace, my legs shaking from adrenalin and exertion.

◆ ◆ ◆

When I got up there Frida was already perched on top of the railing that made a circle around the chimney hole, her feet dangling over the long drop. The railings were made of metal, painted with some sort of rough-textured non-slip yellow paint. If Frida had fallen forward for any reason, it would have been difficult for her to save herself.

While Frida was sitting on the railing, Ava was leaning on it and also ashing her cigarette down the hole. I stepped over to them. The ground looked miles away – a pit of darkness that pulled my gaze to it.

'Get off there,' I said. 'It's not safe.'

Frida laughed – an echoey sound, warped by the chimney – and I blushed.

'When we first met you,' Ava said, bangles jangling on her wrist over the hole, 'Moth said you reminded him of the geeky one from

Scooby-Doo. I wouldn't have taken him for having the hots for . . . what's her name?'

'Velma Dinkley,' Grace laughed, standing next to me, and then stopped when she saw my serious face. 'Oh, don't be so serious, Zo-Zo. I bet you own an orange turtleneck sweater and you rock it.'

'The spirits are lively tonight,' Frida said, from her perch above that endless hole in the earth. She probably didn't know what *Scooby-Doo* was. 'I'm so glad you guys came.'

'Please get off the railing though,' I said. 'It's giving me vertigo. I just came to say that I've decided to leave the island. I'll get the first bus to the station in a couple of hours.'

The air smelled of damp and concrete dust. Frida frowned. Everyone's features were soft and blurry under the bright moon, like pixelated photos. But it was still possible to read the expressions.

'I'm just not cut out for this,' I said. 'I thought I was but I'm not, so let's not make a big deal out of it.'

'The spirts are loud tonight,' Frida said, ignoring me.

'I don't believe in ghosts,' I said. 'Or open relationships.'

'So suburban,' Ava said.

'Don't be a bitch,' Frida said to Ava, and threw her cigarette end at her. Ava moved to the side and let the cigarette burn. 'But Zo-Zo, come on. Tonight is not the time to pick a fight with the spirits. We're meant to be celebrating them. You did so well tonight. Thousands of people engaged with us. We're going to be huge. We're going to be a success.'

I walked over and stood on the burning cigarette end.

'If you say you don't believe in ghosts they might not believe in you either,' Frida said. 'Why would you leave? We're just getting started. We need your conscientious spirit. Your strategy. You are the one who has got us this far, you can't leave. Thousands of people watched us tonight. Ava and I were talking about some cool plans for when we start charging people to come here. Like, more than just meditation.'

'Mindfulness for gardeners,' Ava said, snarky.

'Walking the Path of Gratitude?' Grace said.

'Croquet for inner peace,' Ava said.

'Lucid dreaming,' Frida said.

'Tantric sex,' Grace said.

'Get off the rail,' I said. My words echoed in the chimney underneath. I was prim and stiff, not fitting with the album cover of a girl gang standing here in the dark, cool and strange, smoking cigarettes.

'You are welcome to Frida, Ava,' I said to her quietly. Even quiet words echoed slightly. 'You all deserve each other. I'm going home, back to the real world. There's no such thing as spirits.'

'Hey, come on,' Grace said. 'Everyone's emotional tonight. Let's all go home. Don't say things you can't take back.'

Frida was staring at me, still sitting on the edge.

'Come sit with me,' Frida said. 'Up here. You're not leaving me. You love me. I am not for the faint-hearted, that's true. I am a venture into the uncharted territories of your consciousness, a quest for truth and self-discovery. Come sit with me.'

'You are so full of yourself,' I said. 'I'm leaving tonight. You are not a ley line. You are not a fucking deity. There are no spirits.'

'Don't make the spirits angry, Zo-Zo,' Ava said. 'Say you believe in them or they're going to be mad.'

The air felt thin and cool.

'I'm going.' I turned. I could feel my jaw. All of us just bodies in the cool darkness. There was a savagery to Frida, of course, but right then she looked tender. As she shifted her weight on the railing there was a soft crunching sound.

Just then the moon went behind a cloud and the tower became disorientatingly dark. We were all silent with the shock of this plunging blackness. We couldn't even see our hands, and then there was a fluttering sound. When the moon passed back outside the clouds again, a crow was sitting on the railing next to Frida like a familiar.

It's really no wonder crows have freaked me out since.

'The spirits are right here with us,' Frida said. 'We are all going to change the world together.'

I felt a knot in my stomach.

'No,' I said.

I heard a soft tap, fingertips on the railing. For a moment I thought Frida was going to fall. Her body tipped forward slightly, but instead she swung her legs back to safety and jumped off on to the platform where the rest of us were standing.

'Happy now?' she said.

'Not really. I'm going home.'

I turned away towards the steps. I began to walk down.

'Zo,' she said, coming after me. 'Are you serious? Why would you leave?' I felt tearful, and she put her hand out as I walked. 'Let's go home and talk about it. Just you and me. Your energy is really different. Let's just talk.'

'We can talk, but I'm still leaving. You can't change my mind on that. I'm leaving.'

I didn't turn, just kept walking down the stairs. They shook with the force of our combined march. Frida kept time behind me. She smelled of the fire, and marsh water. Ava and Grace stayed up at the top while we made our way down. We could hear them throwing things into the chimney. Ava hummed some song, I can't remember what.

Then Grace and Ava started to follow us. It didn't take as long coming down as it had going up, obviously. Grace and Ava were laughing and messing around. One of them had taken the other one's pack of cigarettes and was holding it over the stair railings;

the other was reaching. I was only half listening, more concerned with how Frida had managed to slip her hot hand in mine as we walked. I needed to keep my resolve.

I wasn't looking up when it happened. I was listening to Frida's footsteps and concentrating on my plodding feet. Frida and I were on the landing above the ground when we heard a creak above and felt the stairs shift under our feet.

I didn't react at first. This slow creak reverberated off the brick walls. It was long, almost lethargic, a pause in time. Then the air rang out with a sharp, metallic snap, and the entire staircase shifted violently off the wall.

I screamed, grabbing on to the handrail as the structure tilted away from the building. The metal groaned.

'Jump!' I shouted at Frida, realising that falling with the structure would be devastating. She hesitated, but I grabbed her hand and we jumped maybe six feet from the landing down on to the ground, tumbling. Scraped but unhurt, we scrambled up and away.

Above us the staircase had twisted right off the wall from five or six storeys up, tilting at a horrifying angle. Grace and Ava were not on the staircase when we looked up at it from the ground.

◆ ◆ ◆

For a moment, there outside the tower, Frida and I didn't move. The air was cool and the birds were loud. The wind rustled in the trees. My phone wasn't in my pocket – it must have fallen out – but Frida had hers and we turned on the flashlight.

'Grace!' we shouted in the gloom. 'Ava!'

It didn't take us long to find them. They'd been tipped right off the staircase to the floor underneath, not far from where Frida and I had landed. We saw their bodies but couldn't make out their faces for a second: they looked more like part of the abandoned factory detritus than our friends. One had fallen backwards on to a pile of metal tubing and her body was bent the wrong way, stomach raised up. The other body was on its side, facing away from us.

I walked tentatively closer, hoping they would groan and move, but the bodies were as still as the breeze blocks, the metal grating, the beer cans. Frida stood back and I continued forward, crunching over dirt and rocks.

First, the body with a bald head. Her body was all wrong, like a puppet slack in its box. This face had the same shapes and dimensions as my friend's face but the features were limp and the eyes were vacant, pupils staring straight up at the sky. The bald head made her skull-like. I bent down to her. A trickle of blood was running out of her right eye, clotting in the delicate curl of one ear, and I touched her cold hand and put my fingers on her wrist, where there was no pulse. Her laugh had been so big the first time I saw her on the promenade. I remembered her hot pants, flip-flops, huge sunglasses, and the way the men had all stared longingly at her. She had kept touching the space where her hair had been, once it had been shaved off. I thought of how birds had made nests from her thick brown hair. She had been my friend, more so than anyone else on the island.

I didn't want to look away from Grace. But then I thought Ava moved, a shiver or a jump. She had landed on her side. I gagged when I saw that the bone of Ava's neck was jutting out of her skin under her skull, which was no longer entirely attached to her body. The force of the fall had torn the two apart. Her shoulder, too, was not at a natural angle to the rest of her body. Her white bandeau dress was covered in blood and mud. The bangles up her wrists glinted in the moonlight. If there had been movement, it was just breeze in her hair.

Someone told me once that it only takes four minutes without oxygen for the brain to start dying. That's nothing at all. That's the average length of a pop song. That's the brewing time for a strong cup of tea. A microwave meal. Their whole complicated brains, gone in four minutes. All the times someone had hugged them were suddenly not stored anywhere anymore. All their school spelling tests. The feel of their favourite slippers on bare feet as little girls. The taste of Nutella and the suck of a cigarette and their hopes for the summer. The babies they might have had. Their babies. Their swirls of DNA snapping back into the darkness, and gone.

'An ambulance,' I whispered, and I turned to where Frida was standing behind me. She had not come close to the bodies. She lifted her phone and whispered, hoarse with panic: 'No reception.'

Fuck. They looked very dead, but I'd never taken anyone's pulse before. I stood up, feeling dizzy.

'Are they . . . ?' Frida said.

'I don't know. We need an ambulance.'

There was reception out in the estuary. It seemed awful to leave them there in the dark but we needed to call an ambulance. I moved first, grabbing for Frida in the dark. We slipped and tripped our way through the fence and back to the estuary, where the water was up to our thighs now as the tide rose. Once we were there in the water Frida fumbled with her phone and managed to call the ambulance.

'The stairs on the cooling tower at the power plant collapsed underneath us,' Frida said after telling them her name and location. 'They aren't moving, please be quick.'

'I'll wait for the ambulance,' she said breathlessly to me, seeming to regain some composure now. 'Go and tell Nicolae what happened. Quick. Get Nicolae and Alex to come here right now. That is important. Nicolae and Alex will know what to do.'

I ran back to the island, stamping through the rising river water in my wet trainers. My hands were shaking and my pulse was racing, the inescapable smell of algae and concrete and blood clinging to my nostrils. I heard sirens that I assumed were for us. I ran directly to the caravans for Nicolae. The party was over and the fire nearly out, but people were still around, chatting and playing music in tents. I banged on Nicolae's door. Inside, he and Alex and Stefan were smoking on the little built-in sofas.

I stood on the stairs. At first I couldn't get the words out, just pointed at the power plant, but eventually I explained some version of what had happened. Alex and Nicolae shared looks with each other and ran off, then Elena came and sat down next to me on the caravan steps.

'Try to breathe,' she said. 'Drink this.'

She passed me a glass of water and I realised my mouth was dusty. I took a long drink, then another. The power plant wasn't visible from there. It was a long way away. I imagined the paramedics bent over my friends, Frida with a thermal blanket over her, shivering and crying.

As a kid I remember standing in the sea somewhere – Margate maybe – on a camping holiday, and catching bits of floating seaweed. They looked so majestic underwater, twisting. Then you took them out of the water and they were limp and gross. That's what the girls had looked like. The majesty of them was beached and limp. Everything beautiful was just gone.

◆ ◆ ◆

I don't remember anything about the next twelve hours. Elena must have given me something in the cup of water to make me sleep. I woke up in a panic the next day to the sound of seagulls outside the cottage windows, the smell of freshly baked bread in the oven downstairs. Frida was asleep next to me, her hair tangled but clean around her head like a halo. I was wearing a clean white t-shirt, so someone had got me undressed. I smelled clean.

'Frida,' I whispered, waking her. 'What happened?'

'Are you okay?' she said groggily. She was naked – she always slept naked. 'You've been sleeping for ages.'

'What happened? Why didn't you wake me up? What happened with the ambulance?' I asked.

'I didn't call an ambulance.'

'I heard you call an ambulance.'

She assessed me. Dust swam in the triangles of sunlight from the window. Dust fairies, my mum used to call them.

'You and I both know there was nothing to be done. Ava's neck was broken and not attached to her head. Grace was snapped in two at her spine. They fell a long way. Listen to me.' I tried to breathe. Frida tucked my hair behind my ears and I flinched.

'I heard you call an ambulance,' I repeated.

'The paramedics wouldn't have been able to do anything. If the police had come we would have lost everything we've worked for. You and I are doing something amazing here, we're on the precipice of enormous success. Of everything we've wanted. We are going to help so many people. I know that Grace and Ava wouldn't have wanted to ruin that.'

'I heard you call an ambulance,' I repeated.

'But turns out, we didn't,' she said. 'So if you go to the authorities now, there will be questions. You didn't call an ambulance either.'

'There must be cameras or something,' I said.

She shook her head. She reached down under the bed and handed me my waterlogged, ruined iPhone.

'Did nobody hear the stairs fall?' I said.

'Pretty remote out there,' she said. 'That's why it was built there – so not too many people would grow gills. Nobody heard.

And everything has been taken care of now. Alex and Nicolae have cleaned up. We will protect you, and you will protect us.'

'They were our friends. We didn't hurt them. We don't have anything to hide. We can still tell the police.'

'The authorities have never trusted what they don't understand. The public would turn against us. We have woken up with over a hundred thousand followers this morning. We are blowing up. This story would end us just as we're starting.'

'But they were our friends.'

'And they want us to succeed. Their earthside struggles are over and they are now watching over us from another dimension of reality, but an equally valid dimension,' Frida said, squeezing my hand, her weird enigmatic warmth flooding through me. 'I love you. Only you from now on, okay? Nobody but you. And we will appease the spirits and do good deeds in the world.' She ran her hand up my shoulder and cupped my face in her hands. 'We are going to do spectacular things together.'

I felt nauseous.

'It's only you,' she said. 'It should always only have been you, I understand that now. The spirits have told me that I was wrong to upset you. That you are important. That you are a vessel. We are going to do great things together. If you go down for their deaths, so do I. And vice versa. You're not leaving us anymore, are you?'

◆ ◆ ◆

'We must learn to live in the realm beyond space and time, where we transcend our limits,' Frida said online the next day to her hundred and ten thousand followers. 'The spirits say we all shook off our boundaries last night. We all stood, exposed and tender, in the sunshine of our own evolution. Can you feel our ancestors talking to us?'

She smiled.

◆ ◆ ◆

For ten years I have regularly seen Grace in crowds, and then blink and she is gone. I was sure of it one time. I was in a taxi and it was raining so hard that the wipers could barely keep up. We drove past a bar, kicking up dirty puddle water on to the pavements. Past a supermarket and a nightclub, the cab was about to go under a bridge when a group of drunk people came out of the pub on the corner and walked straight in front of the car in front of my taxi, causing both cars to slam on the brakes. My driver swore in Urdu and banged the steering wheel with his hand.

That's when I saw Grace, heading under the bridge. She wore a long leopard-print coat, her black hair loose and wet and grown out since she'd shaved it. The same long neck, delicate jaw, audacious sexuality.

'Pull over!' I said, and the driver looked at me, startled. 'Stop,' I said. 'Here. Right here, please.'

He pulled over to the pavement, but by the time he'd done so I'd lost sight of her in the smashing rain. The drunk people laughed on the other side of the road, offering half-hearted hand gestures of apology. I started walking fast towards the station.

'Grace!' I shouted above the buzz of traffic and rain. 'Grace!'

I saw a flash of her coat disappear in the station. I followed it into the underground, just in time to see her getting on the escalator. I fumbled for my travel card.

Running down the left-hand side of the escalator, I turned right and couldn't see her on that platform so ran to the other, where a train was just rushing into the station. There Grace was, sitting casually on a bench with her legs crossed.

Breathless, I arrived in front of her as she stood up to get on the train.

But when she turned, it wasn't Grace. A pretty Indian girl, yes, but with completely different features.

'Sorry,' I said, panting. 'Wrong person.'

'No problem,' she said with an American accent. My heart pumped loud and my head swam. 'You okay?' the girl said. 'You don't look okay.'

'I'm fine,' I said, and sat where she'd been sitting.

People disappear every minute. They fall in love, find God, have babies and are not the same the next day. They try heroin, or kick it, or believe what their parents say during an argument. None of us are the same people we were ten, twenty years ago. We all disappear from ourselves at some point.

◆ ◆ ◆

Nobody even looked for them, to my knowledge. They were gone before they met Frida. My phone never turned on again after that night – it had landed in some mud, and Nicolae had found it and gave it back but it was completely destroyed. I looked on Frida's phone occasionally, though, and there was no mention of anyone going missing in Essex. Frida's social media was on fire, although I hadn't posted anything since Lughnasadh. Ruth, I think, was in charge of the social media now. I saw her in the garden, bent over her phone, videoing Frida meditating or talking while I was in bed upstairs.

The party was famous. People were calling it iconic, people were pretending they'd been there when they hadn't, and the masks from the party were selling on eBay for hundreds of pounds. Nobody was mentioning that two girls were there at the start of the party but not the end. Frida would tell me the follower count most days. A hundred and twenty thousand. A hundred and thirty thousand.

Frida told the group that Grace and Ava had 'gone on a spiritual journey' and that they would be back in a few months when they had finished 'working on themselves'. Even Moth seemed to buy it. I heard him telling Bella that Grace had needed to do some serious inner work and that she had been dragging the group's energy down. Around fifty people from the party stayed, pitching tents in the fields or bringing caravans. Some were clearly from the commune, but not all.

A few days after they died, I went back to the power plant in daylight but couldn't get in. The fence had been fixed. The cooling tower loomed, indifferent to the events, a timeless mausoleum.

As I walked back to the island, Nicolae stepped out from the trees.

'Don't go back there again,' he said. 'Everything is fine, you didn't do anything wrong, but don't go there again.' I saw he had a knife in the belt of his trousers. 'She is so much more powerful than you even imagine,' he said. 'We must protect her.'

Frida told me more about her childhood while I lay inert in bed. About the vibrant world that she hoped to create here on Bay. How they would all hold hands to watch the sunsets, adults and kids. The dreams. The belonging. More than guilt and confusion, I began to feel constantly sick.

◆ ◆ ◆

Rebecca had sharp cheekbones and sad eyes when she returned to us, just as Frida had predicted. Her baby had indeed died the night she left the island. The week of her return to Bay she didn't leave the house or look up when you said her name but immediately began to work on Frida's 'business plan'.

Rebecca had asked Gregory for a divorce, or maybe the other way around. She would get the house in Devon and he would take the flat in Soho, she said. We could start a retreat in the Devon house, she thought.

Crows came to a looping pause in the field then launched off again towards the forest on the mainland and disappeared. Crows made me uneasy. I kept flashing back to how the crow had arrived out of the cooling tower chimney as if Frida had conjured it.

Everything made me flinch, a knot twisted deep in my stomach. A physical manifestation of guilt, I assumed. I no longer had a phone. Not only was I no longer in charge of social media, I was no longer connected to the outside world.

Caravans were delivered, and others were taken away. Elena watched me, her dreamcatcher earrings swinging like they might catch my nightmares.

Merlin nosed around in the forest. Moth and a new girl meditated and swam together, kissing by the trees.

It sounds odd to put into words, but I started to see a pale child in my peripheral vision. A hallucination of something I didn't understand, but I thought of him as a spirit. When I faced him head on he would be gone.

◆ ◆ ◆

In the weeks after the festival my sense of smell was heightened, as was my thirst. I was drinking litres of water every day. I smelled milk and semen and sweat and every nuance in the air. I didn't know why this could be. I could smell the mushrooms, mud, fumes, rot. The arrows of sunlight through the trees smelled different to the shadows.

Frida held my hand in my sleep, tethering me to her. I dreamed of chillis hanging on their stalks like commas. Jam simmering on the stove. Frida padding over from the bath to our bed, hair dripping, skin warm even in the midnight breeze from the always-open window. The ivy grew inside our room, the plant's claws feeling their way over the wallpaper and trying to peel it off in the corners. I could smell it, growing.

I was at my most beholden to her, despite everything. I did not express any desire to leave. Just going to the toilet exhausted me. When she wanted to have sex we had sex. Sometimes she slept elsewhere but she did not tell me where, or with whom, and the power balance had changed so dramatically that I no longer asked. Over the island, people hung on to her words. She was no longer like a friend to the guests but like a queen.

More and more people were contacting Frida, and turning up with backpacks and sleeping bags. Some with caravans or tents. At some point Frida said there were two hundred people living on the island now. More tents went up. New caravans appeared. She said we had a hundred and forty thousand followers online.

'Welcome,' Frida said to them, 'to the rest of your life.'

People bent their heads to her before meditation. People swam underwater and screamed away their trauma, silently.

◆ ◆ ◆

I felt like, often, I could barely stay awake. It occurred to me that I was being drugged like the night of Lughnasadh. I dreamed of Grace and Ava constantly, feeling increasingly weak and sick when I was conscious. I didn't stay in bed all the time, although more than was healthy. We also picked bullace fruits from the hedgerow and our fingers were purple. We had a bag of hazelnuts, the first of the season, that Elena was going to use to make hazelnut butter. Frida's words filled the air, thick as cigarette smoke. We all worried about where she was, who she was with, what mood she was in. I could hear myself breathing as if I'd just stepped out of the river after a fast, cold swim. My throat itched.

I smelled the rain.

The ghost child watched me with interest. It sounds absurd, but it's true. He seemed very real to me. There was a child just out of my direct vision, and he watched me with big brown eyes.

'Frida is magic,' Moth said to a new person who turned up. 'She makes time run in all directions, she's barely shown a fragment of the truth she is capable of.'

'Are you happy?' I asked him once.

'Of course,' he said. 'Before this I was shooting heroin into the rotting space between my toes. I once slept with a man for a hit. She saved me when she chose me.'

I turned away.

Frida's team of researchers continued without me.

Rebecca watched me all the time. Eagerly. She bought me things. New shoes. Organic moisturiser. I still didn't understand what was going on. I didn't guess yet that there was a baby growing inside me.

◆ ◆ ◆

'We are the children of the next dimension,' Frida said, eyes wild. Ruth filmed her on her phone. 'The world is at the brink of climate catastrophe and you are thinking about your hair or what colour to paint your walls. You think war is something that happens to other people. Bombs and floods. They aren't. Within your lifetime, those disasters will be in your house.'

◆ ◆ ◆

The smell of pretty much anything made me heave. Water. Sunshine. The smell of trees and hedges still wet from the rain. I basically just lay in bed trying not to vomit by this point. No more meditations or swims or chatting. I fell into sticky sleeps like being trapped in a deep wet hole. I sweated honey, which for a while was the only thing I could stomach. I licked it off the spoon. Or wine gums: I could stomach those as well. I listened to the blood running through my body. My mind felt too big for my skull, like it was made of fat Essex mud. Thoughts sank in and never escaped. The smell of laundry drying made me vomit. The smell of the sea. Even the smell of water coming out of the shower made me vomit. Rebecca bought twenty different kinds of vitamins, looking for ones I could stomach.

'Beltane and Samhain are the points in the year where the veil between this world and the Otherworld is at its thinnest, enabling communication between the living and the dead,' Frida said, filming herself now. She had a new phone, the latest iPhone.

'On these days,' Frida said, 'everywhere on Earth experiences roughly twelve hours of sunshine and twelve hours of darkness. Wherever you are, listen to the history of the Earth as I have taught you to do. Listen to continents drift, the echo of natural disasters ruining communities in a click and a bang.'

The last owls called to one another. Boat horns and gulls sounded in the distance. Crows landed in their families, watching us.

'Everything is going to be perfect,' she said to me, getting into bed and running her fingers from my neck to my belly button. 'Don't worry about a thing. We are going to be so powerful.'

◆ ◆ ◆

I woke up in the dark. I yawned and walked to the bathroom to throw up. Frida wasn't in bed with me. I scooped up metallic-tasting water in my hands, but it was disgusting. I was so thirsty and so disgusted by the bathroom water that I left my room for the first time in days. I managed to find my way downstairs through a dark, sleeping cottage.

It was pitch-black but I knew the house well enough not to need any lights. I continued down the stairs, running my fingertips over the old wallpaper, placing each bare foot carefully on the familiar steps, then through the living room towards the kitchen. I was so thirsty.

I put out my hand and the kitchen doorway came faster than I'd expected. I snatched my hand back and tensed it. The hairs on the back of my neck were standing to attention in the dark as I reached for the old leather sofa to the right of the arch, but my hand grabbed at a void and unbalanced me for a second. There was nothing there. I took a step forward and hit my shin on a sharp edge so stopped. I thought of the echoey chimney in the power plant, that stench of salt and chemicals. I was going to throw up.

I pushed the thought of that night away.

I breathed my heartbeat back to normal, like Frida had taught me.

It was okay. I decided to step backwards, slowly, then I would make contact with some furniture or ideally a wall and a light switch.

Back. Back. At every step there was nothing behind me.

After what felt like ten or twenty steps I couldn't be in the living room anymore. I couldn't think how or where I'd started.

A smell wobbled in the darkness. It was Ava's cinnamon lip balm – with no other stimulus to see or hear, it was unmistakable. But there was more, too, around it. Feathers, period blood, snapped sticks after a storm, dead rabbits, Frida's breath, crow feathers. Grace's emollient cream and nail varnish.

'Stop,' I said quietly, to myself, and there was the wettest breeze on my skin in the darkness. It turned my skin cold.

I put my hand on my heart to feel it beating, but fear had taken me beyond panic and there was no heartbeat, no blood, no breath, no body. The air was wet like I was standing right next to the sea. Something was breathing near me. Or someone.

I put my hands out to break my fall because I suddenly felt dizzy, but instead of falling forwards my palms came into contact with a smooth, slightly vibrating surface. I bent forward and used it to ease myself on to the floor and put my forehead to the ground. A few seconds later my head wasn't spinning so fast and I opened my eyes. I listened to a hum in the air and realised it was the fridge and freezer. I fumbled for the handle and opened it quickly, flooding the room with light. I was just a few feet further into the kitchen than imagined, although it was difficult to map out how I'd taken so many steps backwards without bumping into anything. I could taste pennies at the back of my throat, like I'd swallowed the contents of a pocket. I turned to sit down there.

I tried to think of all the things I loved. The mole on Frida's left breast, the weight of stones in my pocket, the smell of rain on hot concrete, my kitten-patterned bedsheets when I was a kid.

My thoughts strained forward, placed into troubling italics, waiting for something.

There was a flicker of light.

I saw the little boy in the corner of the room. He was drawing on the wall. When I turned to look fully at this spirit he was gone again; a trick of light.

Then a face appeared from the gloom.

'Grace?' I said, but nobody was there. I looked out of the window and realised I could run. If I just started running I would reach the causeway before anyone realised, most likely. It could be high tide though.

Then: 'Hey,' Rebecca said in the darkness. 'You're scared. Let me help you.'

She came and hugged me, and I realised she was crying. I smelled her tears before I heard the tight, fast breath. I wasn't sure why she was hugging me but I knew why she was crying.

'I'm so sorry you lost your baby,' I said, and she kept sobbing.

'He's not lost,' she said. 'He's finding a new way.'

◆ ◆ ◆

The Brent geese began to arrive in small groups that didn't stay as summer finally became autumn. I dreamed of tripping over the top step of a tall staircase. Just as I was about to fall flat on my face I would tip my chin upwards slightly, holding my body stiff, and to my surprise the air grasped me. A seagull. A Brent goose. Elated, I would lift off and swoop down the stairs towards the open front door. It wasn't a house from my childhood.

In the garden, fifty people meditated with Frida. Sixty. Seventy. The number kept growing.

One night I said that I needed to see a doctor and she shook her head.

'Oh, Zo-Zo,' she laughed. 'You're fine. You are brilliant. You are personally saving us. You are doing that.'

'How?' I said.

My lips were chapped. My skin was papery from dehydration. I could barely make it to the toilet to throw up.

'We need to tell the police,' I said. 'The families need to be told.'

'You want to go to juvenile detention?' she said. 'Ruin your whole life, everything we started here? You think they'll believe us?'

◆ ◆ ◆

'You, my catalysts, my light. My brothers and sisters. We are here to lead humanity into the next level,' she said.

◆ ◆ ◆

We hit two hundred thousand followers and there was another bonfire party to celebrate, but I didn't attend. I could barely get up without throwing up. Crows sat on Frida's shoulders, and Merlin bared his teeth at everyone but her. I know that I was imagining it, but sometimes when she touched a flower or a tree I thought I saw it growing.

While she was exploding forward I was tunnelling backwards, folding in on myself. I was urgent and delirious. Wet, muddy, thin white legs. Thirsty but couldn't keep water down. I dreamed that my legs were stuck together and I couldn't get up off the floor, like an oil-slick pelican. I slept and awakened, slept again.

She smiled: dazzling, otherworldly.

And I smelled the rain.

And I felt that presence of the spirit child, who I was almost getting used to. I had a sense of him watching me with amused interest. He didn't scare me.

Rebecca brought me water and vitamins and wine gums. She'd bring different foods for me to try. Granola bars. Ginger biscuits. Lollipops.

'You're up,' Elena said, pulling up a chair for me one day when I made it downstairs with an urgent need for wine gums.

'We've been so worried,' said a stranger. I frowned at her, baffled.

A smell of stock and raw potato was turning into a solid knot around my head, and tightening. Coming downstairs had been a mistake. I was going to throw up.

'I lived on ice cubes my first trimester,' another stranger said. 'Couldn't cool down, couldn't eat.'

'My best friend couldn't cut her baby's nails because of a recurring urge to chop off her baby's fingers,' someone else laughed. 'It was wild.'

I wanted to be outside in the fresh air but didn't want to move a limb.

'It's quite all right to think these things,' she said. 'You'll be okay, honey, anyway. I was all on my own in the middle of nowhere with a fat husband sleeping with someone else in London. We'll all be here to help you with the baby. It takes a village, as the saying goes.'

'How long have I been in bed?' I said.

'About a month,' Elena said. I'd almost forgotten about what happened with Moth. It had been so eclipsed by the events later that night.

'Don't worry,' Frida said. 'We've sorted everything out already. You and me, we are the bosses. We are going to do crosswords on verandas, travel the world, help millions of people, and Rebecca is going to get her baby.'

'This baby?' I said, touching my stomach.

'That baby is Rebecca's baby. You are doing a beautiful thing.'

I could smell cinnamon lip balm.

◆ ◆ ◆

'There were monsters everywhere when I was a little girl,' she said in the garden, while Ruth filmed. 'They were under every bed in the house, inside every shadow. I just *knew*, in the same way we sense a person looking at us even without seeing them. I was terrified of these beings until I discovered that real monsters live out in the open, smiling at us on the news or tucking us into bed at night. Don't be scared of the dead. It's the living monsters that you need to watch out for.'

◆ ◆ ◆

Now I knew I was pregnant I could almost feel cells dividing inside me, caught on some invisible primal tide. I held my breath for my period but knew it wouldn't come. I hadn't even realised it was late. My nipples ached and colours appeared deeper around me. The sea was bluer. The air saltier. The baby was the nucleus of a dangerous atom, an abrupt altering of my orbit. He was a little evolution growing underneath my heartbeat, beginning with a bang and quickly nestling into the marshy darkness of my womb to plot his takeover, to split, to lay down cellular blueprints for fingers and spine bones and ventricles. Having his gooey origins tangled inside me and anticipating his growth seemed an obvious advertisement for evolution rather than God, an extraordinary and deeply biological miracle.

An expensive-looking cot appeared in Rebecca's room downstairs. I went down and stared at it, running my fingers over its curved edges. There were bags of organic packaged onesies, tiny mittens and hats.

All minutes and days and years are not created equal. Time doesn't tick forward in the neat steady increments of a clock face; most of it just slips away and only certain moments remain suspended. I remember that summer almost minute by minute, like stop-motion animation watched frame by frame, but as we moved through autumn everything was a blur.

The mud froze and cracked, scummy with pollution. We burnt wood in the fireplaces. The geese came and went.

Frida wouldn't hear of me going to the doctor. She said there was nothing they could do that she couldn't do for me. She lay her hands on me, talking of energy fields and portals, but I still threw up.

I tried to read but couldn't remember anything. The same pages, over and over. I threw up more.

My body hurt. My head hurt. There were flickers of other beings, maybe remembered from the pictures that used to be all over our now-white walls. I was scared.

'It's so *animal*, isn't it?' Moth said to me in the living room one day when nobody else was around. They were all out swimming. 'There's a species of lion that mates, like, twenty to forty times a day when they're in heat. Female pandas are only turned on for a 24- to 72-hour window once a year, at some point between February and May.'

'Stop talking about animal sex. I feel sick,' I said. 'And we both watched the same documentary. It was, like, the first conversation we ever had.'

It felt good to smile and have a semi-normal conversation.

'Such a long time ago. It seems odd there was a time we didn't know each other. Hey. Get this. Penguins are actually the most sexually messed up of all animals,' he said thoughtfully. 'They're necrophiliacs.'

'Stop it.'

'You seem anxious. I don't want the baby to be anxious.'

'It's, like, four cells tall. It's not anxious. Are you thinking about it as a baby? Do you feel . . . connected to it, in any way?'

'Frida says it's the soul of Rebecca's baby, you're just keeping it safe because she couldn't,' Moth said, matter-of-fact.

'But that doesn't make sense.'

'I don't want to look after a baby. Do you?'

'No. I mean, I'd never thought about babies.'

'So, it makes perfect sense for Rebecca to have the baby. She wants a baby, she's got money. She will do anything for a child. Anything. I know you're going through a rough time but it's for a good cause.'

'What is she doing in exchange for my baby?'

'Money. Clout. Contacts.'

'And that doesn't seem kinda gross to you?'

'No. She said she thought about ending her life after the last miscarriage. Frida saved her again, brought her back here. And Frida is going to save millions more people with Rebecca behind her.'

'So you won't have any part of the baby's life?'

'I'm obviously not changing nappies,' he said. 'Spiritually, you and I are barely out of them ourselves.'

I watched a seagull remain near-motionless in the sky outside Elena's greenhouse, wings vibrating slightly with the fun of running headlong into the elements. It reminded me of a postcard I'd seen somewhere of a kid with his chin tilted bravely out towards a spitting sea.

◆ ◆ ◆

'This child is going to have the most wonderful life,' Rebecca said. 'Frida says he will have a birthmark in the shape of a star on his back.'

Chapter Eleven

Leo sleeps next to me, his star birthmark glinting in the moonlight from under the curtains. Oliver never sent me the address where we were supposed to meet and he has not come looking for me. I keep expecting his knock on the door or a ping on my phone. I check the news constantly for his article. Every time Ben comes through the bedroom door I read his face, wondering if there is a picture of me in a newspaper. Perhaps Oliver has decided he didn't need anything more from me; I'd given him enough in the garden that night for him to join the dots and go to press. But nothing has been printed yet. So I wait.

There has been nothing from Frida either. I'd asked her to answer the clue 'theoretical boundary from which nothing can escape', but maybe she didn't remember. Maybe she meant much more to me than I meant to her.

Leo has the most beautiful black curls and I touch one in the dark. He thinks of Ben as his father, and people even say they look alike, but really he looks just like Moth. He's only ten but he's as tall as the average thirteen-year-old. He draws beautifully, as Frida predicted. The sketchbook next to his bed is full of mushrooms, courgette flowers, Lego men and boats. His freckles are dark over his nose, but they have disappeared into the fever flush of his cheeks now. I have never regretted his existence, not for a moment. He blows my mind every day.

My baby boy. He tosses in his sheets and sighs in the days after I was supposed to speak to Oliver. Ben brings home treats for Leo, reminding him to drink lots of water, and he takes Emma to and from school while I stay with Leo. I don't work, lines of code left half written in my study under a painting of a sunflower that Leo did for me last year, and a drawing of our family that Emma made. I read to Leo in the dark while he gets better. Maybe the police stopped Oliver's article from being published, so they could investigate first. Maybe it is the police who are going to knock on my door today or tomorrow, and take me from my children. I inhale the smell of my son.

Leo and I spent the first five years of his life travelling from place to place and only stopped because he needed to go to school. We had slept in the same bed together all that time. Ben knew we'd lived in a van for a while, but I'd made it sound romantic, like a choice. Not the gritty reality of city car parks and free-to-use caravan sites. Back then, Leo and I fell asleep to the constant buzz of traffic. Now there is the sea in front and underground springs and drains all over the fields behind. He goes to a good school. He is loved.

Not far from our little town, the bigger town of Scarborough has one of the highest homelessness rates in Yorkshire – I help out at a soup kitchen once a week. With my double-breasted wool coats and Barbour Chelsea boots, my iPhone and lipstick, the organisers don't recognise me as the woman who, just five years ago, ate there fairly regularly with her son. Now I do the charity's website and social media, raising money for them and helping as much as I can. The homeless guys who knew me back then don't see the same girl serving them soup.

I didn't become a successful coder because of Ben, but he legitimised me. I went from freelancing at the survey data platform to being senior developer at a similar firm, then head of product at an umbrella company in Leeds that ran a whole bunch of apps and sites. I spent a few days a week in a trendy co-working space.

I've done well, and I thought I was only just starting. I have plans. Places I want to go on holiday, things I want to make. I want this quiet life. I fall asleep at night to the sound of water. The springs are natural, the underground drains in the fields are nineteenth century, making a gentle tinkling sound when all else is quiet. A door hinge creaks; a scutter of bird wings sounds outside the window. Leo stirs and murmurs in his fever dream.

Then my phone flashes with an Instagram alert. It's from Frida.

'Intoxicant,' Frida writes in a DM. 'Ten-letter word, one who asks humbly and earnestly.'

'Supplicant,' I type quickly, lifting my phone up, barely having to think of the answer and not letting myself think about whether to reply or not. 'Rift? Six letters.'

'Schism.' Pause. Dot. Dot. Dot. 'To miss. Six letters.'

'Longed.'

I can't believe she is writing to me, after all this time.

'I've missed you too.'

'I didn't tell him anything,' I type. 'We were meant to meet formally but I didn't go.'

'Pinky swear? Seven letters.'

'Promise,' I type.

'I've sorted it out. You won't have to meet him. I told you that you would never have to worry and I always keep my word.'

I frown and put the phone down.

◆ ◆ ◆

While Leo was growing inside me on the island, Frida couldn't find my glasses and I ran out of contact lenses. She said she'd order new glasses but they never turned up. I can barely see without them, so the world became a literal rather than just an emotional blur. I remained in her room, sleeping in her bed, and we still had sex when she wanted to.

'I've never loved anyone like I love you,' Frida said one night. 'You are the only person who has ever really seen me.'

I stared at her. She was all dishevelled and half asleep.

'We should just go to the police. Maybe it's not too late,' I said.

'We are going to change the world, you and I. We're going to do a lot of good. We are going to write books. We are going to control empires. We are bound forever by what happened. If you ever betray me, the spirits will be watching.'

'I don't believe in spirits,' I said, and the ghost child in the room shivered.

'You think your childhood was hard because your mother had a few too many boyfriends? Maybe took her eye off you in the pool on a family holiday? Hearing you moan is excruciating. I did things to survive that you can't imagine.' She paused. 'You don't know trauma. You have no idea of the things that my mother did to me. The people she left me with.'

'I'm sorry bad things happened to you,' I said.

'I'm not. It made me strong. But don't leave me,' she said. 'I love you. Everyone always leaves me. I love you so much.'

'We're in this together,' I said. 'I'm not going anywhere.'

'Just stay, okay, always?' she said. 'For once I'm in control of my life.'

'I'm right here,' I said, and took her hand.

She looked at me. Her level, blue gaze. I expected her to smile but she didn't.

'You're starting to think you want to keep the baby,' she said. 'I can see it in your face. But it's just hormones. Rebecca has wanted a baby her whole life. You probably have never thought about babies at all. They look weird and they cry all the time. This is her time. She is going to donate a great deal of money and time to making us big. In return we will fulfil our promise and give her a baby.'

Frida had a sweaty, glassy look in her eyes. I was too scared to take my hands off hers. Blood rose to my skin. I touched my stomach.

'You can't look after a baby,' she said. 'Rebecca is doing you a favour by taking it. You can barely look after yourself.'

She was right. I'd never held a baby. I'm not sure I'd ever thought about babies. Even as a kid I wasn't one for dolls. I'd never even had a pet.

I would have the baby and give it to Rebecca, then I'd leave the island. But not until the baby was born. I didn't want it, after all. The idea of motherhood was more insane than most of Frida's words. So I couldn't leave with a baby inside me. Where would I go?

'I have a present for you.' She took out a little box with a necklace in it. 'Real diamonds to replace the turtle,' she said, and put it round my neck.

◆ ◆ ◆

I read Jackson's books. Frida brought me a box of them, as well as books of crosswords that we still sometimes did together. I'd hardly read at all that summer compared to before, but now that moving too much made me sick, reading was back in vogue. I read a book about islands, running my fingers over each archipelago as if reading Braille. There was a rabbit island in Japan, home to several poisonous gas factories and thousands of rabbit descendants of the ones brought in to test the poisonous gas.

The house and island were full of activity. Drums and music, cooking and gardening. There were rotas, new clothes, the smell of incense, all while I sat in the cocoon of Frida's bedroom.

The day I nearly lost the baby, the hubbub of the island had quietened because it was morning meditation and everyone – maybe ninety people at this point – was out in the garden. I felt a horrible pressure in my abdomen and then a crushing pain down there. I tried to scream but nothing came out so I staggered up out of my sweaty sheets. Through the window, I could see everyone with their heads bowed. I was scared because Frida wouldn't hear of me going to the doctor. She said I didn't need modern medicine. My body was designed for childbirth, which was a natural process, not a medical procedure. A hospital treats childbirth like a medical emergency and creates unnecessary stress, she said.

But there hadn't been pain before, and so I decided to try to find a phone to call an ambulance myself. There was no way she would call one.

I padded out of the room, holding on to the walls. The hallway was quiet except for the faint creak of the wooden floorboards beneath my bare feet, and I had to stop regularly to ride the pain. I walked down the stairs and looked through into Jackson's room, where four beds were now laid out neatly on the floor for followers I didn't know. There was a trail of burnt incense in a holder, a half-smoked spliff in a glass ashtray, meditation cushions, yoga mats, notebooks. The space pulsed and blurred with the pain but I couldn't immediately see a phone. They probably had them with them, so I continued and stopped at Elena's room. Elena had a very old iPhone that she rarely used. I'd seen her text on it occasionally, but she didn't carry it around with her like everyone else.

I stepped inside, leaning on the wall and gasping. I'd been in there once to deliver washing, and another time to ask her a question about something I was cooking. It was neat and small, smelling of lavender from the little sachets she used to keep moths away. The desk was covered in powders, oils and tinctures. A leather-bound notebook sat open on the desk, the pages covered with notes about plants and symbols.

There was a stone pestle and mortar, stained with green. Candle stubs, polished stone. I opened drawers looking for where it might be, finding books on herbs and medicine, sewing patterns, scrawled recipes, some cheap rings.

It was under her pillow: the old iPhone that pre-dated fingerprint technology. It felt cool and worn in my hand. The screen lit up as soon as I touched it, asking for a password. I glanced at the shelves where jars of dried herbs were neatly stacked, their labels scrawled in a neat, looping script. My mind was foggy after another wave of pain but I tried Frida's birthday, which was the twenty-second of November. Eleven is often considered a 'master number' in numerology, representing spiritual insight, intuition, and connection to higher consciousness. It is seen as a bridge between the earthly and the divine. Twenty-two is also one of the most powerful and spiritually potent numbers, as it combines the energies of both the number two and the master number eleven. But that wasn't the answer.

I tried 1234, which had been my mum's password for years. No. I tried 2222, but no: 'Try again in 1 minute'. I fidgeted, tapping my fingers over the back of the phone, listening to the chanting outside the window. I searched her drawers for her passport, which was under a tube of lotion with Cyrillic writing and some hair ties. It was a British passport, and she was fifty-two years old. I put in her date of birth, but it wasn't that either. There had been a chapter in one of Jackson's books about 'sacred triads' in ancient religions. I typed in 3333, but nothing. Then I tried 1111. Frida had done a monologue on AuraLine once about how the number one was symbolic of unity, origins, and the divine source, but that wasn't it either.

I felt another wave of pain. I wasn't even sure that a miscarriage would be a bad thing. I felt dampness between my legs and was sure that when I put my fingers down there, I would find blood.

I sat on her bed and stared at Elena's locked phone, then slid off her bed, and lay there on the floor with orbs of light floating in front of me. I must have passed out because I woke up feeling a little bit better.

There was a photograph album on the floor under the bed and I slid it over to me. I opened the old-fashioned pages with photo corners, like my grandmother used to have.

There were photos of Elena as a girl. Photos of little girls in front of Christmas trees, and on doorsteps. Photos with friends and family. It was a standard family album, but then a newspaper page fell out of it into my lap.

'SIXTY ARRESTED IN CULT RAID OUTSIDE ROME', it said, dated two years ago. The paper was fragile and dusty. 'In a dramatic series of raids outside Rome last night, the Italian Carabinieri apprehended the leaders of a so-called spiritual community called the Unification of Dacia, believed to be operating as a front for a major organised crime syndicate.

'Hidden deep in the wooded hills, the compound of the Unification of Dacia had long been an enigma to the surrounding community. The arrests come after months of investigation involving the Italian Carabinieri, the UK National Crime Agency and the Romanian Intelligence Service.

'The group attracted thousands of followers across Europe, with their leaders promising a path to enlightenment, financial prosperity, and personal transformation through a blend of spirituality and exclusivity.

'The group is said to worship the ancient goddess Bendis, a lunar deity and protector of nature who they believe took the form of various children, ranging in age from around four to fourteen.

'The breakthrough came when undercover officers infiltrated the group, posing as prospective members. What they discovered during their investigation painted a disturbing picture of coercion, child abuse, manipulation, and criminal activity. According to Chief Commissioner Luca Rossi of the Carabinieri, the group's leaders maintained a tight control over their followers, using psychological manipulation and promises of spiritual rewards to exploit their wealth and labour. The group claimed that children in the commune could predict the future and cure diseases. They dressed these children in white and kept them mostly in solitude, away from their mothers and fathers, where they were forced to heal followers and predict the future.

'"We began to uncover illegal activities that didn't match the group's claimed spiritual mission," Rossi said. "After months of intelligence gathering, it became clear their 'enlightenment practices' were in fact a cover for a vast criminal network, funnelling illicit profits from a range of illegal enterprises." Sixty people have been arrested.'

I heard the floorboard creak but couldn't stop reading. There was a photo of some people getting arrested, and Nicolae's face was in the crowd.

'The remaining members of the Unification Group have been warned to come forward, as further arrests may follow. The investigation remains ongoing, with law enforcement looking to dismantle the criminal network that operated behind the guise of a peaceful spiritual movement.'

◆ ◆ ◆

I must have passed out on the floor again because I woke up back in our bed, with Frida standing with her hands over my stomach. I watched her for a moment.

'I've stopped the miscarriage,' she said.

I didn't reply but my body didn't hurt anymore.

There was a knock at the door and Nicolae appeared. She waved him into the room and he sat down on the bed near me while Frida watched. I tried not to flinch. He smelled of burning.

'How are you feeling?'

'Splendid,' I said, my mouth dry. 'I won't tell anyone about that newspaper article, or what happened to Grace and Ava. You and Frida don't have to worry.'

'You shouldn't have gone digging around,' he said.

'I just needed a phone to call a doctor. I'm really sick. I can't even keep water down.'

'You need Frida, not a doctor. You know, I was wary of you. I thought you were trouble but I also trusted Frida, and she was right. You have started us on an extraordinary path. You taught the group to spread their message in a way I would never have wanted, but can now acknowledge was genius. Her power is going to keep growing because of you.'

'So maybe you should let me go to hospital. I'm not going to tell anyone about the power plant. I was there too.'

'But you don't have as much to lose. Frida is going to be extraordinary,' he said. He smelled of the marsh, and bonfires, outside smells that were too strong in this room. Tattoos covered his muscled arms. 'When she came to the Unification Group her mother said she had the gift but we had no idea that she was the one we were waiting for. We had been waiting so long for a child to come with the power to rebalance the world, as it had been foretold in our texts. And there she was, walking into our commune without any shoes, holding the hand of her druggie mother. We didn't imagine that the mother would be correct. Everyone thinks their children are special. But within weeks of being with us she was bringing the dead back to life. I've seen her summon storms, solve droughts, pour curses on her enemies, and she is only just getting started. You don't need to go to hospital. She will save you.'

I looked over at my friend, standing by the window with a strange look on her face.

'But she can't be associated with the Unification Group,' Nicolae continued. 'Do you understand that? Elena is going to be disciplined for keeping that article. You must forget you read this. People called the group a cult, many of our original group are still in prison, and we can't have people thinking that sort of thing about Frida now.'

'I won't tell anyone,' I said. 'I promise.'

'I know you won't tell. Because we will make sure that you don't. We have eyes and ears everywhere. I want you to remember that.'

'I won't say anything.'

'I know you won't,' he said. 'Because we will be watching you.'

Frida, behind him, smiled sadly at me. I thought there was sorrow in her pretty face, a sort of apology, but also an exit. She was distancing herself. Like she was both the girl doing crosswords with me, learning pop culture references, telling me about kissing cartoon characters, asking about my knickers, and also whatever magical creature these people wanted her to be. She certainly didn't look like herself just then, though, not like the girl I'd fallen in love with.

◆ ◆ ◆

'The leaders shouldn't have gone to prison,' she said to me that night, sitting in bed without touching me. 'It was a beautiful place. Before Rome, I've told you how horrible my childhood was. My mum was a nutcase. Her boyfriends were users. But in Rome they saw my power. Between the ages of ten and fifteen it was magic. When I rang the bell, thousands of people had to stop what they were doing and face west. Even the little ones. Even the babies. Because I knew when the veil thinned and the spirits came out.'

'I found a photo in one of the caravans of you and other children up on stage, all dressed in white.'

'They called us oracles. They believed that the reincarnation of an ancient goddess was going to appear in the form of a child, and so all those children were potential candidates. I am the reincarnation, though.'

'Why didn't Nicolae and Alex go to prison, if others did?'

'They weren't particularly high up the chain so didn't spend long in prison. The main leaders are still there.'

'Did they hurt you? Did they really keep you separate from your mum?'

'That was a blessing. She's in prison too. I didn't see her much after we moved to Rome. There was no question of her having custody of me afterwards.' She paused. 'We were told we could predict the future. We were worshipped.'

'You were abused.'

'You're wrong. I *can* predict the future. The government just doesn't like power they don't control. Do not look away from me.' Her voice was developing a sort of panic as she spoke to me. 'The light you see behind my eyes is not mine – it is *the* light. It is the only flame. I am not asking for your devotion. I am claiming it.'

'I need to see a doctor,' I said to her. 'I'm serious. I'm barely keeping any food down. I can feel the baby getting weaker.'

'I am the only guidance you need. The only safety.'

'He's not going to grow properly without food. He's not growing. I can feel him dying.'

'All you need to do is trust me. I healed you just now and will continue to keep you safe.'

Lying next to her in the night, smelling rotting flowers and salt air, I was struck by how little I had ever known her, or could ever know her.

◆ ◆ ◆

The floorboards creaked, and the curtains rustled like ghosts the night I ran from them. I'd probably still be there if it wasn't for my unborn child. Frida had barely left me alone since the near-miscarriage, whispering things in my ears. *I am the shape of your shadow*, she'd say. *I do not need to be worshipped, you already worship me.* She watched me, she locked the door when she was out and I was asleep, she brought me tea and food and was always saying that she loved me. But I couldn't keep food down. I felt delirious, malnourished, and scared for my unborn child.

Frida smelled of sea water and damp next to me in bed. The moonlight made her skin glow. Leaving didn't even feel entirely a conscious decision. I was led by the ghost child, whose physical form was rolling inside me. My brain wasn't working but the ghost child knew we had to get off the island. He stood at the edges of the water staring over. He hovered at windows and doors. He wanted me to escape.

I unstuck my body from her skin and rolled away from her. The bed creaked as my weight shifted, and Frida stirred, shifting back towards me and laying her hand against the groove of my breastbone. I lay back in the bed. For another few minutes everything was still except the curtain flicking moonlight around in the breeze. Her hair was sticky on the pillow. Moonlight freckled the wall. At one point she muttered something and then smiled, like

I'd told her a joke in her dream, and I used her movement as cover to scoot myself off the bed before giving myself a chance to think.

Out of the window, I could smell that the tide was rising. Looking at Frida's watch by the bed, there were thirty minutes until the causeway disappeared.

I was wearing the expensive necklace she'd given me and I also picked up the watch that Rebecca had brought Frida. I had slept in joggers and a t-shirt, which wasn't unusual, but meant I only needed to pull on some socks and a jumper. My shoes were downstairs.

Keeping to the floorboards that didn't creak, I made it to the bedroom door and tried not to turn back, but then did: her mouth was open, eyes closed. Her naked body curled under the soft cover. My final imprint. I felt sick, thought I might be sick, but then slipped out of the gap in the door.

Downstairs I fumbled against the walls, got some wine gums from the kitchen. I ate a black one and a red one, staring out the window at the vague outline of the tree that Frida had been under the first time I saw her in the flesh. Maybe I was waiting for the light to flick on in the living room, for footsteps on the stairs, for someone's hand on my shoulder.

The air buzzed with messengers. Ghosts, I suppose they are usually called, but not spectral presences. They were impressions and smells, like when you think you're being watched but turn around and there is nobody there.

In my reality the house was silent and still except for a spider building a web in the corner of the kitchen windowsill, spinning. It was close enough for me to see. Beyond it, though, the outside world was a blur.

In other dimensions there were twitches and whispers. Sunflowers and herbs, hanging from the ceiling, quivered. Ava.

Grace. A child? My child. I was struck by a fear that he would stay on the island, but pushed it aside. He was uniquely mine.

I walked over and put on a pair of wellington boots by the mat and one of Jackson's old khaki wax coats, then opened the back door in the kitchen. The door creaked and I paused again. It was a relief to have cold air on my flushed and sweaty skin. If someone came down now, I could still just be getting some air. Just a breath of air, then back to bed.

The watch thudded in my pocket.

The air smelled foggy and the man's coat was heavy across my shoulders. Maybe twenty or thirty dark-bellied Brent geese perched on the exposed mudflats leading towards the power plant. They were white splodges of paint on the canvas of my vision.

They squawked but didn't stop. Another group appeared, and then more. I walked around the back of the cottage, keeping near the walls in case anyone happened to be looking out of their window.

Then I had to change tactics and walk across to the back of the garden in order to avoid the noisy gravel. When I got to the gate I trod lightly on the last remaining bit of gravel and was on the path. In the field, a light went on in one of the caravans – like an eye opening out there – and I slid behind the brick gateposts at the cottage garden. Without my glasses I couldn't guess which caravan it might be. I held my breath for other lights to come on, but nothing happened. The cottage remained dark, as did the other tents and caravans. A moment later the caravan's eye closed again.

I felt Ava there. I felt Grace. But most of all I felt my baby, my son, trailing behind me, with his watchful spirit eyes.

I knew the hedgerows were no longer wildly overgrown with dog roses and honeysuckle as they had been in the summer. It must have been early October, two months since conception. The hedgerows would be thin and bony now, with the field on the left and water on the right covered in a sheet of that bright moonlight. Anyone in the caravans would have seen right through the foliage if they were looking. Gulls hooted. The tides throbbed. I thought I saw curtains twitch in the cottage. I had a strong sense of being watched from somewhere.

Something definitely rustled in the hedgerows and I held my breath. The salty air was wet on my skin, the sea seemed to merge into the sky.

Then I saw a shadow. I wasn't sure if it was human or a tree.

'Please,' I whispered.

Then, after a moment, the shadow dissolved. Either the person turned away or it was just a passing sway of darkness from a cloud. I started running towards the causeway, nearly tripping over a fallen tree branch, tearing my joggers, scrambling up. There was no returning now, this was it. The causeway was covered in a thin layer of water.

Just as I was about to step on to it, a shadow appeared from the hedgerows to my right, holding Merlin by the collar. Merlin strained towards me like the first time he saw me, at the start of the summer.

'Heel,' Frida said to Merlin, then turned to me. 'You're leaving?' Frida said it mock-casually. I nodded. 'In the middle of the night, like a thief?'

'It's not Rebecca's baby. It's mine.'

'Of course you can leave,' she said. 'I didn't know you wanted to. Is it because of the stupid Unification article? So what? You're leaving me because I had a traumatic childhood? I thought you might not understand, and I was right. The arrests and all the press suggest it was all shit, but a lot of it was good.' She paused. 'A lot was bad as well though, because other people were in charge. Now we're in charge it won't be like that again, and I am stronger.'

'I'm sorry,' I said. 'I'm sorry you didn't tell me. If you'd told me maybe I could have understood, but right now I need to leave.'

'Will you be back?'

'I don't know. I need to think. Tell Rebecca I'm sorry.'

'She's going to be devastated.'

'I am genuinely sorry. But I didn't sign anything. Nobody even asked.'

'I will find another way to keep my promise to her. I don't break my promises. I promise you will think of me every day. I promise your baby will have a star-shaped birthmark on his back. He will love to draw and read. He will be a seeker. And you will both come back one day.'

'I loved you.'

'You can't walk away from a love like ours.'

'I won't come back.'

Her eyes narrowed and the muscles around her lips hardened.

'Listen to me now,' she said. 'This is important. If you ever speak negatively about me, or tell people what you know of me or the Unification Group, your son will be taken from you.'

She smiled, tightly.

'He may not be taken from you immediately. It might be later. An illness, a spiritual malady, a terrible fever. Or it might just be a man in the night, scooping him from his bed while he sleeps. But if you ever speak a word against us in public, your son will be taken from you. Do you understand?'

I nodded.

'You will come back to me. I know you better than you know yourself.' She turned away from me before I could turn from her. She let Merlin run in front of her back to the house. She didn't turn back; her blonde hair and shirt and limbs were like flickers of the moon.

◆ ◆ ◆

There were only a handful of people on the bus. Night-shift workers, drunks, a few sleepy teenagers. I probably stank. Without my glasses it was all a blur. My heartbeat became more regular the further from the island I got, but I started to shiver.

The night bus went into Chelmsford. As we filed out in the bus terminal, I asked the bus driver directions to the nearest pawn shop. He asked if he could call anyone for me but I said no, just the pawn shop.

It wasn't open for another few hours so I sat in the doorway and waited. 'GOLD GOLD GOLD,' it said. As soon as the doors opened I pawned the watch and necklace for over a thousand pounds. I put the money under my shoe's insole and bought a Twix bar. Forget about meditation. Forget God. For true bliss have a Twix on a bench in the early morning sunshine, in early pregnancy. I could hear blood humming inside me.

I had to keep asking people about buses and trains because I couldn't see the boards. Mum stored her stuff at the Big Yellow Storage Centre at Staples Corner, near Brent Cross. I'd been there with her before, usually to reorganise between boyfriends. I took a wrong train at some point, heading northbound on the Victoria line, but eventually made it to the Northern line platform at Moorgate – from where I could go up to Brent Cross. Twenty minutes later I was navigating past the roar of the North Circular and cars blurred into a hazy mix. I walked through a convoluted network of roads and bridges, feet aching, then turned the corner to see the flyover at Brent Cross with the Ferris wheel turning in a near-empty fairground. Buses whizzed past. I was starving again so went into the shopping mall.

I was so hungry. I stood, transfixed, in the buzzing food hall, with a dry mouth. It seemed very important to get this choice right: I followed my nose and ended up with a slice of Hasty Tasty pizza, then I ate some McDonald's chips while standing at the railing looking down at the shoppers. Maybe all that time on the island throwing up, all I needed was junk food.

There was a group of people around my age on their phones on the table next to where I was shovelling food into my mouth. I felt much older than them though. They were covered in an armour of plastic tat from Claire's and Accessorize. Older teenagers sitting across the way were laughing at each other. I kept moving. The bins overflowed with polystyrene and plastic that would never biodegrade. Someone bumped into me and I started, but it was just a mother trying to navigate her buggy around a corner. The child stared at me. I couldn't bring myself to smile in return.

I rose on the escalator and stepped into a children's shop. A man was speaking about traction and manoeuvrability to several earnest fathers. Boxes of 'breast pumps' that looked like torture implements. I squinted and picked things up. There was rows and rows of stuff I wouldn't have imagined, like nipple guards and breast milk bags.

The sound of a seagull wheeling outside the high window made me start – it was the sound of Bay. I missed her, in a strange way. I missed the way she laughed at my jokes, and ran her fingers over my skin.

I walked away, towards and then down the escalator. Through clouds of perfume. Out into the polluted air, and this time, stronger from junk food, I found my way to an unmissable giant yellow storage centre.

In the reception a man wore a polyester shirt that matched the yellow walls. He checked Mum's details – my name and photo were on the documents because lots of my stuff was stored there too – then pointed me to a lift. Pop music played at a low volume in sulphurous yellow corridors of identical padlocked doors, as I let myself into Mum's. Inside the stiflingly hot corrugated-iron square was a city of boxes as well as an Ikea swivel chair that cost fifteen pounds to buy yet had probably cost Mum much more to store already. I rooted through for the boxes marked with my name, and had a strong pang of nostalgia for how Mum used to fold my underwear when I was young. I unpeeled a strip of masking tape to reveal a white stuffed tiger with wonky eyes peeking out of a box full of winter clothes. I'd won him in a competition at London Zoo on a school trip and the memory made me feel lonely. I shouldn't have written that email.

I continued my excavation: a watercolour set, worn sneakers, a snow globe with a dancing ballerina my mum had bought me for my tenth birthday, a pile of my favourite t-shirts that smelled of fabric softener and Mum's perfume. She'd packed everything away so neatly. Eventually I found my passport and computer, but the computer wouldn't turn on. I searched around for the charger but instead, with huge relief, found an old pair of glasses. I could see again.

There wasn't a plug socket in the container anyway. I put my computer, charger and a couple of changes of clothes into a rucksack, then searched out my duvet and pillows, with matching blue flowers on them. I changed into grey tracksuit bottoms, a blue t-shirt and a black zip-up top. I found a school project on the end of the world. A section on asteroid impact apocalypse, death by deoxygenation, gamma-ray burst extinction, and antibiotic-resistant plague.

Frida had climbed inside my head and moved everything around. As I came up for air now, my memories weren't in the places where I had left them; my sense of self was new and strange. I felt exposed and confused without her. It felt as if I had to maintain concentration or I would sleepwalk back into her arms. I am sure, now, that if it weren't for Leo's presence inside me I would have gone back.

◆ ◆ ◆

That night in the storage unit under my childhood duvet I heard her in my dream. It was as if we were sewn together at the edges, and after the stitches were unpicked the empty needle holes still ached.

It was early and the sun hadn't come up yet when I walked out of the storage unit. I felt hot and weird, then the world went dark.

I woke up in the Royal Free Hospital with the sound of beeps and whirring machines. My mouth was dry and my head hurt. I was severely dehydrated, and suffering from malnutrition, the nurse said. Very dangerously so. The nurse said that I was lucky to have fainted because it had brought me to hospital. They'd put me on a drip and a food tube. Moth sat next to me, holding my hand territorially. I was too weak to take my hand away, unsure how he'd found me.

They said he'd brought me in. He said that he'd followed me off the island because Frida had an intuition that something bad would happen so he was sent to make sure I was safe. Sure enough, I had fainted in the car park of the storage unit and if he hadn't been there to catch me who knows what might have happened.

'I'm not going back. Where's my bag? My computer?' I said.

'Right here. She just wanted to make sure you were okay. I am just here to make sure you're okay. You don't have to do anything you don't want to.'

'Please leave.'

'We all just want to look out for you,' he said. 'Frida says even if you leave, she will always look out for you.'

'Fuck off,' I said.

He didn't mention the baby. His baby.

I was born in the Royal Free. In my dreams Mum was twirling her hair around her fingers, making lists on the backs of envelopes, dotting her i's with hearts. I smelled mud, dreaming that the baby was taken away from me. Dreams of giving birth, to a crow that swam out of my legs. Sweating through my sheets. Pebbles and shells. Dragons and sea glass. Awake. Asleep. I tried to keep my mind blank, but memories would surface unbidden and make me flinch: the sensation of fingers on my neck, the intense concentration that would settle on her face when we meditated.

I saw that my shoes – with the money under the soles – were there next to my bed.

He stayed though. Later that day a technician put cold jelly on my stomach, then a probe on my tummy. Ten weeks pregnant, eight weeks since conception. The technician smiled at me and pressed some buttons on his computer, squinting, turning the screen so I could see a shifting viscous liquid in a black hole that coalesced into a creature dancing there like an astronaut in space.

I dreamed of Frida. She smiled with her mouth an inch from mine, she slept tangled in sheets, she jumped naked into the sea.

Back in the ward again, a few beds down a girl with a pink streak in her shoulder-length hair, maybe fifteen years old, was holding her phone up as if taking a picture of me and Moth.

'I follow Frida on Instagram and I've seen you both on there with her,' the girl said.

'Love is the greatest weapon against darkness,' Moth said. 'Healing isn't linear but a complex process where destruction turns to evolution. Give us your name and we'll make sure you get a private session with her really soon.'

'Oh my God, thank you,' the girl said.

◆ ◆ ◆

Moth barely left my side, but he sat in a chair outside the bathroom while a nurse helped me wash ash and salt and mud off my body, with harsh blue soap that made my eyes sting. The water turned brown. I was filthy. We cleaned Essex mud from under my nails and I leaned my cheek on my knee. My breath, bouncing back, smelled of rot.

My legs and wrists were impossibly thin, the opposite of every expectation about pregnancy. I was a ball of yarn with a compact and dense centre but loose and easily unravelled edges, all frayed elbows and jutting limbs. In the hospital mirror, gaunt and wild, I was alien to myself.

'Do you need me to call the police?' the nurse whispered in my ear. 'You are obviously scared of that man.'

'Not the police,' I said, my head shaking. 'No. I'm fine. Everything is fine.'

'No police if you're sure,' she said, 'but the police could help you.'

'Please. They won't. What I need to do is get away though. Can you help me with that?'

'The police can help with that.'

'It'll take too long. Please?'

She took a deep breath. 'I'd feel much more comfortable if we went to the police.'

'If you don't help me, I will go back to them. I can't go to the police though. Please help me get away.'

'I'll get you a prescription for some anti-nausea pills and prenatal vitamins. They'll be in the pockets of the trousers under your bed in the morning. I'll ask your guy to sign something outside and you can slip away.'

She did exactly this – a baseball cap, joggers, black hoodie, and my own trainers. The trainers still had the money under the insole. As I was walking out of the ward, the ill girl took my photo.

◆ ◆ ◆

I made it out of the hospital and then doubled back inside and ran to the bathroom. I watched Moth run out of the front doors and towards the bus stop, which is where I would have gone if I'd continued out.

I took the lift down to the basement and walked through a labyrinth until I saw an open fire exit with two orderlies smoking cigarettes and messing around on their phones. They didn't look like followers but I didn't risk it and kept going.

I sat in a store cupboard full of hospital linen and pillows for an hour, paralysed with indecision.

The linen closet had a small high-up window, and I could see people's feet walking on the pavement outside. It was just about big enough for me to climb out of, but I was scared to hurt the baby. So I stepped out of the cupboard into the corridor. Moth was casually waiting for me out there.

'Zo-Zo,' he said, raising his bushy eyebrows. 'I'm not going to chase you. Frida only wants what's best for you. Look, take this,' he said.

'I don't want anything to do with any of you,' I said, and he shrugged his enormous shoulders but held the bag out for me. Timothy, Moth for short. The boy with crazy hair who thought I looked like the geeky one from *Scooby-Doo*. 'It's just to get you started,' he said.

'You know a group of criminals made her think she's the reincarnation of some ancient deity.'

'She is a deity,' he said. 'We both know that. You've brought thousands of people to the knowledge as well.'

'Be careful,' I said.

'You be careful. And don't say a word against her.'

The bag was full of money. I looked at it, then at him.

'Is it yours or hers?'

'Yours. You earned it. The Academy is going to be very successful. It's already well on the way.'

'I can't take it.'

'You made Frida successful. It was your idea to start the social media, your planning and strategy. She wants you to have this. But she wants me to remind you not to speak against her.'

'So she's paying me to stay quiet.'

'She said that she didn't need to pay you for that – you would never speak out against her anyway. She said she is paying you because you've earned it.'

I stood holding the bag.

'How else are you going to survive?' he said. 'Take it for the kid. You might as well.'

He turned and walked abruptly away, up the stairs, turning to smile a little bit just as he went around the corner. I waited for a while, listening to the clicks and creaks of the hospital. Wheels on plastic tiles, elevators, machinery. Then I walked up the stairs after him, and he was gone. I held the backpack of money in my hand, then put it on my back.

I got on the C11 bus and got off at a hostel near the Finchley Road. This was the area where I grew up. The ice cream parlour where I used to work, the McDonald's I used to hang out in.

I couldn't think straight. The money was a bribe, a peace offering, or maybe a payment. It was a lot of money – twenty thousand pounds, it turned out. The guy on reception at the hostel was staring out of the window and I slipped past. On the stairs a group of Italian teenagers were dragging backpacks up the stairs, laughing and shoving each other. *Scusa, scusa*, they giggled, and I looked away. I kept thinking people were staring.

◆ ◆ ◆

'Our loneliness and anxiety come from being untethered from our surroundings,' Frida said online to two hundred and twenty thousand followers. 'We've forgotten how to listen. I was taught to sit still for hours, as a young girl. At first my foot itched, I was thirsty, my stick dolls wanted to play with me. Boredom overwhelms, the mind wanders, but you stay. There was nothing to do but try and listen as instructed. There's the first layer of obvious sounds: where I grew up it was the birds, the boats, the tides licking the mud. But sink. Listen deeper. You'll hear the bristle worms, the bivalves, the mud snails, the slurp of wading birds' feet on the sand and the sidling of crabs. The hustle of samphire and the whisper of sea lavender roots, wiggling down through the silt and the mud. You'll hear the mud itself. The soft stuff, the tarry stuff that is eating the plants and animals and forcing it to decay. When you get good enough at hearing the Earth you'll hear the bacteria sucking in oxygen and then, like a can opening, you will no longer have to try anymore and the Earth will pour out its story. The hurricanes and storms, the wars, the explosions. Four billion years of life on this planet, two billion years for life larger than single-celled organisms. It will all come at you, releasing inside you, telling you everything. I don't go a day without listening now, and you shouldn't either, even if you're in a big city. Especially if you're in a big city.

'You talk at each other rather than with each other. You are so urgently trying to persuade others of your worth, or your point of view, that you've forgotten how to listen. This clamour of noise out there, all of you shouting, waiting for your turn to speak.

'I grew up with strong physical boundaries, but I listen. I had never been to a theme park as a kid.' She smiled. 'Or watched a Disney movie. But when anyone spoke I listened to so much more than their words. I want you all to be able to hear what I hear. I want you all to sense the multitude of dimensions available to us. There is not just one life for you. We are infinite.'

◆ ◆ ◆

Over the following months I travelled, zigzagging across Europe, spending as little as possible. I stood in food shops and stared at the aisles, transfixed by whether I needed to eat cereal or chicken. I jumped at sirens, thinking Frida would have told the police what had happened. I cried on the pavement because I made the wrong choice of food, starving but incapable.

The Unification of Dacia had been reported in most papers, but not extensively. I googled it regularly. The more I read, the more nuts it was. Polygamy, purity rites, offerings, underage sex. Children forced to participate in rituals involving 'sensory deprivation pods' where they sat for days. They believed their child leader could pause time. Split dimensions. The followers gave up all their worldly possessions to live within the cult's isolated compound.

I felt sick the more I read. Sick that Frida had gone through something like that, and sick that she still believed she had some large spiritual power. But I also felt sick because some part of me also believed she was magical.

I should have gone to the police. I know that. I did call Grace's parents. They said that they didn't have a daughter. When pressed they said they hadn't spoken to her in twelve years and had no idea where she was.

I ate ravenously. Craved hamburgers. Craved yoghurt and honey. Craved fish. Fresh white apricots. Mint. Lemons. I ate lemons raw, sliding them into my mouth. I couldn't even think about onions, or beetroot, or oranges. The sight of oranges made me throw up. I dreamed of Grace and Ava most nights.

As Frida once predicted, there was a bad storm on the east coast of England and the seawalls broke. The island became uninhabitable for all but a few hours of the day, and the cottage was ruined by flooding. She moved to somewhere tropical for a few months, then to an island off the Welsh coast.

'Most cultures have a flood myth,' Frida said to her three hundred and fifty thousand followers. 'A divine retribution. A deluge. The primaeval waters of creation. The bursting of pent-up energy. Mother Nature showing us that she cannot be tamed or trampled. Soon this flood will take the form of different natural disasters. A deluge in the form of a man-made virus, followed by a mental health crisis that will scar a generation. We're all just searching for some truth, a few bits of connection and joy, to get us through.'

Chapter Twelve

Whenever Leo is sick I think of Frida's words about him out on the causeway: a spiritual malady, a fever. After Frida DMs me back the first crossword clue, we keep messaging each other. At first, just clues and answers. An underwater valley, four letters. Feline monarch, seven letters.

Leo's hot breath is on my neck while I write to her, or steam from the stove as I make him soup. He still has flushed cheeks, shivers even in the heat, and dry skin flakes on his cheeks. I press cool towels to his forehead and lie beside him through the night. Ben says it is just a fever, one of a thousand things they might pick up at school, but I sit up and watch him sleep.

Frida often spoke of finding truth. These days I reckon the truth is closing your eyes when you stand in a patch of sun. It's the loaf of bread out of the oven, and the smell of your kids after a bath, a flower uncurling. The small things are the only things that matter.

'Have you missed me?' she writes one day, the message waiting when I wake up.

'Not really. Why have you been having me followed?' I reply to her.

'Don't flatter yourself,' she writes. 'I don't have someone camped out in that godforsaken seaside town all the time. But there's a woman there who checks up on you occasionally. What are you wearing right now, Zo?'

Ben is getting ready for a morning shift in the other room, careful not to wake us but my heart is thudding fast. Ben is not perfect, in case I have made him seem so. He has a past, he also has a woman he once loved – the surgeon – who I know he still thinks of and sees occasionally. I think he's even slept with her since we've been married, but in a way I understand. He belongs to me, but there was also her, before me. I love him no less because of this. My feelings for him are bigger and more important than my feelings for Frida.

Ben's grandmother's sheets feel hot and itchy against my skin.

'Does she work at Costa?' I write to Frida.

'No. LOL. She's at the school gate.'

'A mother at the school gate?' I write. 'That's creepy.'

'She says you're just as gorgeous as you always were. You still wear your hair short to frame your face, like I cut it on the island. You should go back to blonde, though.'

Ben kisses me and then Leo on the forehead to say goodbye and I make sure he doesn't see the phone screen. I will make it up to him. Atone for this moment for when he feels guilty for working on a Saturday, but it is me who is sinning. I wonder whether, behind every perfect wife, there is a sin or a secret being fixed with pie crust and home-made lasagne.

'How long have you known where I am?'

'Not long. You did a pretty good job of staying under the radar, but one of my followers moved to your town and recognised you.'

'How? You took all the photos of me down.'

'I've looked for you on and off,' she says. 'I've asked followers to look out for you. I never meant you any harm, but I've wanted to talk to you over the years, and I've posted the occasional photo wondering if anyone knew where you were.' She paused. 'I never thought the name Zoe fitted you. I'm surprised you kept that up over our summer.'

The front door closes and latches downstairs as Ben leaves.

Emma is supposed to go to a party today, but I intend to cancel. The birthday present is wrapped with a bow, perfectly chosen. I let the idea sink in: Frida has been looking for me.

'Katie doesn't suit you either, though. So demure and childish. I think I'll keep calling you Zo.'

'Does Moth have any interest in Leo?'

'None,' she says.

'Thank you for that.'

'Does he have a star birthmark?'

'Yes.'

'What are you wearing? Do you still wear knickers to bed?'

'I thought you were psychic.'

'You made that joke the first time we spoke.'

'It's kind of a classic one, surely.' I pause. 'Leo isn't very well.'

'What's wrong with him?'

'Just a fever.'

'I'll put in a good word with the spirits,' she writes. 'I'm sure it'll clear up. Did you tell the journalist anything? Be honest.'

'You know they found the bodies,' I reply. 'They've found glitter and feathers that might tie the deaths to that night. My turtle necklace.'

'It doesn't matter,' she responds. 'They were troubled girls. I have a follower on the force, and they've already found evidence of drug abuse, and school friends saying they'd been into the power plant to get high with Grace and Ava throughout their teens. I'm not interested in what he knows of those girls, I'm interested in what he knows of my childhood and the Unification Group.'

'He doesn't know enough. He wanted me to help him.'

'But that won't happen,' she says.

I lie back in bed, watching Leo breathe.

'He hasn't got back in contact. I was meant to meet him.'

'You did the right thing. We will always look out for each other, Zo. We're bound together.'

She didn't explain, just then, why Oliver never got back in contact.

◆ ◆ ◆

People say she predicted Covid. People shared the video from the summer of her predicting how the world would stop and foxes would take control of the cities, and it went, well, *viral.* Frida's success skyrocketed during the pandemic when people were physically cut off but minutely connected online. Three hundred thousand turned into just shy of a million.

Planes were grounded, the industrial bustle muted, the giant metal cranes stopped bending over the scrubland, and on computer screens Frida promised connection and happiness. Kids were off school. Businesses were failing, people were losing their jobs, humans had time on their hands.

Bored school kids watching her in their bedrooms, sharing Frida's words with their other lonely friends. Everyone trapped in their houses. Her casual, intimate way of talking proved alluring.

Parents let their kids watch her. Of all the things these scared kids could be watching, adults thought this wasn't the worst. Stranded university and high school students came together online for global meditations where they focused on healing the Earth, they decided to stop eating meat, they spoke about being fearless and brave and trying their best. Sure, she spoke of not trusting the government. Yes, she spoke with apocalyptic language, but not that often and only with reason – the Earth was being slowly unpicked at the seams by human nature right then. The Earth was burning, polarising, bubbling with virus and conspiracy. She just used it.

She posted pictures of her lithe, perfect body performing yoga firefly poses, all set to music. Of course I watched her during Covid. Up late at night, trying to earn some money fixing broken links and slow-loading landing pages, I watched her. I stayed in Livadia, central Greece, for Covid. My baby grew and I began to waddle like a sea creature on land. Nothing fitted and I was alien to myself.

I lived in a shared house with some young women who were out of work for the duration. Tourism stopped. They took me to the archaeological site that Frida would have loved, a site of divination devoted to an oracle renowned for cryptic and unsettling experiences. Meanwhile, Frida's following grew and she led live global group meditations.

'Experience Frida Rae live to understand your purpose, unlock your happiness, and transform your life', said an advert that would come up on my computer with Frida's benign smile there, even though I only watched her through a virtual private network. I was tongue-tied and milky. I still dreamed of Ava and Grace most nights, waking in a hot sweat. Frida had deleted every mention of me on her grid. The whole summer had been wiped from her history. Grace. Ava. Me. Frida's teeth were white by this point. Her nose straight. Her skin was clear.

I loved the creature swelling inside me, turning from ghost to corporeal being. I did not speak out against Frida because I loved him.

◆ ◆ ◆

'How did the very first atom emerge from a vacuum? The little things are the big things,' Frida said to her army of followers.

◆ ◆ ◆

I gave birth to Leo in May, at the height of coronavirus. The day he was born I woke up with an animal smell in my nostrils, like blood on hay. The muscles of my stomach were contracting as if a corset was being tightened under my skin and then released as I headed to the whitewashed general hospital. My body had been doing this occasionally for a few weeks, but that day it was stronger. In the hospital I was put in a waiting room full of blue curtains that didn't go far in dividing the handful of trapped, panting women from each other. I meditated and I breathed through the pain. Leo was born a few hours later. He tore through me, and I remember fragments: his body reaching for me as they passed him up between my legs, the smell of him. It was nothing like I'd expected. He wasn't cute like babies in pictures. He was majestic and utterly himself. Covered in blood and body fluid at first, it looked as if my heart had been torn out and handed to me.

I felt that if I looked up, Frida would be there.

But she wasn't. I felt disappointed, despite everything.

I wasn't surprised though that Leo had a birthmark in the shape of a star, over his right shoulder, just as Frida had predicted.

That was the trouble with Frida – her ambiguity. Like her almost-smile, she was never entirely one thing. Not devil or angel, saviour or con artist. All of them and also none of them, depending on the angle you looked at her and what she wanted you to see.

◆ ◆ ◆

'In the beginning there was water,' she said. 'We began as water and we will become water again. It is not long to go now, till the singularity.'

◆ ◆ ◆

'But he seemed like such a nice man,' Mum said while I sat on a balcony, tanning my legs in the Greek sunshine. I called her occasionally. She didn't know where I was. 'He works at an advertising firm. So polite and well educated. He said you'd left without any explanation and he wanted to be a part of Leo's life.' She paused. 'You so wanted a dad growing up. Your biological dad never gave me a penny or had any interest, but I would have jumped at the chance. Your kid will want his dad, like you did.'

'Please say you didn't tell him anything,' I said.

She paused. I could hear her tapping her nails on the kitchen counter.

'Mum?'

'I don't know what the problem is. Did he hit you? He seemed so nice, and, frankly, posh. That accent, geez. Very hot.'

I felt like this might be the only time Mum had ever been impressed by me. A rich man!

'You have no idea how expensive a kid is,' she said. 'I didn't tell him anything because I don't know anything. I have no idea where my daughter or my grandson live.'

'Nothing?'

'I said you'd had the baby. I showed him the picture you sent me in the post.'

I looked back at that photo, wondering what information Frida might glean from it. I'd almost told Mum where we were a few times, and was thankful that I hadn't.

◆ ◆ ◆

'We are polluted by negative vibrations of separation. It is up to you, the revolutionaries, to correct this imbalance. This is the start of the rest of your life,' Frida said online. 'The climate apocalypse is coming. An asteroid that will raise sea levels and force the chosen few to higher ground. We must be ready, but it is not the end. There is no such thing. We are all connected and we will walk through to a new dimension.'

I moved away from Livadia when Covid restrictions eased. I flew into Manchester with Leo.

'When the flood comes,' Frida said on my screen, 'people will be driven out of the cramped cities where they have congregated. It will turn us all into refugees.'

I kept silent about Grace and Ava. I was guilty. I fed my baby. I let Frida grow through little squares on the screens, as she preached.

'I am not a prophet of doom,' she said, when I scrolled, despite telling myself I would never look at her. It was just so hard not to. 'I am merely a witness to the undeniable truth that we are hurtling towards an ecological apocalypse. We are on the precipice of something far worse than a mere change in climate, a mere virus. We are on the brink of the collapse of ecosystems that have been in balance for millions of years. The time for waiting is over. The time for action is now. Let us rise to the challenge, not with fear, but with hope. It is the end of the world as we know it.'

She was right and wrong. Truth and lies. I bought a caravan from a dealership in Derbyshire. For years I never let Leo out of my sight. After Covid abated she performed to five thousand people at a holistic festival in Bath, which apparently sold out and had people begging for tickets just because they wanted to meet Frida. Then she sold out more events, filling stadiums across the UK. She closed the retreat in Wales and opened a much bigger one in Bali.

Meanwhile, I coded and looked after my baby. I jumped at the sight of crows and seagulls and stray dogs. I earned just about enough money. I had a herb garden on the windowsill. A room. A bed. A stove. Fennel for stomach cramps, feverfew for a headache. Hyssop for a cold. Rosemary to stimulate the memory. Lavender to calm down. I never put down roots. Leo was my roots. I had the odd liaison, never a relationship. A kiss once with a pretty, dark-haired Hare Krishna girl with a pink sari, after Leo and I started going to get free food from them on Saturdays. A brief flirtation that went nowhere with another single mother who lived in a caravan that parked near us for a bit. A smile for a man who didn't understand why I wouldn't let Leo out of my sight.

She became so legitimate in the world outside my head. Business leaders, fashion icons, even European royalty followed her.

'Where you choose to put your attention is who you choose to be,' as she said. I wanted my world to be the curve of Leo's cheek, the proud look he got when he did something difficult, his thrill in how light makes patterns through trees.

◆ ◆ ◆

'If the Earth's 4.5 billion years of existence were just a day, humans would have been here for three little seconds,' she said on stage at the Palais des Congrès de Paris, after raising her hands to pause the applause. She had 1.5 million followers on Instagram then.

Leo was about to turn five, and while the Paris event streamed on my phone, Leo played in a playground. He would need to go to school soon. I would need to stay in one place and give him a proper life. He swung on the monkey bars, shouting at me to watch him.

Frida smiled on my screen, still wearing a similar white t-shirt to when we first met. The same blonde hair and blunt fringe. The same girlish smile mixed with wise blue eyes that seemed much older than her years. I needed to stop watching her. Not just try to stop, but stop for Leo's sake. Leaving her standing there on the island was only half that battle.

'When humans are done on Earth,' Frida said on stage, 'cities will return to the foxes and spirits. Light will still fall through oak trees.'

I told myself I would turn it off before she finished her speech.

'We are just a blink of an eye, my followers. Do not be scared of the end, because there is no such thing as endings. Just transformations.'

I turned her off, and raised my eyes to watch Leo on the monkey bars.

Chapter Thirteen

Oliver never messaged me again after he left my house that warm night. A few days later – after Leo's fever had broken – someone from the charity that I worked for mentioned the tragic case of a man found dead in his car. He'd taken an overdose.

It had happened the night he left my house to find his car, scrappy and tipsy with his creased shirt and razor-burnt throat. His death hadn't even made the local news. I found out at the soup kitchen that the dead man had been a digital journalist but had lost his job and ended up with a drug habit, living rough. No kids or significant other, but he'd had an oddly large amount of heroin in his system and more in his glove compartment. Nearly five hundred pounds' worth – a lot for a homeless guy.

So now I sit in my beautiful house, watching the sea. Don't scroll, I tell myself. I can only guess that she made sure he came into a large amount of heroin that night. Maybe it was in the stolen car when he picked it up.

I will keep my promise and never tell a soul what I know of her origins or rise, or what happened at the power plant.

I spin my wedding ring and get ready to pick the kids up from school. I fill my mug of tea and scroll through her grid sometimes, although I tell myself that I won't ever do it again. But then she DMs me with a crossword clue and I itch to answer, unable to concentrate on anything else until I do. I run on the cliffs with my husband. I dance with my children in the kitchen, and help them with their spellings, and grow vegetables and try to pretend that I don't think about her.

But everyone you love leaves parts of themselves in you. The way they wave with just their fingers, or bite their lip when they concentrate. There's no escape from these little ghosts left inside us: how we sigh, or come, or lick our fingers. Our bodies remember.

So I will forever placate crows and jump at the sound of seagulls. I will always sleep with a light on. I do not believe that we can walk between dimensions, or that she has predicted when the world might end. But when she asks for the answer to a crossword clue, I find myself answering. Aurora. Nero. Infinite.

BOOK CLUB QUESTIONS

When I was nineteen I inadvertently joined a cult. I had booked a seemingly well-priced hostel bed in New York's East Village for the summer, but on arrival it turned out the building was run by a powerful religious movement.

I won't name the movement (for all the fearful reasons discussed in *Follow Her*) but I was beguiled and stayed for the summer. These people were doing genuine good, more good than I had ever done – feeding the poor, offering refuge and giving meaning to people who had lost themselves. Yet the group was also indoctrinating these vulnerable people, and worshipping a deeply flawed but charismatic leader.

I know the moment that I had the idea for *Follow Her*, many years before I started writing it. After a group meditation I was watching a video sermon of this dubious spiritual leader and I thought: You were a kid once. What circumstances led to you believing all this about yourself? And I knew I wanted to write about the early years of a cult leader.

I've had a complicated relationship with spirituality, and the wellness industry, ever since. I've worked as a telephone psychic. I've been on retreats. I believe in something beyond, but am scared of it, and I hope this nuance comes across in this novel. *Follow Her* is, at heart, a love story about all the places we find meaning in this complicated world.

1. It's never entirely clear if Frida has a genuine gift, or if she's a con artist. She helps people, but also gains power and money through helping them. Have you ever been to visit a psychic, and do you believe they are real?

2. The narrator notes that brilliant empaths often grew up dealing with trauma: if your safety depends on pre-empting another person's emotions, you become good at it. As a reader did you have sympathy for Frida? And if you did: did your sympathy grow or decline through the book?

3. Might you follow Frida on Instagram, if she were a real guru? Do you think you could take the good things from her without falling under her control?

4. In an increasingly anxious society, social media is shown as both alienating and as a way of connecting. There's bad and good to it. Frida uses social media to help people but also to manipulate them, but isn't that what everyone does on social media? What makes her actions so bad?

5. Were you rooting for Zoe/Katie and Frida to stay together, or for the protagonist to get out before she was consumed?

Follow the Author on Amazon

If you enjoyed this book, follow Anna Stothard on Amazon to be notified when the author releases a new book!
To do this, please follow these instructions:

Desktop:

1) Search for the author's name on Amazon or in the Amazon App.
2) Click on the author's name to arrive on their Amazon page.
3) Click the 'Follow' button.

Mobile and Tablet:

1) Search for the author's name on Amazon or in the Amazon App.
2) Click on one of the author's books.
3) Click on the author's name to arrive on their Amazon page.
4) Click the 'Follow' button.

Kindle eReader and Kindle App:

If you enjoyed this book on a Kindle eReader or in the Kindle App, you will find the author 'Follow' button after the last page.